ONCE THEY WORE THE GRAY

ONCE THEY WORE THE GRAY

JOHNNY D. BOGGS

SAGEBRUSH
Large Print Westerns

First published in Great Britain by Gunsmoke
First published in the United States by Five Star

Published in Large Print 2014 by ISIS Publishing Ltd.,
7 Centremead, Osney Mead, Oxford OX2 0ES
by arrangement with
Golden West Literary Agency

CIP data is available for this title from the British Library

ISBN 978–0–7531–5357–4 (pb)

Printed and bound in Great Britain by
T. J. International Ltd., Padstow, Cornwall

In memory of a cousin, 1st Lieutenant Terry Graham, Killed in Action March 28, 1969

CHAPTER ONE

An icy February wind from the Mississippi whipped between the metal bars of the coffin wagon, which creaked and groaned on its preposterously laggard journey toward the railroad. Thirty men had been crammed into the vehicle — which trailed a wagon hauling another thirty men — with nothing but their rags and lice-infested long hair to protect them from the cold. A few stared blankly outside at the drab Illinois sky; others huddled among themselves to keep warm.

"Sergeant?"

Gil Metairie looked up. He crawled weakly to the rear of the wagon, over long legs and soiled clothes, and stared sadly at the youthful private whose head was cradled in the thick arms of redheaded Irishman Peadar Flann. Death's pallor had replaced the sooty tone of the Alabaman's face. He lay shivering, lips trembling, ice already forming on the ends of his sweat-soaked curly blond locks.

"I think the lad's dying, Gil," Flann said in a choking brogue.

1st Sergeant Gil Metairie, 15th Arkansas, Govan's Brigade, bowed his head. Gray salted Metairie's thick

1

brown mane and unruly hair, his pale eyes were hollow and bloodshot, and his face and hands felt leathery, hard. He looked tired. Ancient. Yet he was barely thirty-one years old.

"It don't seem right," Flann said. "Not now."

Gil nodded. It wasn't fair. He looked through the barred door at the end of the wagon, saw the guards in their blue greatcoats and mufflers, and shouted. He attempted to yell, at least, but his scream seemed barely audible. Metairie swallowed, tried again.

"Hey! Stop this thing!"

The wagon crept along. Metairie moved to the door, pulled himself up. "Stop. We got a sick man here!" The soldiers ignored him. Gil turned, saw an artilleryman from North Carolina nearby. He tried to think of the gunner's name. "Rogers," he said. "Hand me your brogan."

Rogers answered with a curse, and Metairie lashed out at him. "Now, Private. I want that brogan!" The Carolinian drew up, frightened. Metairie knew why. Peadar Flann once told him: "A body can see death in your eyes when you're riled, Sergeant." Rogers quickly unwrapped the putrid woolen cloth around his left foot, pulled off the rotting piece of leather that once resembled a high-ankle shoe, and tossed it to Metairie. Gil pounded the heel against the metal bars, ringing them as loud as he could, and screamed at the tormentors.

"Stop!" he pleaded. "Stop this now. You have to stop!" He kept at it until he felt as though he had been lung-shot, and collapsed against the door. But the

2

coffin wagon had halted, and as Metairie slowly turned, he looked into the cold black barrel of a .44 Army Colt.

"You're gonna shut your lousy Reb yap, or I'll shut it for you, damn it!" the mustached lieutenant barked. "You're takin' orders from this man's army now."

Metairie jerked his head at Flann and Private William James. "The boy's sick," Gil said hoarsely. "Needs a doctor bad."

The officer's black eyes glanced at the Alabaman. He holstered the revolver and backed away from the door, withdrawing a ring of keys from inside his greatcoat. "Corporal!" He barked out a few orders, and the troopers behind the wagon dropped from their saddles and cocked the long Springfield rifles.

"Stand back!" the lieutenant ordered the prisoners, and slowly unlocked the door. "Anyone of you sons-a-bitches moves, dies." The officer nodded at Metairie. "You and the Irishman haul that boy out. The rest of you stay put."

Snow crunched under Gil's bare feet as he laid William James on the side of the road. He heard the lieutenant curse, then whisper to the corporal: "Why did they let this piece of secesh trash out?" Metairie dropped to his knees, felt the dampness and cold of the ice, and pushed the wet bangs off the Alabaman's forehead. William James opened his eyes.

"Hey, Sergeant."

"Hello, Billy."

The private's eyes flickered, lighted on Flann. "And good mornin' to you, Corporal Flann." The lucidity passed. James cried out for his mother, shook his head rabidly, and screamed: "The Yanks! The Yanks. Oh, for the love of God, General Johnston's dead!" He began babbling something insensible before falling into welcomed unconsciousness.

Metairie glanced at the officer in charge. "Can you send one of your men back, Lieutenant? Fetch a wagon to haul this boy to the hospital?"

"What for?" the Federal replied. "He'll be dead in ten minutes."

Flann barked out a curse. "Mother of Mary, sir, show some decency. Some compassion."

The officer held out his left arm, revealing the stump where a hand should have been. "My compassion," he said bitterly, "died at Stones River."

"Gil?"

Metairie looked down at the boy, awake, coherent again. James smiled. "You don't mind if I call you Gil, do you?"

"No, Billy."

"Can you do me a favor, Gil?"

"Sure, Billy. Anything."

"Sing to me, Gil."

Metairie smiled. "I ain't got much of a voice, Billy."

"Sing."

Gil bowed his head. He hadn't sung in a long time. Stones River, the Federal had said. Gil knew that well. He had been there, too, with the 15th. The Yanks had fallen in northwest of Murfreesboro, and would attack at dawn. But on this night, December 30, 1862, it was the bands of both armies doing the fighting.

4

Union strains of "Yankee Doodle" cut through the cold Tennessee night. General Bragg's brass countered with "The Bonnie Blue Flag." Louder, trying to drown out the Confederate horns, "Hail Columbia" blasted from the Union camp. The Rebels trumpeted out "Dixie." "When Johnny Comes Marching Home" was answered with "The Secesh." Suddenly the Yankee bands started another song, but this one was different, softer, sweeter. Gil stared into the faces of the men warming themselves by the fire. One began to mouth the words. "Home Sweet Home." The Confederate bands joined in, and the music carried across the river, blending beautifully.

Metairie rose then, leaving the fire, and walked toward the banks of the river. He inhaled, breathed out slowly, and, when the bands let the last cords of "Home Sweet Home" drift away, he sang:

> **Should auld acquaintance be forgot,**
> **And never brought to mind?**
> **Should auld acquaintance be forgot,**
> **And auld lang syne.**
>
> **For auld lang syne, my dear,**
> **For auld lang syne,**
> **We'll tak a cup o' kindness yet**
> **For auld lang syne.**

Across the river, a Federal soldier joined in. They weren't trying to out-sing the other. It was a duet — sweet, soft, low. They finished, and Metairie returned to the fire in silence, remembering the voice of the unseen Yankee who had harmonized so well, wondering if they would kill each other in the morning.

Gil realized he was singing now, although his once pleasant baritone cracked dryly. It hurt to sing, but he did anyway, staring into the eyes of a smiling Private William James, 16th Alabama, seventeen years old. Metairie stopped, swallowed, realized Billy was dead. He closed the soldier's eyes and rose, helped to his feet by Flann.

"Get back in the wagon," the lieutenant ordered.

"You can't leave him here," Gil said.

"I can and I will. He ain't goin' nowheres, and you've got a train to catch. Move!"

Metairie felt the flash of anger. He spun, eyes blazing, and probably would have charged the Federal, knowing it would mean his death, but Flann's strong paws grabbed his shoulders. "Let it go, Sergeant," the Irishman said softly. "Young William's in a better place."

Gil waited until his heart slowed, letting the anger pass. "You shouldn't treat him this way," he told the officer. "Us this way."

The one-handed soldier spit. "Get in that wagon, mister. You're still Rebel trash to me, no matter how many oaths you take."

"Come on, Sergeant. It's not worth it."

"And you're not a sergeant no more. Remember that."

Slowly Gil climbed back into the wagon and leaned against the cold bars. Flann dropped beside him, and the door slammed shut, was locked. The wagon lurched forward.

"Is this what it's going to be like?" Gil asked.

6

Flann shrugged. "Probably. For a while I guess."

Metairie sighed. "Maybe we should have stayed at Rock Island."

"And died? No, Sergeant, this is for the best. It was our only choice, really."

"Call me Gil, Flann. The Yank was right. I'm not a sergeant any more. We're in his army now, the Yankee Army."

CHAPTER
TWO

Metairie and Flann were among the first to arrive at Rock Island Prison in December of 1863. They had been held in Louisville before being shipped north to the Mississippi River island between Davenport, Iowa, and Moline, Illinois. Gil still suffered from the shock of a mortar shell at Missionary Ridge. The fact that the Confederates had lost that battle seemed incomprehensible. Missionary Ridge and Major General Patrick Cleburne were impregnable, invincible. But here Gil stood, a prisoner of war, and General Cleburne would be dead within a year, falling in front of his men during the slaughter at Franklin, Tennessee.

The captives had been told that Rock Island was ready. But Metairie knew that wasn't the case as he marched in snow to his knees, teeth chattering, miserable, and hurt. It was thirty-two degrees below zero, Peadar Flann and many others had smallpox, and the mastermind who planned the prison compound had forgotten to build a hospital. So, sick and healthy together, they crammed into the shanties that were supposed to be barracks, tried to stay warm, tried to stay alive. Flann recovered, but many didn't. Within days, while carpenters built a hospital, Metairie and others dragged the dead into the snow to await burial. By February more than three hundred rested in the cemetery.

Metairie stared at the compound, tried to think. He had joined Cleburne's 15th early in 1862, just in time for the march north from Corinth, Mississippi, where the Confederate and Union Armies bloodied each other on the banks of the Tennessee. He "saw the elephant" at Shiloh, tasted battle again in Kentucky at Richmond and Perryville, and at Murfreesboro, Tennessee. By September of 1863, he has risen to the rank of first sergeant. But late that November, while providing a rear-guard action to cover his army's retreat, an explosion rendered him unconscious, and when he woke up, he found himself staring at the dirty canvas of a Yankee hospital tent.

Guards walked along the high planks behind Rock Island's stockade palisade, ten or twelve feet high, and sentries stood at their posts, watching, waiting. There were two gates, thick sally ports, on the east and west ends. Beyond the fence stood guardhouses at each gate.

Escape? Even if he could get past the compound, there was the Mississippi River to contend with, not to mention the Yankees from the nearby arsenal, and a brutal journey south, maybe five hundred miles to Confederate lines, if he could even find the battered Army of Tennessee. But Gil Metairie tried. At night in Barracks Number Forty-Two, he and his prison mates tunneled. By day, they would walk across the grounds, letting the soil fall down trousers legs, spreading the earth nonchalantly and praying no sentry would notice.

In mid-June, they pushed up behind the south wall. Eight men went through the tunnel first, and Gil followed with Flann right behind him. Metairie took a deep breath of the humid, free air and ran — only to stop twenty yards from the opening. Flann cursed. Metairie spun around to see the big Irishman struggling to pull himself free. He was stuck.

Metairie sprinted back and dropped to his knees, frantically digging like a hound around the corporal's thick chest. "Get out of here, lad!" Flann said. "Leave me."

"Not a chance," Metairie said. "Be quiet."

Flann groaned. "Oh, for the love of it all. I'm this close to tasting my first good mug of beer since . . ."

"The beer's why you're stuck now, Flann."

He heard the alarm, looked up, saw the Yankee fire the musket, felt the ball whirl past his head. "Run, Sergeant!" Flann snapped. "Get out of here while you have a chance!"

Metairie sighed. Soldiers poured from the guardhouse. Other sentries fired. He stood quickly, raising his hands above his head, hoping the Yanks wouldn't kill him anyway. Of the eight who made it out, five were herded back to Rock Island and thrown into the sweatbox with Metairie and Flann. One drowned in the river, his body washing ashore four days later. And the other two? Maybe they made it, but Gil would never know.

Strong hands pulled Metairie from the box. He cried out from the sunlight, blinded, and was shoved forward. He stumbled, tried to rise, but a musket's stock slammed into the small of his back. He felt himself being dragged. How far, he couldn't tell. He tasted blood and dirt, was jerked to his feet, and thrust through a door.

"Have a seat, Sergeant Metairie!" a voice called out.

Metairie didn't move, couldn't until his eyes focused. He stared at a Union officer, a white-bearded major he had never seen. The man motioned to a high-back chair, and Metairie studied it awkwardly. He hadn't seen a piece of furniture in eight months. He sat, found it uncomfortable. His back throbbed.

"You served under Cleburne, correct?" the major asked.

Gil nodded. The officer studied him. "And before that?"

He shook his head.

"You look familiar," the major said. "Where are you from?"

"Alexandria, Louisiana," he answered. It wasn't a lie, although he hadn't seen Louisiana since he was nineteen.

"Yet serving with an Arkansas regiment?"

"My moth . . . I have relations in Helena."

"Never been to Missouri or Kansas?"

"No, sir."

The major scratched his beard, studying Gil's face. "Would you like to?"

"Sir?"

The Yankee cleared his throat. "Are you familiar with President Lincoln's Amnesty Proclamation, Sergeant?"

So this was it? Metairie nodded. He knew about the amnesty. Swear an oath to the Union and enlist in the Yankee Army. Some prisoners had already done so, being assured they would be stationed out West, would not have to fight against the Confederacy, just Indians.

The major uncorked a bottle, poured three fingers of brandy into a glass, and downed it. Metairie could smell the liquor. He saw the fresh bread on the table behind the Yank. His mouth watered.

"It's a chance to get out of this . . . this . . ." The major shuddered.

"I'm not a traitor, Major," Gil Metairie said flatly.

The major frowned, set the glass down heavily. "You are a traitor, Mister Metairie, to the glorious Union. But have it your way, for now."

So he went back to his barracks to rot. The James brothers arrived two months later, Billy and Thomas, a pair of Alabamans too young to shave. At roll call each morning, the Federals made a pitch for volunteers. More and more Confederates seemed to comply, despite the threats of the loyal Rebel prisoners. Metairie couldn't blame those who deserted the Southern cause. Stay here? Fight over rats for supper? He often thought about taking the pledge himself, but couldn't do it, although he felt his resolve weakening. By September, Billy James had developed a hacking cough and intermittent fevers. His older brother fared worse, watching his teeth fall out and fingers turn black. Metairie smelled the gangrene, yet couldn't convince Thomas to go to the hospital.

"Ever'body I seen go to that buildin'," Thomas said, "gets hisself buried. Not me."

On October 10th, Flann and Metairie carried Billy James to the hospital. They returned to the barracks, ate their cornmeal and half-raw, half-spoiled bacon, and rested. Thomas pulled himself to his feet and stumbled toward the door.

"Where are you heading, Tommy?" Flann asked.

"To see a damyankee 'bout somethin'," James replied. "Y'all take care of Billy."

Five minutes later, Metairie heard the gunshot. By the time he and Flann reached the fence, two guards were dragging Thomas James's lifeless body to the dead house.

"We're going to die here, Sergeant," Flann said softly. "Mother of Mary, we're all going to die."

Gil Metairie stood in front of a bespectacled doctor and besotted captain.

"You been sick, suffered from disease, or had any fits?" the doctor asked.

Sick? Would that include the fever from infection after the shell slapped his forehead with a chunk of hot steel? Fits? What exactly is a fit? Metairie wished he could laugh. "No, sir," he said in a near whisper. The doctor nodded, made a mark on his pad, and read from his list of questions.

"Ever suffered a head wound?"

Metairie nodded. "Missionary Ridge. Mortar. I recovered."

The doctor adjusted his glasses, chewed his pencil, glanced at the captain.

"He looks all right to me," the officer said. The doctor nodded and made another mark.

"How about drinking? You got the habit?"

Metairie wondered if Peadar Flann answered this question honestly. He shook his head. The doctor nodded, scratched with the pencil, and continued with a series of questions of a personal nature. Finally the doctor nodded and told the officer: "He passes the physical examination, Captain. He's all yours now."

The officer straightened as if called to attention, and despite weaving drunkenly, never slurred his words. "Gil Metairie," he said, "do you desire to take an oath of allegiance to the United States of America and enlist in the U.S. Volunteers, Second Regiment, and be stationed on the frontier for a period of not less than one year?"

Metairie sighed. "I do," he said.

He repeated the oath, signed the agreement, and moved to the crammed barracks for the volunteers. "Galvanized Yankees," a guard called them, and that was one of the nicer terms. "White-washed Rebs," "deserters," and even the word Metairie had spoken months earlier: "traitor."

That had been in December, yet two months passed before they moved out of the Rock Island barracks. By then it was too late for Private Billy James.

CHAPTER
THREE

A false spring greeted the galvanized Yankees as they stumbled out of the cattle car that had carried them across Iowa and Missouri. Awaiting the fifty-nine volunteers stood a black-bearded second lieutenant and twelve armed guards, their Springfield rifles at full cock. *We're soldiers,* Metairie thought, *but still treated as prisoners.* They hadn't even been properly clothed.

"Glory be, Gil," Peadar Flann said, "look at that fine thing of beauty awaiting us, lad."

Metairie saw the Army ambulance, an open-air wagon like those he had seen too often in Tennessee and Georgia; only this one wasn't hauling wounded soldiers or empty litters. A Union private in a dress uniform, brass buttons gleaming like gold, and not a speck of dust on the dark blouse, and a dark-haired sergeant helped a woman wearing a green dress inside the back of the canvas-covered transport. Did Flann mean the wagon, or the woman? Neither. Gil smiled as the ambulance pulled away and parked in front of three covered wagons. He had a clear view of the building now:

Duine's Saloon
Fine Cigars . . . Beer . . . Whisky
If you're a blessed Irishman, be
aoi a bhfuil failte roimhe

"Control your thirst, Flann," Gil said. "What's the bottom line mean?"

"A welcome guest. Oh, Gil, don't you think these Yanks would let us have a wee taste?"

"No, and they'd fix it so you'd never enjoy a drink again."

"Keep movin'!" a guard barked.

Metairie let the sun warm him while he walked to one of the covered freight wagons, as directed by the Union escort, and climbed in the back. When the last of the Confederate volunteers seated himself, the lieutenant stuck his head in and said: "I got leg irons ready if any of you boys need 'em. I've also got orders to shoot anyone who tries to desert. Remember that."

A yoke of oxen began pulling the vehicle away from the railroad station, following the two other covered freight wagons and the ambulance. Each wagon, even the ambulance, had a driver and guard. Eight soldiers, all on duns, rode behind the wagons while the rest of the escort, led by the lieutenant, took the point. Twenty-one Yankee soldiers and one woman against almost sixty former Confederates. Gil wondered how many of his colleagues were thinking about those odds.

The wooden planks rubbed uncomfortably against Gil's back, and the driver seemed to make sure the wagon hit every pothole on the road — if this were even a road. Wagon traces and spurs jingled. The driver spit and swore at the oxen.

"I don't know about you fellows," Rogers said quietly, "but I aim to depart this damyankee army first chance I get, and light a shuck home. Anybody who wants is welcome to join me."

Arthur Bealer, a balding, bespectacled man who had served, surprisingly, with the 15th Mississippi Battalion Sharpshooters, said: "Rogers, you ain't even got a notion where we are. How you gonna even find our army?"

"I'll find it. Don't you worry none about that."

"What about the oath you gave at the prison?" Flann asked.

"My word to them damyankees don't mean a damn' thing. I gave my oath to the Confederate States of America four years ago. Hell, so did you, Flann. So did all of us. I ain't forgetting that, or what them bluebellies put us through at Rock Island."

Metairie couldn't debate that, even had he felt like arguing. No one could. They sat in silence for a few minutes, staring at each other, thinking. Finally Bealer asked: "Anybody see a sign at that train dépôt? Anybody know where we're at?"

Gil waited, but when no one spoke, he said: "We're in Kansas."

Everyone stared at him now. He continued. "The big river we crossed is the Missouri. We're moving north, along the river. My guess is we're being taken to Fort Leavenworth."

"How do you know that?" Rogers asked.

"He must know Kansas," Bealer said.

Metairie's laugh was mirthless. "Yeah," he said. "I know Kansas."

Bealer blinked. "So you could get us back home?"

"No." Gil shook his head. He had vowed never to touch Missouri soil again, but he had said the same thing about Kansas, too.

Flann nodded. "You boys get caught in Missouri, you might be mistook for Moon Montulé's devils. Yanks would shoot you on the spot."

Gil tried to swallow, couldn't. He let Flann continue.

"Gil's right. Besides, we ain't got decent clothes for . . ."

An Arkansas private laughed. "Corporal, we ain't had decent clothin' in a coon's age. Even Sergeant Metairie ain't worn shoes since Chickamauga."

Gil smiled weakly. So did Flann. "Yes, lad, that's true," the Irishman said. "But we need horses."

"I reckon the United States Army can loan us a few mounts," a South Carolinian offered, and the Confederates laughed again.

"So we wait," Rogers said. "Until the first chance we can steal some horses. Then we desert."

No one spoke until Flann chuckled and said: "Well, I'm not quitting this man's army until I've sampled some Kansas whisky."

When the laughter subsided, Bealer took charge. "I reckon not all of us wants to go home." His brown eyes, magnified by the glasses, leaped out at Metairie. "For whatever reasons. Anyone who wants to honor that oath to the Yanks, well, that's your choice. But no one sells

18

out any of us who wants to go home, rejoin our Army. We won't tolerate no traitors. Agreed?"

Metairie nodded. "Agreed," echoed down the wagon.

They still had not been fed when they reached the Missouri River bluffs and rode into the sprawling Fort Leavenworth compound. Dusk fell as the men huddled around fires, surrounded by Union pickets and the black-bearded lieutenant. Gil hadn't tasted food since the guards had tossed in a couple of canteens and a bucket of molded cornbread during a water stop right before they disembarked the train for Leavenworth. He ran his fingers through his hair and pulled at the massive beard.

"Gil," Flann said, "I must be dreaming. Or have died and am looking at a angel. Which is it?"

Metairie marveled at the woman crossing the parade ground. He blinked. A black cape partially covered the same green dress, embroidered and laced with ruffles and bows that she had worn at the dépôt. It had been years since Gil had seen a dress like that, or a woman so striking. Well, perhaps she wasn't that beautiful. Some might call her plain, maybe pretty, but it had been years since Gil had even seen a woman. At least, it seemed that way.

She stopped by the lieutenant, smiled briefly, and tried not to gawk at Metairie and the other men. She couldn't help herself, though. Gil looked at her brown hair, pinned up in a bun. Her face was round, soft, and the firelight reflected in her eyes. He couldn't tell the color.

19

"Gil?"

Metairie shook himself. "She's a dream, Flann. You haven't died. No angel will greet you when you're planted, my friend. Just old Beelzebub."

The Irishman sighed. Gil strained to hear the woman's voice.

"Who are those men, Henry?"

"Rebel deserters, Becky. A most miserable lot. Unfortunately, they're my company. I'm ordered to escort them to Fort Zarah along with yourself. We didn't get to talk much at the dépôt. How was Boston?"

She ignored his question. "These are the volunteers, then? That Father wrote me about. Shouldn't they be fed, clothed?"

"They're deserters, Becky, from their own army. They don't deserve nothin'."

"They're volunteer soldiers," she said harshly, adding: "And they're men." She turned and walked purposefully away from the officer. The lieutenant glared at her fast-moving back, turned, and spit.

"Reckon she told him off," Flann said.

Metairie smiled. "She's not finished. Bet you a whisky she'll be back."

Flann laughed. "I can't lose with that bet, Gil. I either get a taste of me Irish or see that *aingeal* again."

She returned in less than fifteen minutes, followed by a gray-haired major with a close-cropped beard and two orderlies who had trouble matching the woman's stride. The lieutenant threw up a laggard salute, which the major did not return. He considered the

Confederates briefly, then wheeled around at the lieutenant.

"Mister Russell," he said. "Miss Rankin says these men are volunteers, the last of the Second Regiment, I am informed. Is that correct?"

"Yes, sir. Company B, sir."

"Then why are they in this condition?"

Lieutenant Russell smiled. "I reckon they're out of uniform, Major. I'll see they get fined a month's pay for this."

"Lieutenant!" The major almost screamed. "If you ever get smart with me again, if you even show the slightest disrespect, I will personally testify at your court-martial and see that you suffer a lengthy stay in our prison here. Is that understood?"

"Yes, sir."

"These men should have been outfitted properly before they left Rock Island. I know Colonel Caraher is not aware of their condition. He would not tolerate this. Nor will I. Lieutenant Russell, you will personally see that these men are fed, that they are given uniforms, that they may bathe and shave. I'll make sure the store is open tonight until you are finished. And I will inspect these men before you leave for Fort Zarah in the morning. If I am not satisfied, Lieutenant, you will not be leaving with these men and you will never command in this army again. Is that understood?"

"Yes, sir," Russell seethed.

"Then get to it, mister."

Russell's salute snapped this time, and he spun around and barked, "Sergeant Elliott. Get these volunteers up and march them to ... to ... find a place and get these men cleaned up, then fed, and meet me at the quartermaster's store in two hours."

"Yes, sir!"

They marched past the officers and the woman. Metairie paused briefly, bringing his right hand up as if to tip his hat. He wore no hat, though, and hadn't since Missionary Ridge.

"Thank you, ma'am," he said quietly.

"You're quite welcome."

Her eyes, Metairie noticed, were brown.

CHAPTER
FOUR

"This ain't no damned hotel, mister," an officer barked. "Get out of that tub so the others can get a bath."

Metairie pulled himself up and caught the towel Flann threw him. He felt forty pounds lighter with the dirt, excess hair, and beard finally removed, although he had kept his mustache and goatee. Metairie moved down the line behind Flann, followed by Arthur Bealer. A quartermaster issued each man underwear, blanket, uniform, and overcoat, as well as some tack and cookware.

"The charges will be taken out of your first three months' pay," the man told Flann.

The Irishman laughed. "Well, it's good to know that the U.S. Volunteer Second Regiment is the same as the Fifteenth Arkansas and the grand British Forty-First Regiment of Foot and all the armies before them."

"Shut your Irish trap and keep moving."

"That's no way to be addressing a man fortunate enough to be born in County Cork."

"Move! Get dressed and get some grub."

The thought of food shut Flann up.

Metairie took his pile without comment, stuffing the extra socks and tinware into the Army-issue haversack.

The brogans felt strange. He realized it had been some time since he had worn shoes. The kepi seemed a half size too small, the navy woolen shirt scratched uncomfortably, and the trousers would have easily fallen down if not for the canvas suspenders.

"How 'bout a rifle?" Bealer asked.

The quartermaster glared at the Mississippian. "Weapons have been issued to Lieutenant Russell, who will disperse them among you soldiers in the morning. The rifles, too, will be charged to you over your first six months of service."

Smiling, Bealer pulled on his long johns and told Metairie: "Ol' Flann won't have enough money left after our first pay day to visit the nearest saloon."

Metairie replied: "I doubt that."

Gil fell in line with the other volunteers as the sun crept its way above the bluffs. Every man looked clean and refreshed except Rogers, who seemed prejudiced against washing his face. Flann stood sharply at attention, his uniform buttons straining to hold in his ample gut — and Peadar had dropped probably fifty pounds at Rock Island, the only time Gil had ever known the Irishman to lose weight.

The major walked down the parade ground. Gil looked for the woman, and, when he didn't see her, he frowned.

"Company B!" Russell barked. "A-ten-shun!"

Metairie stood erect. Others fell into a haggard stance; the Army of Tennessee had never been the most military of soldiers. The major didn't seem to mind. He

24

and the lieutenant exchanged salutes, then the major said — "At ease." — and began talking.

"Here comes the speechifyin'," Bealer whispered.

"Welcome to the Department of the Missouri," the major said. "You men are now volunteers in the United States Army. The headquarters for the Second Regiment are at Fort Riley. Company B, that is you, however, will be stationed at the new Fort Zarah on Walnut Creek. You will guard wagon trains and offer protection along the Santa Fé Trail for settlers and merchants."

The major cleared his throat. "I must warn you men, that this is a different type of war. Kiowas, Comanches, and other red vermin are your enemies, and they are savage. This is not civilized warfare. This . . ."

Metairie swallowed. The major had stopped in midsentence and was marching toward him. Did the officer recognize him? Gil cursed himself. He should have left the full beard. His eyes searched the grounds for a horse. He'd have to run. He'd . . . Metairie sighed, relaxed. The Federal stood in front of Peadar Flann.

"Soldier," the officer said sternly, "is there something I have said that amuses you?"

In the corner of his eye, Metairie saw Flann's wide grin. "Well, Major, darling," Flann answered, "it's just that I was having a hard time trying to recall anything civilized about our little scrape at Shiloh Meeting House."

"Amen," someone said softly down the line.

The major chewed his lower lip for a few seconds, told Flann to wipe off his grin, and turned around. "As I said, the Comanches and . . ."

They saw the galloper racing down the parade ground, his horse lathered in sweat. The rider's eyes were red-rimmed, his face ashen. He threw up a salute and dropped wearily to the ground. "Major Larson," he said, gasping. "Captain O'Brien sends his compliments, sir, and regrets to inform you that Moon Montulé has attacked the detachment at Atchison, sir. Captain O'Brien requests any assistance."

The major spoke hurriedly to Russell: "You will have the volunteers elect four sergeants and eight corporals. Then you will issue each man a rifle before beginning your march to Fort Zarah."

"Very good, sir."

"That is all. Good luck." Major Larson ran as he spoke, firing questions at the exhausted messenger.

"Good luck to you, Major."

Metairie, Bealer, Flann, and a foreigner from Memphis named Van Boskirk were elected sergeants. Their first duty involved issuing the rifles to the volunteers. Metairie hefted the first rifle from the wooden crate and stared. He had expected to pull out a heavy .58-caliber Springfield muzzleloader like Lieutenant Russell's guards carried, but this was a carbine, .52 caliber with a twenty-two inch barrel. Stamped on the top of the breech was: **Spencer Repeating Rifle Co. Boston, Mass./Pat'd March 5, 1860**.

"Bealer?"

26

The sharpshooter removed his glasses and whistled. He took the Spencer gently, thumbed back the side hammer, and, after testing the carbine's balance, nodded appreciatively and slammed the butt against his shoulder. Aiming at the flagpole, he pulled the trigger. The heavy hammer snapped loudly.

"I've heard of'em," Bealer said as he returned the Spencer to Metairie. "But this is the first I laid my eyes on. It's a repeater. Loads cartridges in a metal tube through the butt. Kinda like that Yankee Henry rifle, you can load her on Sunday and fire all week long."

Metairie saw the opening in the buttstock. One of the guards called for Russell. "How come they get those Spencers, Lieutenant?" the Federal asked.

Russell's face reddened. "I don't know, Corporal. Make sure they are not given any ammunition. Keep all of the powder and cartridges locked up. I'm not about to march to Fort Zarah with a bunch of Rebs that can outshoot us."

Gil stood by the fire, alone. His feet ached. It had been a long time since he had been put on a forced march. They had left Fort Leavenworth late that morning, shouldering their empty Spencer carbines as they followed the ambulance and three other wagons. Supplies, including locked boxes of cartridges for the Spencers and black powder and percussion caps for the Springfields, loaded down the wagons. The girl rode in the ambulance, although Metairie hadn't seen her.

The sun sank, looking like a grassfire in the distance. The far horizon blazed orange, while the clouds reflected yellow, red, more orange, even a little purple. Beautiful. He never thought he would think of Kansas that way, but here he did.

"Hello."

He turned, saw her, and stepped back, startled. She wore a plain blue dress now, and a wide-brimmed, low-crowned hat the color of a dun horse covered her hair. Smiling, she offered a hand. Gil shook it uncomfortably, looked around at the soldiers as they ate their supper. No one noticed him, or the girl.

"I'm Rebecca Rankin," she said.

He nodded and waited, before realizing he stood like an oaf. "Oh," he said. "I'm Gil Metairie, ma'am." He tried to smile, and quickly corrected himself. "Sergeant Metairie, I mean."

"Pleased to make your acquaintance. I was hoping we could talk some. With your beard gone, Sergeant, I almost didn't recognize you. Anyway, I'm glad to see you and your volunteers looking fit."

She didn't like the goatee. He could tell. "Thanks to you, Miss . . . ?" He had already forgotten her name.

"Rankin. But you may call me Becky. Miss Rankin sounds, well, awful."

He rubbed his hands together. The fire crackled. Neither spoke for a few minutes. Finally she asked: "May I ask you a few questions?"

Gil nodded. Rebecca Rankin was quite forward. He wondered if all Kansas women were like this. Or was she from Kansas? Back at Fort Leavenworth, the lieutenant had mentioned Boston. And what was she

28

doing here, going with an infantry company all the way to Fort Zarah, wherever that was?

"You're the first Rebel I've met," she said.

"I'm not a Rebel any more," he said.

"You know what I mean."

"Yes. I guess I do."

"My mother was an abolitionist, so that's all I've ever known. I don't believe my father cares one way or the other. The Army is all he ever considered. I find slavery morally wrong, as did my mother. Anyway, I would like your views on the issue. After all, you are fighting to keep the Negro in chains."

So this was it? Metairie removed his kepi, ran his fingers through his hair, felt as if he were some caged animal. *Friends. See the ex-Confederate soldier. Ten cents per man. Five cents ladies and children. Step right up.* Yet he couldn't get mad at Rebecca Rankin. Her soft brown eyes assuaged any anger.

"Miss Rankin, Rebecca . . . Becky . . . I never owned a slave. Don't know many folks who did. I guess I'm like you. I wouldn't cotton to owning a person, don't think it's right. But I'm not . . . wasn't I mean . . . fighting for slavery."

She frowned. "So you're using that pathetic argument of states's rights? Really, Sergeant Metairie." She paused, shaking her head but grinning. Her teeth were white. The smile quickly vanished, and, when she spoke again, her voice sounded strained. "Well, at least you served in a real army, not with Moon Montulé's raiders. Did you hear that he attacked Atchison?"

29

Metairie's stomach knotted. "Yes," he whispered, staring at the fire.

"He killed my mother," she said hollowly. "When he raided Baxter Springs in Eighteen Sixty-Three. Butchered twenty people . . . women and children."

Gil wanted to change the subject, talk about the Kansas sunsets, ask her a few questions. Lieutenant Henry Russell prevented that. He stepped up, put his hand on Rebecca's shoulder, and said sternly: "Becky, you shouldn't be here."

"I was just talking to Sergeant Metairie," she said, pulling away from the officer's grip.

"It's dangerous." Russell spoke to the woman, but his eyes locked on Gil.

"Oh, Henry," she said, exasperated. "You're not my keeper. I can take care of myself."

"I am in charge of this company, Becky, as well as your well-being. I insist that you return to your quarters and do not leave it until breakfast. I'll post a guard if need be."

Her eyes lost their softness, but she relented. "Very well, Henry," she said. Gil watched as she allowed Russell to guide her back to the ambulance. Metairie felt relieved, glad that hard-nosed Yankee had butted in, even if it meant he would probably not be able to talk to Rebecca Rankin again. Russell would see to that.

Gil didn't want to talk to her about the war. He wanted to leave that back East. He closed his eyes. Moon Montulé. Why him?

CHAPTER
FIVE

Sunday, September 22, 1861. Gil Metairie would never forget that date as long as he lived, although he had often tried. Earlier in the day, he had been sitting in Lohman's Saloon, nursing his second and last whisky, and listening to the excited voices of the men of Osceola, Missouri. Major General Sterling Price's Confederate militia had defeated the Federals at Wilson's Creek last month and was now marching north through the state. At Lohman's, zealous Southern sympathizers jeered Unionists while Mal Prudhomme, the radical abolitionist, sang from a pickle barrel that "God's will will be done." Gil figured he was like a lot of Missourians. Union or Confederacy, neither meant much to him.

Later that afternoon he stood, fists clenched, a bayonet inches from his chest, and watched helplessly as Jim Lane, the "Grim Chieftain," watched his miserable jayhawkers run from store to store, filling their saddlebags with booty — mostly liquor and money — and splash coal oil on the walls of each building.

"You can't do this, Lane!" Collin Evans yelled at the wild-haired Indianian.

Lane twisted his bony frame around in the saddle. He had a prominent nose, strong chin, thin lips, and a couple days' growth of beard. "Fifteen hundred men say I can." Lane smiled, revealing his rotten teeth. He had discovered weapons and supplies in a warehouse shortly after arriving in Osceola, declared that he would clean out Missouri of anything disloyal to the Union, "be it a Shanghai rooster or a Durham cow."

This wasn't war. This was plunder, outlawry. The jayhawkers torched the first building, a bank. Women and children wailed, so did several men, and, when a dog lashed out at one of the thieves, the Kansan shot the animal and left it dying in the street.

"Lane, stop this!" Evans ducked under the hitching post and shoved a soldier aside. He stared up at Lane. "You miserable bastard. You have no right."

Gil jumped at the gunshot. He had been staring at Lane, who never moved. Metairie's eyes found Evans, saw the young man stagger, clutching his chest with both hands, and weave his way toward the boardwalk. Blood spilled between his fingers, soaking his Sunday white shirt. He paused, swallowed, reached out for Metairie with a trembling hand.

"Gil," Evans said in a dull voice, "I think I'm killed."

The nearest jayhawker swirled, his musket still smoking, and buried the bayonet into Evans's side. Metairie cursed, hurdled the hitching post, and shoved the soldier out of the way. He turned, caught his friend, and fell backward, crashing to the street with the bloody body of Collin Evans on top of him. Gil sat up, cradled Collin's head in his lap, stared at the lifeless green eyes. How? He and Collin had played poker just last night, had sat on the back pew at church this morning before retiring to Lohman's. Metairie looked for Jim Lane but saw only the butt of the jayhawker's musket as it came crashing down.

When Metairie woke with a start, flames ripped through Osceola. Lohman himself dabbed Metairie's cut and bruised forehead with a whisky-soaked bandanna. Groaning, Gil sat up. He watched the flames, the thick smoke blackening the evening sky, and sighed.

"Lane's gone," Lohman said. "Stole just about every horse and mule in town . . . wagons . . . even liberated a passel of slaves. The bushwhacker even took Miss Sue's piano for himself. And Gil . . ." Lohman dropped the rag. "Them jayhawkers was heading toward your pa's place when they left."

Gil half ran, half stumbled his way through the darkness. His throat was raw by the time he topped the hill and stared below. The jayhawkers had torn down the fence, killed the milch cow, and burned the barn. For some reason, they left the house alone. Dazed, empty, he walked through the field, past the smoldering hayricks to the elm tree near the well. A rope swayed from a sturdy limb. Below that lay a body. Someone had cut the man down and covered him, although scuffed brown boots, pointing skyward, stuck out from the bottom of the woolen blanket. Gil dropped to his knees, closed his eyes, and pulled back a corner of the cloth. Metairie forced his eyes open, cringed, and quickly covered the face of his father.

"Gil?"

He turned, recognized the clean-shaven face of neighbor Bass Leigh warmed by the lantern held at his side. His other hand gripped a shotgun. Bass was sweet on Gil's sister, Arianne. A good man. Gil was glad to see Bass here. Arianne and Ma would need him.

"It was Jim Lane's men," Bass said.

"I know. They burned Osceola, killed Collin Evans, I don't know how many others."

Bass followed a prayer with a curse. "I saw the fire and come running, but was too late. It was all over by the time I got here. Your mother says they rode up here right before supper. Your pa stepped out, and one of the jayhawkers asked if he was for the Union or Confederacy. Your pa said he was for God, said the men were welcome to any water, but he didn't think he'd have enough flour to feed all of the boys. They laughed at him. You know how that went. Half the time I couldn't understand Baptiste. Always amazed you shucked your accent. One of the bushwhackers said . . . 'Where you from, mister?' Baptiste said he was Cajun, had left Alexandria in 'Fifty-Three for Missouri. Another fellow says that he reckoned anyone from Louisiana was a slave owner and anyone living in Missouri was a wolf or a devil."

Bass paused, glanced at the elm tree and blinked back tears. "They hung him, Gil. Made your mother and Arianne watch. Shot him while he swung. Then they . . . oh . . . Gil . . ." He fell to his knees, dropping the shotgun, and almost tipping the lantern over before

34

resting it on the ground. Bass wailed like a wild man, tried to speak but couldn't.

"Why did y'all leave him out here, Bass?" Gil asked. It sounded as if someone else were talking, someone far, far away.

"Your ma," Bass choked out. "She wanted . . . wanted you to see what they done. I told her it's best to cut his body down, was the Christian thing. She agreed to that, but . . ." He turned toward the house, called out Arianne's name, and fell face-first on the ground, writhing in agony. Gil rose, mouthed a silent prayer, and left Bass Leigh alone. He stopped on the steps, saw the delicate body wrapped in a quilt. Arianne and Grandma Susan had made that quilt, right before Grandma died.

He felt the boiling rage, could not control it, kicked the wooden railing savagely, and screamed. He didn't remember finding the flowerpot and smashing it on the ground, but the bits of clay crunched underneath his boots when he left the house. Everything went black. For how long, he didn't know, but he realized he was kneeling over Arianne's body, sobbing uncontrollably, when he heard his mother's voice from inside the house.

Gil rose, pushed through the door, and saw his mother rocking slowly by the fireplace, clutching her shawl. Odette Metairie had always looked old to Gil, but now she appeared ancient, a sunken-eyed skeleton in gray flannel, dipping snuff but not enjoying the flavor.

"Ma," Gil said, and dropped to his knees, taking her cold right hand in his own but too scared to squeeze it lest it shatter.

Odette found her spit can and sent a stream of juice splashing against the tin. "You seen what them Yankees did to your pa, boy? And your sister?"

Gil nodded, tried to hold back his tears.

"Promise me, boy. You promise your old ma that you'll see that them Yankees pay for what they done here. 'The candle of the wicked shall be put out.' Don't you forget that, Gil Metairie. Don't you forget nothin'."

He walked out of the house, found Bass Leigh washing his face from the well bucket.

"Bass," Gil said. "I know you'll look after Pa and Arianne, see they're given a good Christian burial. I want you to take care of Ma, too." Bass nodded slightly. "She has a sister in Helena, Arkansas," Metairie continued. "I'd like for you to see that she gets there. I don't want her staying here after . . . this."

Bass's head bobbed again. Gil wanted to say more, wanted Bass to speak, but that didn't seem likely. He walked down the road, toward Osceola, and did not look back.

He met Toby Greer in Jarrette's Store near Sedalia. A flat-crowned black hat topped Greer's rectangular head, and he wore a brace of Navy Colts tucked butt forward in a wide black belt. The brass buckle was stamped **US**. Greer said he took it off a dead Kansas bushwhacker. "Jim Lane's less one killer," he said flatly.

Greer was as thin as a fence post. Curly brown hair covered the top of his huge ears, and he sported a neatly trimmed mustache and unruly goatee. Sheathed in one boot top was an Arkansas toothpick, while the other boot held a single-shot .50-caliber pistol. Greer lit a cigar, smiled down at Gil, who sat on a bench, chewing the last of his dinner of bread and cheese.

"Jarrette says you aim to join up, fight the Yanks and murderin' jayhawkers." Greer puffed on the cigar, waited for an answer.

"Yes."

"Why?" Greer smirked.

Metairie brushed the crumbs off his pants leg. "Osceola," he said.

Greer's smile vanished. He cursed savagely and sat beside Metairie. "That's about as just a reason as there is. I'm with the Blackwater River Guards. If you want to join up, I'll take you to see the captain."

"Let's go," Metairie said.

The man didn't look like any captain. He sat on a camp stool, legs crossed, holding Remington .44 revolvers in both hands. Gray trousers were tucked in knee-high boots, and he wore a matching frock coat and a black brocade vest with rounded lapels. A yellow sash was wrapped around his waist, the ends dangling over the seat, and he wore a fancy black cravat and white shirt. His hat was black, the right side held up with a lady's stick pin with a wilting rose stuck in the leftside hatband.

Black hair hung past his shoulders, and a thick mustache and goatee hid his lips. His nose was straight, his eyes blue and far apart, his face and hands pale. Captain? He looked more like a riverboat gambler.

"I'm Captain Moon Montulé. You wish to join our forces and drive the Yankee tyrants from Missouri?" His voice had a feminine quality, yet his eyes were hard, bitter.

"Yes, sir," Gil said. "I'm Gil Met . . ."

"Smith," Greer interrupted and stepped forward. "He's Gil Smith." Toby winked. "I'm Toby Greer to my friends, but Toby Smith in the Blackwater River Guards. You'd best be Gil Smith from here on out. Them jayhawkers or Yankee swine find out your real name, they can make it hard on your family."

Metairie nodded. "I'm Gil Smith," he said.

Montulé smiled. "We have a lot of Smiths in the Guards. Welcome aboard, Private Smith. Vengeance shall be ours."

They were a miserable, rough lot, these Blackwater River Guards. Each man carried at least a brace of revolvers, and some lugged as many as four, not to mention the knives, dirks, hatchets, and muskets they bore. Moon Montulé also owned a long stiletto whose blade was sheathed in a wooden cane.

In the brush along the Boonville Road, they waited, watching the approaching dust. Metairie wet his dry lips, tried to steady his breathing. He swore he could hear his heart pounding against his rib cage. The Third Model Dragoon Colt in his right hand weighed four pounds, almost twice as much as most revolvers, but now felt like a bag of gold. His hands were clammy.

"Easy," Toby said. "Cock that piece now so the Yanks don't hear it."

The heavy double-click of the Dragoon sounded like thunder as the first soldier topped the hill, about two hundred yards away. Fifteen others followed. The United States banner flapped in the November wind.

"A regular Army patrol," someone whispered. "Real soldiers. This is gonna be mighty fun."

A blond-haired lieutenant headed the squad. Gil could see his pockmarked face now. The officer sat in his saddle reading a letter, smiling. Several of the soldiers whistled. One stuffed his mouth with a turkey leg.

"Perfect," Montulé whispered, and fired.

Gil ducked at the first shot, looked up, saw the lieutenant twist in his saddle. Dust popped off the dark blouse as bullets tore into the body. The letter and envelope dropped to the ground as the horse galloped wildly off the road. Twenty yards away, the officer fell from the saddle. The horse kept running.

Gunshots ripped apart the quiet afternoon. The sickening smell of powder smoke burned Metairie's nostrils, and his ears rang. A screaming wail pierced the brush as the Guards poured onto the road, firing, hacking, shrieking as ambushed soldiers and horses fell, died. Gil realized he hadn't fired his Colt, that he was alone in the brush. Montulé, Greer, and the others ran down the road, dodging panicked horses, shooting recklessly. One Yankee suddenly rose from the dirt and, gripping his shattered left arm, sprinted into the woods, only a few feet from Metairie.

"Get him, Gil! Don't let him get away."

Metairie swung around, aimed, but couldn't pull the trigger. The soldier crashed through dead brambles and vines and disappeared. Gil cursed himself, stood, and sprinted after the Yankee. Ducking under a limb, he saw the soldier. The dragoon bucked in Metairie's hand. Bark flew from a tree. The Federal screamed, ran on. Gil had missed. He swore again, ran, his boots crushing twigs and leaves, saw the trail of blood the Yank was leaving.

Gil gained on him quickly. The soldier turned, saw Gil, screamed, and tripped over a fallen tree. The Yank crawled backward, crying, his left arm dragging uselessly against the rotting leaves and timber. Metairie stood over him, thumbed back the hammer, and shouted: "Stop, Yank!"

He was just a boy, really, much younger than Gil. Tears flowed down the Federal's cheeks, and he lifted his good arm above his head. The boy's lips trembled, and he mouthed the word please.

The Colt shook in Metairie's right hand. He brought up his left to steady the massive revolver. Gil waited, unsure, realizing he couldn't move. Footsteps sounded behind him, but Metairie wouldn't take his eyes off the Federal. He didn't know why. The soldier was unarmed, no threat, and certainly wasn't going anywhere. The boy was as scared as Gil Metairie.

"What have we here?" It was Moon Montulé's voice. Slowly Gil eased down the hammer on the dragoon and lowered the barrel. He turned toward the smiling Missourian and said: "I got a prisoner, Captain."

"I see." Montulé stepped over the fallen tree, and shot the Federal in the forehead. The body snapped back at the bullet's impact, and the boy's right arm crashed to the earth as he let out a faint sigh. His sightless eyes stared blankly at Gil. Montulé cocked the Remington again and pulled the trigger. The lifeless body jerked. Montulé fired again and didn't stop until the Remington's hammer snapped on an empty chamber. The captain of the Blackwater River Guards waited for the barrel to cool before slipping the .44 into his sash. He stepped over the log, looked at Metairie, and said coldly: "We don't take prisoners, boy."

Gil should have left then. These Guards were no better than Lane's jayhawkers, but he told himself he owed his father and sister more, that he had vowed to his mother their deaths would be avenged. That's why he followed the Missouri raiders across the border and into Kansas in mid-December.

On Christmas Eve, they rode into the front yard of the Olathe Baptist Church. A tall man with a thick brown beard stepped out the front door. "May I help you men?" he asked uneasily.

"Are you the Reverend McCright?" Montulé asked.

"No, sir, I am Deacon James W. Lincoln. The reverend is inside, preparing for tonight's services. It is Christmas Eve."

Montulé nodded. "I am told that Jim Lane attended services here recently, am told that McCright doesn't believe in slavery or the South's just cause."

The deacon closed the door, and walked halfway down the steps. He was pale, sweating despite the stiff Kansas wind. "Sirs," Lincoln said pleadingly, "the Reverend McCright is an abolitionist, certainly, but he is a just man, a man who preaches against violence."

A Clay County man named Blevins wheeled his horse in front of the deacon. "Then how come he let that butcher Jim Lane in here? Osceola!" Several others picked up the horrible battle cry. Gil remained quiet.

Lincoln tried to keep from shaking. "As for Senator Lane," he said, "all men are welcome in our church, providing they are unarmed. We invite you to our services to celebrate the glorious birth of Jesus Christ if you leave your weapons outside. Please, gentlemen . . ."

Montule cut him off. "I do not care for the good reverend's politics," he said. "To let a man like that cutthroat Jim Lane into a house of God is sacrilegious. And as for you, Deacon, I dislike your surname."

He pulled the .44 and killed James W. Lincoln on the doorstep. Metairie watched in horror as the Guards dismounted and stormed into the church, screaming "Osceola!" Stained glass shattered amid the muffled gunshots, and, when the last of the Missourians fled the church, smoke and wicked flames poured from the broken windows.

"Where you goin', Louisiana?"

His father had called him that. Toby Greer hadn't known that, but somehow he had also labeled Gil with the nickname. Metairie dropped the reins to the claybank and faced Greer. They had ridden hard since

Christmas, dodging jayhawkers and Federals for weeks. The whole country seemed armed and angry over the Olathe, Kansas raid. Moon Montulé would be accursed like Bloody Bill Anderson and William Quantrill — or Jim Lane, for that matter. A full moon lit up the Missouri sky, reflecting off the snowy ground, and Gil had chosen tonight to desert the Blackwater River Guards. In this light, he could ride all night.

"I'm leaving, Toby."

Greer smiled, tucked his fingers inside the leather belt, close to the well-oiled, often-used Colts, to fend off the January cold. "Captain Montulé wouldn't like that, my friend. Yankees get a-hold of you, you'd scream for your life, tell them all about me and Moon and the boys."

Metairie shook his head. *Captain of what?* he thought. *A cold-blooded, black-hearted murderer who led those of his mercenary ilk.* This wasn't an army, but a ruthless gang. The Federals had already offered a reward for Moon Montulé's head, and the Army had orders to hang any of the Blackwater River Guards caught on sight. If Montulé gave no quarter, the Yankees wouldn't either.

"I'm going to see my mother in Arkansas," Gil said softly. "Then I'm going to join the Confederate Army. A real army, Toby."

Greer frowned. "You ain't goin' nowheres, Louisiana."

Toby's hands flashed, reaching for his revolvers, but Gil was already moving. He slammed his right shoulder into Greer's stomach, and the two crashed into the snow. Gil sat up, straddling Toby's thin chest, and backhanded his face before drawing the dragoon. He cocked the revolver quickly and stuck the long barrel under Greer's nose.

"I ain't killed nobody, Toby, and don't want you to be the first. But I've had it with this outfit." His gun hand didn't waver. With his left, he pulled the Colts from Greer's belt and tossed them into the snow. Gil rolled off Toby, found the long knife and boot pistol, and pitched those as well. He stood, staring down at the unmoving, unsmiling Missourian.

"I could kill you, Toby. But I'm not. I'm riding out of here, but if you move, say one word, I'll blow your head off. And if Moon comes after me, y'all may kill me, but I'll take a lot of you yellow scum with me."

Greer blinked. "By jingo, Louisiana. I believe you. You might be a damn' killer, after all."

Gil mounted the horse, shoved the Colt into the pommel scabbard.

Greer was on his feet now, but he didn't appear to be a threat. Toby smiled again. "Be seein' you, Louisiana."

"No, you won't," Gil said, and spurred the claybank into a lope.

His mother ripped the snuff from her gums and cursed. Gil had never heard his mother swear before, but she lashed out at him and stained his shirt with the contents of her spit can. "You coward!" she shrieked. "You forgotten what them Yankee swine done to your pa, your sister? They've made your poor ma a widow, boy. Why did you desert the Guards, boy? Why?"

Metairie turned away from her livid face, stared out the window at Helena's streets. "That wasn't an army, Ma. And I haven't forgotten anything. I'm joining the Confederate Army. Patrick Cleburne's from here. I hear he's a colonel under Hardee."

"Bosh! Those boys are fightin' in Tennessee and Kentucky. Your home's in Missouri. That's where you should be! It's the Kansans that killed your family, not some Ohio Yankee."

He sighed. Had he stayed with Montulé's men, he would have become one of them. And that, he could not do. His father would understand. So would Arianne. The only thing waiting for him with Montulé and Greer was death from a Yankee bullet or hangman's noose. Perhaps he would die serving with Patrick Cleburne, but at least there his death would be honorable.

"I'm sorry, Ma," he said as he headed for the door. "But I'm doing this my way."

He tried to block out her curses as he stepped off the porch and unfastened the hobbles and mounted the claybank. But even as he rode east, he heard his mother's words.

"I have no son. Do you hear me, boy? I have no son. He's dead . . . like the rest of my family!"

CHAPTER
SIX

Two weeks out of Leavenworth, the company reached Fort Riley. They had averaged twelve miles a day, which proved too much for several of the new Yankees. Weak from their stay at Rock Island, eight men collapsed during the march, and Lieutenant Russell refused to let them ride in the overloaded wagons. They buried Private John Davis, a man Metairie never knew, on the banks of the Vermillion. Metairie and Flann helped carry one of the remaining sick soldiers the rest of the way to Riley.

"Look at them," one Riley officer remarked. "Hard to believe them Rebs been able to whip our boys for so long."

Gil ignored the remark and rested by the stables. The fort had been established in 1853 on the Kansas River at the junctions of the Republican and Smoky Hill. Headquarters of the United States Volunteers, 2nd Regiment, had been established here, but Gil knew Company B would be moving out at first light for Fort Zarah, another one hundred and twenty miles away, he had been told.

Russell stepped out of the headquarters building, his ears crimson. Metairie smiled. He could only guess, and hope that the lieutenant had been severely chastised for bringing his volunteers to Fort Riley in such a wretched condition. "Corporal Crook!" Russell screamed.

The soldier sprinted across the parade ground to the officer and fired a salute. "We're movin' out at dawn. We will march only eight miles a day. That's an order from Colonel Caraher. The seven sick men are to remain here. Anyone who cannot make the march during our journey to Fort Zarah will be allowed to ride in the wagons. You will see to these orders, Corporal."

"Very good, sir."

Russell saw Metairie's smile. He glared and turned around, marching hurriedly toward the officers' saloon.

Rebecca Rankin rode in the ambulance to Fort Zarah. Gil had expected her to remain at Riley. He had not talked to her since their first night out of Leavenworth, and Gil wasn't sure of his feelings there. He would have enjoyed talking to her, but only about certain things. Maybe it was better this way.

Ten days later, Russell stopped the march at mid-afternoon and issued orders to make camp on the banks of the Little Arkansas. "Our volunteers look plumb tuckered out, Corporal Crook," the lieutenant said. "Sergeant Elliott and I will take a detachment out and scout for Indians."

A wide grin spread across Crook's sunburned face. "Very good, Lieutenant."

"You'll stay here," Russell continued. Crook's smile turned upside down. "Pick two men to help you guard our volunteers."

Crook squatted by the cook fire, cradling the Springfield against his thighs. Metairie filled a cup with coffee and offered it the corporal. Crook stared at the drink and Gil suspiciously.

"It's just coffee, Corporal."

Crook didn't move.

"Corporal, you have three guards, including yourself, with single-shot rifles against fifty men. If we wanted to attack, we wouldn't need to slip poison into your coffee."

Flann grunted. "Aye, lad. It's about time you darling soldiers learned that we have volunteered to fight with you boys now, not against you."

"Lieutenant Russell says you'll desert the first chance you get," Crook said.

Metairie nodded. "I suppose some feel that way. Not all of us." He lifted the cup. "It's burning my fingers, Corporal."

Crook smiled and took the coffee, took a sip, and made an awful face.

Metairie laughed. "Sergeant Flann isn't known for making good coffee, Corporal."

The soldier shrugged and leaned back, relaxing. Crook was clean-shaven with dirty blond hair, hazel eyes, and a cleft in his chin. Calluses covered his big hands, and, although he wore the double stripes of a corporal, his blouse still bore the outline that said he had once been a sergeant.

"Where you boys from?" Crook asked. "I mean, what outfit were you with?"

"Fifteenth Arkansas, Flann and me," Metairie replied. "Most of us were with the Army of Tennessee. Flann and I were captured at Missionary Ridge."

Crook sipped the coffee. "Y'all seen the elephant much?"

"Too much." This time Flann answered. "Shiloh . . . you Yanks called it Pittsburgh Landing . . . and Murfreesboro, Chickamauga, Lookout Mountain, Missionary Ridge, Richmond, Perryville. Seen a lot of men fighting, a lot of good men die."

"Blue and gray," Metairie added.

"Amen."

Crook shrugged. "I never seen much fighting out here, against Rebs. Was sick with dysentery last fall during Price's raid, so I missed that. But I've traded shots with Indians before."

"That makes us even," Gil said. "Flann and I have never fought Indians. What outfit are you with?"

"Eleventh Kansas Cavalry. We're all with the Eleventh, except Lieutenant Russell. He's all yours. I'll be glad to get back to Fort Zarah and be shuck of him."

"This Fort Zarah," Flann said. "Might a soldier buy a drink there?"

Metairie smiled and poured himself a cup of coffee as Crook began citing the virtues of life at Fort Zarah, off duty, that is. Gil checked the sun, guessed it was mid-afternoon. Russell and his patrol had been gone for two hours now. Gil sipped his drink — it was horrible — and looked around the camp. Most of the volunteers sat around their own campfires, frying bacon and heating coffee, trying not to break their teeth on

49

hardtack and jerky. A cavalryman stood guard at each end of camp, but they scanned the plains, not the former Confederates. For the first time, Gil didn't feel like a prisoner.

The tarp covering the ambulance flapped, and Becky Rankin stepped outside. She had let her hair down, and it flowed past her shoulders. After putting on her hat, she looked around the campground before spotting Gil. She smiled and began walking toward him.

"Corporal Crook!"

Becky stopped. Crook jumped up, spilling his coffee, and looked to the west where the Kansas trooper waved his slouch hat and pointed across the plains. Gil also rose, shielding his eyes with his right hand, and made out the approaching riders. Crook swore softly and ran toward the sentry.

"Flann," Metairie said, "get Bealer and come with me. Have Van Boskirk keep everyone else in line."

Metairie didn't hear the Irishman's reply. He picked up his Spencer carbine and walked after Crook, telling Becky — "You'd best get back in that ambulance." — but not stopping. By the time he reached the edge of camp, Crook and the sentry were talking excitedly, and Gil could see the three riders clearly. Two stopped twenty yards from camp, while the other rode in easily on a high-stepping pinto.

He was a thin man, carrying a Sharps rifle, wearing only a breechclout with long flaps, a plain buckskin shirt with long fringe, and a hair-pipe breastplate. His black hair was long, parted in the middle, with two braids wrapped in beaded tubes that fell to his waist.

50

He wore one-piece moccasins with the front seams beaded. His face was round, with a prominent nose and full lips. He smiled as he approached, raising his right hand while his left held the Sharps and the horse's hackamore.

Gil studied the two other riders as they tried to control their dancing horses. Each wore the same style dress, but their heads had been shaved, leaving only a long, centered tuft of hair stiffened with grease and paint, and a braided scalp lock in the back. Both men carried rifles, while one had a quiver of arrows and bow and the other held an oval shield painted red and black.

"Who are they?" asked a woman's voice.

Gil fought back a curse and turned angrily at Becky Rankin. It was too late to send her back, though, because the Indian had seen her. Bealer ran up to them and stopped, with Flann puffing his way behind.

"There's only three of them," the sentry said.

"That we can see," Crook corrected.

The Indian stopped his horse. "Ho-ho," he said in guttural English. "Soldier friends! I good La-ko-ta. Come in. Make trade. Want cof-fee!"

Crook swore again, faced Metairie. "Sergeant, get your men ready. Make them show off their weapons, but don't let the Indians find out they're not loaded."

Gil turned, studied Flann, his chest heaving, hands on his knees. "Did you hear that, Peadar?"

The Irishman panted. "Yes . . . Gil."

"Spread the word."

"But, Gil . . . you want me . . . to run . . . all the way . . . ?"

"Move!" Metairie spun around. "How about getting our ammunition, Corporal?"

Crook shook his head. "The boxes are locked. Lieutenant Russell has the keys."

"We can shoot the locks off," Bealer said.

"And blow ourselves halfway to Texas?" Crook cursed again. "Those crates are full of powder. Shit! Sorry, Miss Rankin."

The Indian stood by, waiting impatiently, no longer smiling.

Gil glanced at his empty carbine, sighed, tried to think. "How soon do you think Russell will be back from his scout?"

Crook snorted and spit. "Scout! He took the boys to a hog ranch ten miles south of here. Why you think some of them had to ride double? They won't be back till morning . . . hung over."

Bealer spit. "I wondered about that. But figured that lieutenant just didn't have no brains."

Becky gestured toward the Indians. "Maybe all they want is coffee."

"No, ma'am," Crook said. "Because that ain't no Lakota Sioux. He's a Pawnee."

"Ho, soldiers!" the Indian cried. "You no friend to La-ko-ta? You no trade us cof-fee?"

Crook sighed. "I guess we should parlay with them, hope there's only three and they ain't hostile." He looked at Metairie, licked his lips, and shrugged. "What's your name?"

"Gil Metairie."

"Gil, I'm Ben Crook. Thanks for the coffee, Sergeant. It might be the last I ever have." He turned, raised his right hand over his head, and called: "Lakota! Come in. We have coffee to share."

CHAPTER
SEVEN

"What's goin' on, Sergeant?" an Alabaman asked.

After wetting his lips and explaining the situation, Metairie barked out a set of orders. Flann would take twenty men and surround the rope corral that held the livestock. Right shoulder arms. Four corporals would pick two men and find sentry positions around the camp, north, south, east, west. The rest of the men would circle the three visiting Indians, act friendly, but don't let them touch your carbines. After serving coffee to the Pawnees and once Corporal Crook started his parlay, Van Boskirk and two men would sneak into the wagons and get those crates opened and ammunition distributed. "Quietly," he said. "Any questions?"

The Alabaman grunted. "We s'posed to guard them horses with empty carbines?"

"Poker. It's called bluffing, Private," Metairie said. "Move out."

Leaving their pintos near the ambulance, the Pawnees walked to the campfire where Corporal Crook filled three mugs with Flann's coffee. Metairie cringed. Peadar's coffee would either kill the Pawnees or start a bloodbath. But the Indians weren't served until Becky brought Crook a tin of sugar and the soldier liberally added cubes to the strong concoctions before serving the guests. It didn't help.

One of the Pawnees with a shaved head gagged and said: "No good. No good. Too bad. Much bad."

"Tobacco, then," Crook said, and pulled out his clay pipe. First Shaved Head nodded excitedly, pitched the mug of coffee into the grass, and took Crook's offering. Second Shaved Head held his steaming cup of coffee and seemed to be staring at the fire, but Metairie knew he was looking at the corralled oxen. At least all of the horses were gone. Gil had heard how Indians loved to steal horses. He didn't know what they would do with oxen. The third Indian, Long Hair, never took his eyes off Becky. Metairie didn't like that at all. He waited until First Shaved Head fired up the pipe and started to pass it around the fire, then backed up a few steps and eased his way to one of the wagons.

Peering over the tailgate, he asked: "How's it going?"

Van Boskirk muttered something in his foreign tongue — German? Swiss? Russian? Metairie didn't know — and shook his head. "Slow," he answered.

"If shooting starts, just break open the damn' things," Metairie said, and walked back to the fire.

"No whisky," Crook was saying. "Tobacco and coffee only. No whisky."

First Shaved Head grumbled. Long Hair gestured with his hands and said something in a deep guttural voice. Metairie moved closer to the fire, tossing another buffalo chip into the flames, fascinated by the conversation taking place before him between Long Hair and Corporal Crook. Both men talked in their native tongues, translating their messages with their hands. For soldier, Gil learned, Crook brought his closed fists in front of his chest, thumbs touching, then moved his hands right to left with the horizon. Most of the other words went too fast for him.

Talk became animated. Long Hair frowned, drew his flat right hand across his neck as if chopping off his own head. He said: "La-ko-ta."

Crook, however, shook his head. First he held his left hand out flat and rubbed it back and forth twice, then brought his right hand to his shoulder, extending two fingers, and moved his hand up a few inches. "Pawnee," Crook said.

Long Hair brought his hands to his sides, spit into the fire, and did not move. Crook's eyes met Metairie's. "They want to trade for whisky and guns. I told him we have neither. He asked what was in our wagons. I told him food and supplies for our soldiers. He said he's hungry. I told him we could trade some salt pork and coffee. He would prefer rifles or whisky. He insists he's a Sioux. I told him I knew he was a Pawnee."

"Which is worse? Sioux or Pawnee?"

"Depends on which is scalpin' you." Crook smiled. "If they just wanted to trade, be peaceful, he wouldn't have lied about the tribe."

Gil looked at the Indian. "Can he understand what we're saying?"

"A little bit, probably. But I don't give a damn. I've already told him he's a liar."

Metairie heard the shouts behind him, jumped up, and pushed his way through the crowd. Rogers had

56

mounted one of the pintos, whipping its sides with the hackamore as he raced west out of camp. Gil cursed, heard the Pawnees scream.

"That son-of-a-bitch!" Bealer cried. "He's desertin'."

"You yeller bastard!" another soldier shouted.

First Shaved Head sprinted, aimed his old musket, fired, missing. Spinning around, the Indian knocked a Mississippian off his feet and jerked the rifle from the soldier's grasp. The Pawnee brought the Spencer's stock to his shoulder, heard the snap of the hammer after pulling the trigger, cocked the carbine, realized the gun was empty. He spun around, grabbed Bealer's Spencer, and pulled the trigger just as Crook tackled him.

The Pawnee screamed, raising the unloaded carbine over his head. Second Shaved Head fired, blowing off the top of a private's head, then swung his rifle like an axe. Gil heard the crunch of bone as another soldier dropped. Metairie spun, shoved Becky to the dirt, looked for Long Hair, and saw him sprinting to the south.

"Aiyeeeee!" Second Shaved Head screamed.

One of the Yankee sentries ran to the fire, leveled his Springfield, and said: "This one's loaded, you red bastard." The shot lifted the Indian off his feet and sent him crashing to the earth ten feet away. Another shot echoed.

"Boskirk!" Bealer shouted. "Get them crates open!"

First Shaved Head rolled on top of Crook. Gil swung his carbine savagely, catching the Indian at the base of his neck. The Indian quivered, purged his bowels, and dropped in a heap. As Crook hurriedly climbed to his feet, the piercing scream cut through the plains.

"Oh, dear God!" someone yelled.

Gil saw them — thirty mounted warriors from out of nowhere had surrounded the fleeing Rogers, cutting him off. The pinto went down. Rogers screamed, tried to make his way back to the camp.

"Poor bastard," Crook said. "They caught him alive."

"Here they come!"

The Indians charged. The Yankee sentry reloaded his Springfield. Another shot cracked. Gil grabbed Becky's right hand and ran to the nearest wagon. He shoved her forward, and she tripped over the wagon tongue. "Get under the wagon and stay there!" he yelled, and looked inside.

"I need those crates open!"

Hoofs thundered past. A few muskets popped. Like a cavalry charge, Metairie thought, and for some reason recalled the infantry soldier's joke: You ever seen a dead cavalryman? Nope. But the yips of the Pawnees would never be mistaken for a Yankee hurrah. He heard the thud, saw the quivering arrow driven deep into the side of the wagon.

"Boskirk!"

The crate cracked. The corporal squatting next to Van Boskirk suddenly fell back, an arrow piercing his neck, blood pumping like an artesian well, spraying the crate and the other soldiers. Van Boskirk reached over, pushed the dying soldier aside, and pried off the lid.

Metairie turned. "Bealer!"

The Mississippian sprinted across the camp, dodging a Pawnee's battle-axe. Metairie was handed a long metal tube, realized it held rimfire copper cartridges. He handed it to Bealer, watched as the sharpshooter slid the tube into the buttstock of the Spencer, levered the carbine, aimed. The Spencer boomed.

Metairie shouted at Van Boskirk. "You see how he did that?"

"Aye."

"Get your weapons loaded."

Bealer was gone, chasing the fight, firing, crouching, running. Metairie grabbed a handful of tubes and ran, handing out the ammunition. He tripped over a body, glanced at it, saw it was one of his men, looked ahead. The Pawnees were gathering to the east, shouting. One dismounted, lifted his breechclout, flashed his genitals toward the soldiers. The Indians laughed. Long Hair raised a captured Spencer over his head, whooped, tried to control his dancing pony.

"They'll hit us again."

Metairie recognized Crook's voice. Blood leaked from the corporal's nose, mingling with the black powder on his chin.

"Bealer!" Gil yelled.

The sergeant had lost his hat, and the sun reflected off his balding head. Bealer shoved a fresh tube into his Spencer, cocked the carbine, considered Metairie. Gil pointed to Long Hair. "Can you hit him from here?"

Bealer guessed the range, shook his head, then saw a Sharps rifle beside a dead Pawnee brave. He tossed his Spencer to Metairie, picked up the rifle, smiled upon realizing the gun was fully charged, ready to fire. "Now I can," he said, and dropped to a knee.

The rifle cannonaded. Long Hair jerked, surprised, toppled from the high-stepping pinto. Several soldiers let out their own whoops. One yelled: "Take that you red son-of-a-bitch!" Shouting stopped. The Pawnees charged again.

Crook swore. "I'm out of powder."

Metairie tossed him his Spencer, threw Bealer's back to the sharpshooter, ran back toward the supply wagon. Gunfire resonated once more. A horse cried, his neck burned. Gil brought his right hand up as he ran, felt the warm stickiness, hoped it was only a scratch, looked in the wagon. Becky was inside, helping Van Boskirk load the Spencers. The other trooper lay dead, a tiny hole below his open right eye.

"Toss me a rifle," he said before the breath exploded from his lungs. The wagon spun past him. He crashed hard to the ground, felt hot breath on his face as he tried to roll over. He blinked to focus, knew a man sat atop him, saw the mohawk and hideous eyes of a rabid Pawnee. He freed his right hand as the Pawnee drove a knife forward. Gil caught the Indian's wrist, stopped the blade. The Pawnee's left hand covered Metairie's throat, pressing down, crushing him. He couldn't breathe. The knife moved lower. The Pawnee jerked, went limp, fell to his side. Gil rolled over, fought for breath, pulled himself up, saw Becky Rankin holding the smoking Spencer.

He took the carbine from her, levered in a fresh cartridge, leaned against the wagon, fired. The Pawnees swooped through the center of camp again, lifting the dead and wounded Indians off the ground. Amazing. Gil had never seen such horsemanship, or bravery. The Indians thundered off toward the west, stopped briefly near where Rogers had fallen. One dismounted, fell to his knees, hacked. When he stood, he raised something into the air, too big for a scalp. Gil shuddered. It was Private Rogers's head. The Pawnees whooped, then disappeared. Gil turned. The only Indian left behind was the one Becky had just killed.

He looked to the east, found the oxen, every one dead. Six horses littered the camp. One lifted its head, cried pathetically. Crook stood over it, frowning, placed the muzzle of the Spencer against the animal, and pulled the trigger. Gil tried to count. Two dead men in the wagon. He spotted more blue bodies on the ground. How many? He would have to report to the lieutenant. Was it a victory? Were the Yanks in retreat? He slid to the ground, leaned against the wagon wheel. Sweat and powder smoke burned his eyes and nostrils. His chest heaved. How many dead?

"Sergeant?" He couldn't see the face. "Gil, lad, can you hear me?" He recognized the voice, the Irish accent.

His head bobbed. "Yes, sir, General Cleburne," he said softly.

"Ten dead, fifteen wounded." Crook shook his head. "Plus, those red bastards killed every one of our oxen."

Gil sat up stiffly, gently touched his bandaged neck. He asked for water. His brain told him it was dawn.

Crook spit. "I'll see Lieutenant Russell court-martialed for this."

Flann filled a cup from his canteen and handed it to Gil. He drank greedily, then asked for more.

"We buried our dead, Sergeant," Crook said. "And I left that Pawnee buck with our oxen for the wolves. Son-of-a-bitch!"

Gil remembered the officer at Fort Leavenworth talking about a savage kind of warfare. He wasn't used to this, Crook's hatred of the Pawnees. In the Confederacy, they had respected their enemies. He smelled soup, turned, and saw Becky Rankin kneeling beside him.

"Try this," she said softly, and held a spoon to his lips.

Metairie swallowed, smiled.

"Corporal Crook!"

The cavalryman rose. Metairie saw the soldiers riding in, knew it was Russell returning from his "scout." Becky brought forward another spoonful, but Gil pushed it aside, apologized, and pulled himself to his feet. He weaved, fought off the dizziness, and slowly followed Crook to meet the lieutenant.

CHAPTER
EIGHT

"Pawnees? Corporal, are you sure they were Pawnees?" Lieutenant Henry Russell turned pale, and his bloodshot eyes made him look even more sickly. He wet his lips as Crook answered angrily. Russell could foresee a board of inquiry, a court-martial, perhaps a return trip to Fort Leavenworth, this time in manacles. If Russell weren't such an ass, such a fool, Gil Metairie might have felt sorry for him.

"Well." The lieutenant forced a smile. "You all seem no worse for the wear. I'll . . ."

The corporal exploded. "We buried ten men, Lieutenant. Ten! Fifteen are wounded, five of those can't walk. The Pawnees killed our oxen, all because you wanted to poke some two-bit whore."

"That's enough, Corporal. How many hostiles were killed?"

Crook shrugged, still fuming. "They took their dead with them, all except one. Best guess is a dozen killed, a few more wounded."

Russell considered Crook's report for a moment. Finally he nodded, and said: "That's twelve Pawnee bucks that won't be ravagin' and scalpin' any Kansas settlers, Crook. The major will find this good news, despite our losses. You play your cards right, and I'll see that you get that sergeant's stripe back. That's what my report to the major will say when we reach Fort Zarah."

Becky Rankin cleared her throat. "Do you want to know what my report will say, Henry?"

Russell turned slowly, nervously, his eyes pleading, lips trembling. "Becky," he said in a timid whisper. "There's no need for . . ."

She stood firmly. "Who do you think the major will believe, Henry? You, or his daughter?"

Daughter? Metairie glanced at Becky. Her brown eyes trained on the lieutenant like the bores of a battery of three-hundred-pound Parrott guns. He hadn't really noticed her military bearing until now. She stood erect, shoulders back, head up, tall, determined. Yes, she was a major's daughter. That would explain her military escort, why she was heading to Fort Zarah. Gil turned to face Russell once more. For an instant, he read the pending court-martial in the Yank's eyes, but the lieutenant was strong-willed, too, and he snapped out of it and met Becky Rankin's hard stare.

"You may tell your father anything you wish, Miss Rankin." He was in control again, cocksure, a career military man. "My report will state that I led a patrol on a scout looking for signs of any Indian movement, and, while I was gone, a band of renegade Pawnees, claiming to be Sioux, attacked the encampment of white-washed Rebs, three enlisted men of the Eleventh Kansas Cavalry, and Rebecca Rankin, daughter of Major John J. Rankin. During that fight, Army casualties totaled ten killed and fifteen wounded while the Pawnees suffered more than two dozen killed and wounded. Rather than pursue the hostiles, I decided it prudent to proceed to Fort Zarah, thinkin' of the safety of Miss Rankin and our wounded, hitchin' most of our horses to the wagons since the Pawnees had killed our oxen. I remind you, Becky, that I am an officer, and an officer's word is golden in this man's army."

Russell had made his point. No one could prove he had gone to a hog ranch instead of on a scout. His men certainly wouldn't admit to it and face Russell's wrath plus months in the guardhouse at hard labor, and, even if the Army investigated the matter, what would come of it? Go to the brothel? Take a whore's word over that of a so-called officer and a gentleman? That wasn't likely. The fight with the Pawnees had resulted in an equal amount of casualties. Technically and strategically, it would be called an Army victory. They had held their ground. Besides, most of the Army casualties were only those galvanized Yankees.

Henry Russell smiled. That was a mistake.

Metairie felt the blood rush to his head. Losing control again. His heart pumped, and he clenched his fists, about to step forward when Arthur Bealer spat and said: "Beggin' the Yankee lieutenant's pardon, but we really don't care much for bein' taken for fools, for bein' left to fend for ourselves with empty guns against a bunch of savage Indians." He eared back the hammer of the Spencer. Russell's stare fell on the carbine. Bealer grinned. "It's loaded now, sir."

The Yankees shifted uncomfortably as Van Boskirk, Flann, and other former Confederates hefted their weapons. A Springfield was cocked. "Secesh trash," a hung-over Yank mumbled. The lieutenant reached to unfasten the holster flap covering his revolver. Ben Crook looked confused, his loyalties divided between the officer he loathed and his duty as a soldier against these Confederates, his sworn enemy. A war was about to break out here, Metairie thought, and Becky Rankin would be caught in the crossfire.

Gil took a deep breath to regain control and moved in front of Russell. His eyes bore into the lieutenant, unblinking, and he spoke evenly. "Sergeant Bealer, lower your carbine."

"I don't think so, Metairie."

Gil never took his eyes off the lieutenant. Russell's right hand seemed frozen over the butt of his revolver. If he went for the Colt, Metairie wouldn't be able to stop a bloodbath. More than likely, he and the lieutenant would be the first to die. "Sergeant Flann!" Gil called out.

"Aye?" Peadar's voice had turned uncertain.

"If Sergeant Bealer doesn't lower his carbine in three seconds, blow his head off."

"Aye, Gil."

"One," Metairie counted, and turned to face his men. Peadar Flann had trained his Spencer on the back of the Mississippian's balding head. Van Boskirk had already lowered his weapon, and the rest of the Confederates stood anxious, confused. "Two." Bealer lowered the hammer and shouldered his carbine. Behind Metairie came the sighs of several of Russell's men.

"Killing each other won't do us any good," Gil said, trying to ease the hostility of his men, his comrades who had suffered together with the Army of the Tennessee and then at the hell hole called a prisoner of war camp. "We'll need all the men we've got and certainly all of the powder and shot if those Pawnees hit us again."

"All right, Metairie," Bealer said. "But Mister Russell better watch his back. He might get hisself accidentally shot."

Russell swore. "Damned if I'll put up with a mutiny." He had started to pull the Colt when Metairie spun around. Gil took two quick steps. His left hand caught Russell's forearm, stopping the draw, and his right balled into a rock-hard fist and slammed upward, catching the officer just below the jaw. The revolver flew one way, and Henry Russell the other. He landed hard, the breath rushing from his lungs, and he rolled over a few seconds later, trying to breathe.

Metairie looked at Russell's soldiers for a moment before glancing at Bealer, a smiling Flann, and the other Rebels. Sergeant Metairie, a peace-keeper. The boys back in Govan's Brigade would never believe that. Gil had a little trouble believing it himself. He picked up the Colt, blew off sand and grass, and rotated the cylinder until he rested the hammer against the nipple without a percussion cap. Henry Russell was safety-minded, carrying only five loads in his six-shooter. Most of the soldiers in the 15th Arkansas, those fortunate enough to carry sidearms, had never cared much for such precautions. Six beans in the wheel, they would say. Better to kill six Yanks than five. Metairie turned and approached Russell, now sitting where he had fallen, breathing again, and testing his scraped jaw. His face flushed as Metairie towered over him, reversed the Colt, and handed it to him, butt forward.

Russell snatched the revolver, cocked it, and aimed at Gil's chest. "I don't know what they teach you in that Rebel army, mister, but strikin' an officer will allow you to feel fifty lashes on your back . . . if I don't kill you myself."

Two cavalry troopers who had gone on Russell's "scout" ran to the lieutenant. Metairie just stared at the officer. He wasn't afraid. Gil had looked into the eyes of many men holding guns, and he knew Henry Russell wouldn't shoot him. Slowly the Colt sank, and one of the soldiers helped Russell to his feet. He holstered the revolver, brushed himself off, and barked out an order.

"I want this man arrested! He is to be shackled and forced to walk behind the wagons to Fort Zarah."

"He's injured," Becky Rankin protested.

"He seems healthy enough to strike an officer. He can walk. We'll see how healthy he is after fifty lashes and a month in the sweatbox for strikin' an officer and insubordination. Take this piece of Rebel scum away."

Metairie felt himself being shoved forward by the Kansas boys. He smiled as he went past Becky Rankin, and she smiled back. Peadar Flann gave him an overly exaggerated wink. Gil wouldn't mind the manacles. Iron cuffs had rubbed his wrists and ankles raw before. He had never been whipped, but that didn't scare him. What could Henry Russell do to him that hadn't already been done by Jim Lane or the Yankees at Rock Island? If he had to spend the rest of the war in a guardhouse at Fort Zarah, so be it.

As Gil marched toward the wagons, Russell barked out another order. "Corporal Crook, I want these Rebs disarmed before we move out for the fort."

Ben Crook cleared his throat. "Lieutenant, just who's gonna disarm them?"

Russell considered this for a minute. "Very well," he admitted. The Kansans were outnumbered. Armed with Spencers, one Union volunteer could match the firepower of seven cavalrymen holding Springfields. Russell refused to admit defeat, however, saying: "I guess it's best the Rebs keep the carbines. We might need them if we run into hostiles again. I want the horses watered, then hitched to each wagon."

"These aren't draft animals, sir," Crook said.

"I'm well aware of that, Corporal. But there are wounded men, and we can't leave them here. It will be slow goin', but this is the humane and gentlemanly choice. You have your orders, Corporal Crook. See that they are carried out."

"Yes, sir."

Gil had sat that evening, chained to a wagon wheel, guarded by one of the Kansas troopers. He had just drifted off to sleep. His head fell forward, and he jerked awake. Sleeping in this seated position with the metal rim of a wheel for a pillow would be difficult. His feet hurt from the day's travels. He wasn't used to marching in shoes, and his brogans still were far from broken in.

Well, he thought, he'd probably sleep better than Henry Russell. The lieutenant would be worried to death about Arthur Bealer's threat and facing Major Rankin. Hell, that ass probably wouldn't get a wink of sleep until they reached Fort Zarah. The chains rattled as Metairie shifted around to find a better sleeping position. His guard ignored him. Gil rested his head against the wagon wheel and closed his eyes, which opened when he heard Becky Rankin's voice.

"No visitors allowed for the prisoner, ma'am," the Kansan said. "Lieutenant Russell's orders."

"I'm bringing his supper."

The sentry shuffled his feet. "Ma'am, the lieutenant will tan my hide if he catches you here."

"And my father will have you in the stockade for a month if you don't let me pass. Who would you rather answer to, mister, Lieutenant Russell or Major Rankin?"

The soldier mumbled something, and Becky Rankin walked past him, carrying a tray. She knelt beside Metairie, looked at the handcuffs. "Can you eat in those?" she asked.

"Yes, ma'am."

She placed the tray on his lap. A bowl of soup or stew. Cup of coffee. Some hardtack. Metairie's stomach grumbled. He found the spoon and tasted the food. He still couldn't tell if it was supposed to be soup or stew, nor did he want to guess the kind of meat used. The coffee was bitter — so strong and awful it had to be some of Peadar Flann's — and the hardtack would have broken his teeth if he hadn't dipped it in the coffee first.

"It's not much," she said softly.

"Beats kush," he said honestly, and tested the soup/stew again.

"Kush?"

Gil swallowed and took a sip of coffee before explaining. "Back in Tennessee, we'd take cornmeal and bacon, throw it in a pot of water, and boil it till the water was gone. That's about all we had to eat, Miss Rankin."

"Becky."

"Becky. Called it kush. It wasn't exactly mashed potatoes, ham, and apple cobbler." Better than what we had at Rock Island, though, but he kept this to himself. He dug into the food again. She let him eat. She didn't speak again until he had finished. Soup and coffee dribbled down his goatee. Using the hem of her skirt, she wiped his mouth and face. Then she checked his neck wound.

"You'll live," she proclaimed.

Their eyes met and held. Gil finally looked away, remembering Becky's mother, killed by Moon Montulé at Baxter Springs. He had left the Blackwater River Guards long before then, but how could he explain to her that he had once ridden with those men? What right did he have to be in her company? What the hell was she doing here anyway?

"Would you like me to bring you some more coffee?"

He shook his head. "No, thank you."

Becky picked up the tray and rose. She bid him good night and turned. About five yards away, she stopped, turned, and asked: "Why did you step in today?"

71

"I don't understand."

"You could have let your friends kill Henry and the rest of us, then taken the horses and fled, returned to your glorious Confederacy. Nobody could have stopped you."

He looked away. In truth, he had considered that briefly before stepping in front of the pompous lieutenant. Bealer and the others, probably everyone but Flann, had thought of this, too, and probably hated Gil this evening. It might have been days before the bodies had been discovered, and by then the Rebels would have been to Missouri, or dipped south to Texas. He exhaled and faced Becky again. "I'm not sure about that, Miss . . . Becky. We would have had to watch out for the Pawnees, and we're not used to this country. We would have been caught, shot, or hung. I think your father would have trailed us to the gates of hell if we had harmed you."

"So you were protecting me?"

"I didn't say that. More likely, I was protecting my own interests, and my friends."

She nodded and a few seconds later asked: "Would you have let that Irishman shoot the other sergeant . . . to protect me?"

"No," he answered immediately. "I was bluffing."

Becky Rankin smiled. "You're a poor liar, Sergeant Metairie. But you're right about one thing. Father would have killed every last one of you if you had hurt me."

CHAPTER
NINE

A collection of adobe huts, dug-outs, and corrals, Fort Zarah stood on the east side of Walnut Creek near the small parasite hamlet that seemed to spring up overnight around these frontier posts. Neither the town nor the fort looked to be permanent. What surprised Gil Metairie was the fact that both burg and fort bustled with activity. Muleskinners cursed as they hitched their freight wagons, infantry soldiers drilled on the parade grounds and churned up thick clouds of dust, cavalry troopers groomed their horses in a series of fence and adobe corrals, while other Yankees, under guard, dug a drainage ditch away from what Gil's nose told him was the fort's latrine. Metairie spotted two small cannons at the east and west ends of the open compound, and an American flag flapping in the breeze atop a pole made from two cottonwoods. The town consisted of an adobe way station and corrals, one rawhide-looking saloon, a store, café, and a few hard-scrabble dug-outs and privies. Conestoga wagons and oxen far out-numbered the town population.

Becky Rankin was coming here?

Fort Zarah had been established a year earlier by Major General Samuel Curtis for protection along the

Santa Fé Trail and named after Curtis's son, Henry Zarah Curtis, killed in the Baxter Springs raid when Quantrill and Montulé stormed the town in October of 1863. *Moon Montulé again*, Gil thought. He could never escape that butcher. Metairie didn't have much time to consider this because, as soon as the wagons rolled into the fort, Lieutenant Russell barked an order and Gil, still in chains, was shoved into a dark, damp, one-room guardhouse. The door slammed shut, the bar dropped, and Metairie stood alone. He peered through the iron bars in the lone window, became bored, and searched for a cot or slop jar. Finding neither, he finally rested on the dirt floor, and with his kepi for a pillow soon fell asleep.

Tall and wiry, Major John J. Rankin, 2nd Colorado Cavalry, had the build of a telegraph pole, with a bronzed face partially hidden by a thick mustache and flowing Dundreary whiskers. His graying dark hair had begun to recede, and his gray eyes burned. He wore high black boots, blue trousers and dust-covered blouse, and held a fat cigar between long, bony fingers on his right hand. A blood-stained, white handkerchief was wrapped around his left hand. Gil Metairie could see no resemblance between the major and his daughter.

Metairie had spent the night in the guardhouse. That afternoon, the other prisoners were herded inside, most of them boys from the 7th Iowa, Gil learned, who were imprisoned for various offenses, ranging from drunkenness to murder. Those unfortunate enough not to be assigned the backbreaking duty of carving blocks from a sandstone bluff to build better quarters had to work on the latrines. They brought the smell back with them. Supper had been moldy bread and tepid water. One of the Iowans had introduced himself to Gil, but when he found out Metairie was a former Confederate, they avoided him as if he were a leper. Gil didn't mind. By now he was used to it.

The next morning he expected to be marched to the latrine pits, but instead he found himself escorted to headquarters. Headquarters? One would never have guessed that. It was a dug-out on a hill on the banks of Walnut Creek with a gunny sack for a door. Gil was shoved through the opening, where he met a red-haired cook holding a cleaver. "Next room," the cook said, and Metairie, chains rattling like one of Dickens's ghosts, ducked through another dusty sack and faced a bearded infantry captain.

"You're Russell's prisoner?" the officer asked in a bored monotone.

"Yes, sir."

"Next room. The major's waiting."

Another gunny sack. Another cramped quarters outfitted with three wooden chairs, a small cuspidor, and a camp desk, although this room was at least brightened by a couple of lanterns. Major Rankin, who was standing, studied Metairie for a full minute, then took a long drag on his cigar and slowly exhaled.

"Salute the major, you insolent son-of-a-bitch!" a voice bellowed. "And take off your hat, mister."

Henry Russell. Metairie hadn't noticed the lieutenant when he entered Rankin's quarters. The officer stood in the corner like a dunce. Gil glanced at him before returning his attention to Major Rankin. "It's hard to salute properly in these, sir," he said evenly, holding up his cuffed wrists, before removing his kepi.

Rankin's face disappeared behind blue tobacco smoke. Maybe he had smiled. Gil wasn't sure. The major removed his cigar and tapped the end, dropping a long ash onto the sod floor. "Lieutenant Russell," he said, "do you have the keys to release the prisoner?"

"No, sir. I left them in my quarters, sir."

"Fetch them. I'd like to see if the prisoner can salute me properly."

"Yes, sir."

As soon as Russell had left, Rankin sat behind his desk. "You're at ease, Sergeant Metairie," he said, and shuffled through a stack of papers. Gil waited. Rankin didn't sound like his daughter, either. In fact, his accent seemed almost Southern, a rich drawl that lacked the twang of the Carolinas or Texas, perhaps from one of the border states like Kentucky or Missouri.

Without looking up, Rankin continued: "I have heard and read Mister Russell's report. Striking an officer is a most serious offense, even in the Confederate Army. You should know that."

"Yes, sir."

"You served under Cleburne I am told. Is that correct?"

"Yes, sir. Fifteenth Arkansas. Govan's Brigade."

"I have heard nothing but praise about the late General Cleburne. I'm sure he would not tolerate your striking a Confederate lieutenant."

"No, sir. He wouldn't."

"What was your rank in the Fifteenth?"

"First sergeant."

"And you were voted a sergeant for the volunteers, I see. Sergeants must keep discipline."

"Yes, sir."

Rankin tested his cigar again, pushed the papers aside, and at last looked up at Metairie. "Lieutenant Russell's report is most damning, Sergeant. Yet, I have also heard testimony, unofficially of course, from my daughter. She says your actions against the Pawnees undoubtedly saved many lives. Becky thinks you should be commended, not disciplined."

"I don't know about that, sir. I just did what I had to do. Corporal Crook, Sergeants Flann and Bealer, they probably did more than I did against the Pawnees, sir. Bealer, especially. He killed the leader of those braves. And your daughter, sir, Miss Rankin, she actually saved my life."

Rankin nodded. This time he smiled. "I taught Becky to shoot myself." The smile vanished. His face hardened. "Yes, I talked to Corporal Crook. He also praised your coolness under fire. And I must admit I am not overly pleased with Lieutenant Russell's report. Taking several men out on this scout with many soldiers forced to ride double is not sound military strategy. Nevertheless, he is an officer, and I cannot permit an enlisted man, especially a sergeant, to be

77

engaged in fisticuffs with a lieutenant. Why did you strike Mister Russell?"

Metairie hesitated. He lowered his gaze, thought about the consequences, and met Rankin's stare again. "Permission to speak freely, sir?"

"Certainly."

"Lieutenant Russell is an ass. Again, I did what I had to do. If I had not hit him, the likelihood is that one of my men would have shot him. That would have resulted in a shooting scrape between your cavalry boys and my . . ."

"Your Johnny Rebs."

Gil fell silent. Rankin took another long pull on his cigar, knocked off the ash, and stood. "I am not an idiot, Sergeant Metairie," he said. "I am well aware of that notorious brothel near the site of your engagement against the Pawnees. I commend you for your bravery, especially for your help in keeping my daughter alive. I did not want her to come out here anyway, but as you might have learned, she is quite strong-willed. However, I am not sure about your loyalty to the United States of America. You've worn the gray. Once a Rebel, always a Rebel. Once a traitor, always a traitor." He held up his injured hand, showing off the dried blood. "We are in hostile territory, Sergeant. I don't have enough men, enough experienced soldiers to protect the wagon trains and settlers around the Great Bend of the Arkansas. I ask for more recruits, and I am sent Rebel prisoners. Perhaps you prevented a mutiny, perhaps even murder, but that doesn't mean you won't desert as soon as you get a chance. Then what do I do?

Send a patrol after you, risk the lives of the settlers and merchants I am sworn to protect? You put me in a bind. If you do desert, Sergeant, I will consider that cowardice in the face of the enemy. Your judgment will be summary. You'll be shot on sight. Am I clear?"

"Yes, sir."

Russell pushed his way past the sack, saluted, and held up the keys.

"Release him, Mister Russell," Rankin ordered, and flipped the cigar into a spittoon. He dipped a quill into an inkwell and signed a paper.

As soon as the manacles were off, Metairie flexed his wrists and rubbed the tender spots gently. Russell stepped away, holding the chains, waiting anxiously. Gil put on his kepi, and, as soon as Rankin looked up, he saluted sharply. The major returned the salute nonchalantly, rose stiffly, and handed the order he had signed to Henry Russell.

"Sergeant Metairie, you are charged with insubordination and striking an officer. You have pled guilty. Do you have anything else to say?"

Gil didn't remember actually pleading guilty, but he would have. No sense in denying it. He answered negatively and stood at attention. Out of the corner of his eye, he saw Russell grinning.

"I sentence you to one night in the post guardhouse and forfeiture of a month's pay. Since you spent last night confined, that will suffice for your imprisonment. You are hereby released to return to your company for further orders. Sergeant Metairie, you are dismissed."

"Sir!" Russell cried out above the rattling chains he held. "I must protest."

Rankin turned sharply. His voice rattled the quarters so much that dust floated off the walls. "Mister Russell, you left men charged in your care with no way to defend themselves knowing you were in hostile country. I could have charges of dereliction of duty, perhaps murder, preferred against you, and I would if I weren't short-handed of experienced soldiers out here. You went on an alleged scout with many of your horses carrying double with a stupid explanation that you wanted more men to get experience in the field. What kind of experience is that, Lieutenant? Don't play me for a fool, mister. Ten men are dead, another fifteen wounded with seven of those unfit for active duty. What's more, you risked the life of my only daughter, and, if she had been harmed, we would be meeting on the field of honor, regulations be damned. Now get out of my sight."

Russell's face reddened. He turned quickly to leave, and almost knocked over the bearded captain who hurriedly was entering the room. Russell swore and backed away.

The captain straightened, panting, and said between gasps: "Begging everybody's . . . pardon . . . but Major Rankin . . . I think you'd best . . . step outside."

Metairie followed the officers into the sunlight. A crowd had gathered at the parade grounds, officers, enlisted men, laundresses, even Becky Rankin, as a train of supply wagons stretched for about a quarter of a mile. Everyone stared at the convoy as if they had never seen a wagon train. Even the prisoners at the latrine had stopped digging and watched. Ahead of the wagons rode a long-haired man in buckskins and a flat hat. He would stop about every twenty yards, rear his white stallion, whip a Navy Colt from a red sash, and snap a shot into the air. Then he would shout, although Metairie couldn't make out his words. People standing in front of the saloon and store broke out in cheers as the wagons and rider passed. Then the post sentries began yelling. They dropped their muskets and broke into some sort of jig. The stallion reared once more; the man fired his pistol and yelled.

This time Gil Metairie understood. The words turned his stomach. "Lee's surrendered! Lee's surrendered to Grant! The war is over!"

CHAPTER
TEN

He sipped a glass of rye in the smoke-filled saloon where a couple of drummers well in their cups sat on the far end of the bar, one playing a mouth harp, the other a fiddle, and led the throng in singing "Battle Cry of Freedom." Bar? It was nothing more than two warped planks, ten inches by two, nailed atop a pair of empty whisky kegs. The chorus resonated loudly in the small confines of the soddy.

> **The Union forever**
> **Hurrah, boys, hurrah**
> **Down with the traitor**
> **Up with the star**
> **While we rally 'round the flag, boys**
> **Rally once again**
> **Shouting the battle cry of freedom!**

Well, not everyone sang.

Arthur Bealer, Van Boskirk, Metairie, and Flann sat alone at a table. Silent. Major Rankin had given everyone at Fort Zarah a pass to celebrate the Yankee victory, even the 2nd U.S. Volunteers, but not before explaining in no uncertain terms to the men of

Company B that they had enlisted "for a period of not less than one year," and that had not changed. If any galvanized Yank deserted, he would be tracked down and shot. The war was over, or it would be as soon as the other Rebel armies surrendered. Hell, as slow as the news spread, Johnson and the others had probably followed Bobby Lee's example and taken the oath of allegiance.

Bealer swore and topped his shot glass, then refilled Metairie's. If the Mississippian harbored any anger toward Gil after the incident with Lieutenant Russell, he didn't show it. Maybe he had turned his anger to something else by now, like the United States of America. The saloon's revelers swung into the third verse:

**We will welcome to our numbers
the loyal, true, and brave
Shouting the battle cry of freedom!**

"Vish they shut up dat damyankee song," Van Boskirk said.

Peadar Flann wiped his lips and grinned. "You lads do remember we had our own words for that tune?" He smiled, waited for the soldiers, townsfolk, and travelers to begin the chorus. And when they started "The Union forever," Flann stood up and sang:

**Our Dixie forever
She's never at a loss
Down with the eagle**

83

Up with the cross
We'll rally 'round the bonnie flag
We'll rally once again
Shout, shout the battle cry of freedom!

Of course, only the three other galvanized Yankees heard him above the Federal din. Flann crashed heavily into his chair, laughing, and downed his whisky. "I admit I lack the voice of my good friend, Gil Metairie, but . . ." He sighed, emptied the bottle, and opened another on the table. "I will say one thing about this fine saloon. They give a soldier credit."

"That's because they don't know you're a Reb." Bealer cursed again. "Four damn' years fightin' these sons-a-bitches, and it's all for naught. Hell, we should have stayed at Rock Island. We'd be free now, free to go home."

We'd be dead now, Gil thought, but he said: "I thought you planned on going home anyway, Bealer. Borrowing a cavalry mount and lighting a shuck for Mississippi."

Bealer refilled his glass, took a sip, and shook his head. "That was before them Injuns hit us. I don't fancy losin' my hair alone on that damned prairie. No, sir."

That prompted Peadar Flann to laugh so hard he sprayed the sod wall with whisky. Snorting, catching his breath, the Irishman reached over and removed Bealer's kepi, then rubbed the sharpshooter's bald head. "What hair did you think you might lose, Arthur, me boy?"

The Mississippian slapped Flann's hand and slammed the cap back on his head. "You're drunk, Flann." Still, he smiled slightly.

"Aye," Peadar replied. "But not drunk enough."

Metairie knew Flann would stay. Now Bealer said he would, too. He looked at Van Boskirk. "What about you, Sergeant?" he asked. "You plan on running home or fulfilling your enlistment?"

"Vat home? Sherman burned it. And you hear vat de major said. Desert and be shot. They say the scout with de vagon train . . . he shootist. Big man-killer."

Bealer pulled out a tobacco pouch, carved off a chew, and pushed it into his mouth. "What's your interest in us, Gil?" he asked. "You ain't plannin' on desertin', are you? Change your mind?"

Metairie shook his head. "I'm like Van Boskirk and Flann. Nowhere to go. Might as well stay here."

"Some of the boys will run as fast as they can," Bealer said. "No reason to stay."

"I wish them luck," Gil said, nodding in agreement. Someone fired a gun into the ceiling. A cloud of acrid smoke drifted across the room. Glass broke. The makeshift band began "When Johnny Comes Marching Home." Metairie wondered what would face any of the U.S. Volunteers who did desert and reached their homes in the South. Would they be welcomed home, or shunned as traitors to the Cause, branded a Yankee and coward? He had lived in the South long enough to know that answer. Proud people would not admit defeat, and they certainly would never forgive a Confederate soldier who had worn the blue. They just could never know what it had been like to rot in a place like Rock Island, that their only choice had been to enlist in the Union Army to fight Indians, not their countrymen, or die. It didn't matter. Gil Metairie had no home, no country. No family, either. His mother's words echoed in his head again, and he cringed.

I have no son. Do you hear me, boy? I have no son. He's dead . . . like the rest of my family!

Van Boskirk disappeared in the haze to find another bottle of rye. Metairie didn't feel much like celebrating, or drowning his sorrow in forty-rod whisky. He felt torn, glad the slaughter had finally ended, saddened for the Lost Cause. Arthur Bealer had been right. Four years all for nothing. Metairie's father and sister dead by Jim Lane's cutthroats, himself disowned by his bitter mother. Men like Lane and Moon Montulé would go unpunished for their crimes. Well, maybe not Montulé. He had chosen the losing side, and now he and Quantrill were sure to be hunted down and killed like Bloody Bill. Maybe Gil would be tracked down, too.

He finished his whisky and rose.

"Where you going, Gil?" Flann shouted above the din. "Van Boskirk's fetching us some more scamper juice."

"I need some fresh air, Peadar," he said. "See you gents later."

Outside, Gil rubbed his eyes and pulled on his kepi. The celebration had spilled into the streets. Several freighters passed a jug around a bonfire. Someone sang inside the store, and the café overflowed with soldiers, travelers, and townsfolk, keeping the hash-slingers and waitresses busy. Metairie stepped over the passed-out body of a cavalry trooper and looked at a white stallion tethered to the hitching rail in front of the café. It would be easy, he thought, to walk up to the horse, climb into the saddle, and lope out of town. South, he thought, to Texas, and to hell with the Army and the Pawnees. He'd take his chances. Who would notice on this evening? Everyone was drunk, or getting there in a hurry. But what would he do in Texas? Drift? Run for the rest of his life? Besides, he recognized the stallion as the horse the wagon train scout had ridden, the man Van Boskirk heard was a gunman and killer.

The door to the café opened, and Metairie caught the aroma of coffee and fried beef. His stomach growled. The coffee had to be better than anything Peadar Flann ever made, and the Army's supper of boiled beef and boiled potatoes certainly didn't smell as good as what drifted across the street. Then again, he had no money, and would be forfeiting his first month's salary. His stomach would have to wait. Best if he just went back to the post and turned in. He'd probably be the only soldier who didn't have a hangover tomorrow morning.

He rounded the corner and slammed into a body. A man swore and staggered into the shadows. Metairie had begun his apology when two hands grabbed his shirt. He was pulled forward and slammed against the dirt wall of the saloon.

"You fool. You . . ." The moon suddenly appeared from behind a cloud, casting a faint glow on the land.

Lieutenant Henry Russell released his grip on Metairie's shirt and backed up. Metairie finished his apology and straightened his shirt. He was about to leave when Russell whipped out his Colt, thumbed back the hammer, and pressed the barrel against Gil's throat. The moon disappeared again.

"I can blow your head off, Reb," Russell said in the darkness. "Say I shot you while you were desertin'. The major's orders, you know. They might promote me a full grade. And you? You'd be famous, the last secesh traitor killed."

Russell slurred his words. Metairie didn't have to see the soldier's eyes to know this time the lieutenant would pull the trigger. He could tell by the voice. Metairie could do nothing. If he moved even slightly, Russell would kill him.

Two singers hurried down the street, staggering, clutching each other for support. But they didn't notice the two men in the shadows, and, even if they had, they likely wouldn't remember a thing come dawn. A horse snorted. Hoofs sounded on the well-packed dirt of the Santa Fé Trail. The cloud passed, and Metairie looked into the officer's hollow eyes. Russell laughed. His breath stank of whisky and cigar smoke.

"I'll see you in hell, Reb," Russell said.

The horse snorted again. Gil looked past the drunken lieutenant and saw the rider staring at the two men. A match flared, revealing the mustached face of the Army scout. He lit a cigar, shook out the flame, and called out, friendly and homespun: "Whoa there, boys!

We're supposed to be celebratin' the biggest victory we'll ever see in our short lifetimes."

"Mister," Russell said, intense eyes still on Metairie, "you best mind your own affair, or you'll be seein' Saint Peter as soon as I'm done with this Reb."

The scout crossed his arms until both hands rested on the butts of two revolvers stuck butt forward in his sash. "Mister, you best turn around." He spit out his cigar. The voice had lost its friendliness. So had the scout's face. "You've already filled your hand, but I'll kill you before you can spit. I said turn around."

Russell's lips trembled. He tried to swallow but couldn't. Slowly he took two steps back from Metairie and turned to face the scout in buckskins. "Lieutenant Russell?" the scout said, only now recognizing Metairie's assailant. The officer could only nod. He kept the barrel of his revolver pointed away from the stranger.

The shootist said: "It's your play, Russell."

The lieutenant slowly shook his head.

"Then I'll take an apology," the scout continued, "and so will that fella."

"I'm sorry," Russell told the scout. The man nodded toward Metairie. Russell faced Gil. "My apologies," he said in a strained voice, holstered the revolver, and took off in an awkward run. He never looked back.

Gil Metairie breathed again. He stepped into the street, picked up the cigar, and handed it to the gunman. Up close, the man looked more like a dandy than a killer, fair-skinned with pale blue eyes and long, curly hair that smelled as if it had been washed in perfume. The scout's eyes fell briefly on the dirty cigar, then locked on Metairie.

"I don't fancy smokin' cigars that have been layin' on a street full of hoss apples, pard," the man said, his eyes and voice friendly again.

Metairie pitched the cigar away. "Sorry," he said. "Don't know what I was thinking. I do owe you."

The scout nodded. "You do, indeed. And Mister Russell owes me a cigar. Buy me a drink?"

"I don't have any money," Metairie answered. "And I'm not sure they'll give me credit."

"They will, if you're with me."

He turned the stallion and rode the short distance to the hitching rail in front of the saloon. *Well*, Metairie thought, *I guess I'm not going back to the fort, after all*. He met the stranger on the crude boardwalk in front of the saloon. He towered over Gil, and Metairie wasn't short, and looked like a cover engraving on one of those half-dime novels. The black hat was new with a low crown and five-inch brim, the white buckskins brilliant with the pants legs tucked into shining black boots outfitted with nickel-plated spurs and big rowels. And the guns? The revolvers were engraved, also with nickel plating, and smooth, polished ivory grips.

Metairie held out his hand. "Sergeant Gil Metairie," he said, "Company B, Second Regiment, U.S. Volunteers."

They shook. "Hickok," was all the man said, and he walked into the saloon.

CHAPTER
ELEVEN

Becky Rankin thought her father would pull his mustache right off his face he was tugging on the ends so hard. Ears burning, he sat at the breakfast table and listened to the report of Captain Bernard O'Connor, 11th Kansas Cavalry, as he informed the post commander that seven men stole horses, tack and supplies, and deserted at some point during the night. Privates Abbott, Melvin, Burke and Scott, and Corporal Hardee of Company B, 2nd Volunteers, and Privates Godich and Roden of Troop C, 7th Iowa. "Sorry to disturb your breakfast, sir, but I thought the major should know right away," O'Connor said to conclude his report.

Rankin freed his mustache and leaned back in his chair with a heavy sigh. Blaming himself, Becky thought, thinking he should have never allowed a celebration last night, should have doubled the sentries in anticipation that the volunteers would desert now that the war had ended. He said something, but his voice was so quiet the captain had to ask him to repeat it.

After clearing his throat, Rankin asked: "Where is Lieutenant Russell?"

"On the sick list," O'Connor replied. "We have a lot of officers and men at the post hospital this morning, sir." The captain tried not to smile.

"All right." Rankin stood, leaning his rail-thin body forward and placing both hands on the table. "Form a patrol and go after those men. You choose the men. It might be good to send Corporal Crook. He knows what these Rebs look like. Take three days' rations and fifty rounds of ammunition for each man. See if Hickok will scout for you, if he's sober. Have the Officer of the Day double the pickets tonight." He straightened, tugged on his mustache once more.

"When we overtake them, sir?"

Rankin's eyes flared. "Bring them back, Captain. Shoot them if they resist."

"It's unlikely that the Johnny Rebs traveled with the two Iowa troopers, Major, at least not for long. Even the Rebs will probably split up, make it difficult to follow them all."

"Use your discretion in the field, Captain."

As O'Connor turned to leave, Rankin thought of something. He called out, and the captain stopped with his hand on the door. "Captain, take five of the Rebel volunteers with you. Sergeant . . ." He snapped his fingers, trying to think of the name.

"Metairie," Becky told him. Her tone was bitter.

Rankin glanced at his daughter but said nothing. "Yes, Sergeant Metairie and four others."

O'Connor turned around. "Sir, you want those Johnny Rebs to help track down their comrades?"

"I do, Captain. They must not forget that they are soldiers in the United States Army now. If a trooper from the Eleventh deserted, we wouldn't question sending a patrol of the Eleventh after him, would we?"

"No, sir, but . . ."

"We'll make an example of these deserters, Captain. At the same time, we shall challenge those who didn't go over the wall to keep their oath of allegiance."

"Very good, sir."

O'Connor left, but Becky knew he didn't like the idea. Rankin sat down and tested his coffee. It had turned cold. So had the bacon and biscuits. He tried the food anyway, but didn't feel like eating. Becky stared at him, her food also untouched. The major drank his cold coffee, refilled the china cup, and said without looking at his daughter: "You do not approve."

"I believe you owe the Confederates the benefit of . . ."

Rankin looked up suddenly. Becky stopped in midsentence. "I owe those Rebels nothing, especially my trust. I trusted them last night, and they stole government equipment and ran for home. I should have known better."

"Like you said, Father, two cavalrymen from Iowa also deserted. It wasn't just the Confederates."

Rankin shook his head. "Five last night, how many tomorrow? This is some fool's idea in Washington. He has no idea what it's like to try to keep the peace on the frontier. I'm supposed to be protecting the Santa Fé Trail, but with these Rebs I'll have to become a warden, too."

"Father, I think you'll find most of these men to be soldiers, good men. If you could have seen the conditions these poor souls were in back at Fort Leavenworth . . . They were wretched, barely even human. I felt pity . . ."

He exploded, slamming both fists on the table so hard the coffee pot overturned. So did both cups. Becky jumped back but not before the coffee stained her white dress. Her father didn't notice.

"Pity?" He rose furiously. "Lest you forget, Rebecca, those Confederates murdered your mother."

"Not them. Those men weren't soldiers."

"Silence! Good men? Pity? What kind of fool are you, girl? Once these men wore the gray. Once a traitor, always a traitor. That's what I told that sergeant you seem so infatuated with. Jesus, perhaps I should have given that man the whip. You shouldn't have come out here, Becky. I wish to God you hadn't. Haven't you learned anything?" He paused for an answer.

Becky had never seen her father like this, but she hadn't seen him since her mother's funeral. When he had been ordered to Fort Riley and later Fort Zarah, John Rankin sent his wife and daughter to live with his sister in Baxter Springs. He thought they would be safer there than on the frontier, but he didn't count on Confederate guerrillas to raid the town. After the funeral, Becky's aunt took her to Boston, away from the slaughter going on in bloody Kansas and Missouri. But after a little more than a year, she knew she belonged with her father. Today, she wasn't so sure. She

94

met her father's cold stare. No tears. Not from her. John Rankin had raised her better than that.

"You taught me a lot, Father," she said quietly but firmly. "You taught me that to earn respect and trust, you must first give them. It's too bad you seem to have forgotten that."

She left him standing there alone.

The wind had turned cold for May, maybe because there didn't appear to be anything to stop it from the North Pole all the way to Texas. Oh, you'd find some cottonwoods along the riverbanks, and maybe a few ash and blackjacks, but for the most part the only thing that grew on these Kansas plains was tall grass. And buffalo.

Gil Metairie had never seen so many buffalo. From a distance, the herd of shaggy beasts, now shedding their winter coats, looked like a rolling sea of coffee. He reined in his horse as soon as he spotted the dead cow, held up his kepi, and waved it over his head until Hickok and the others saw him.

The patrol had split up shortly after leaving Fort Zarah. Two sets of tracks turned northeast. Those would belong to the two troopers from the 7th Iowa. Captain O'Connor decided not to pursue, and Metairie couldn't fault his reasoning. Godich and Roden had enlisted in Cedar Falls. If they were dumb enough to go home, they would be caught, court-martialed, and sent to the prison at Fort Leavenworth. And even if they didn't go to Cedar Falls, they were heading toward civilization, not to mention other Army patrols, and stood a pretty good chance of being captured. The other five deserters were making a beeline south, and they would likely find plenty of help in the former Confederacy to hide from provost marshals, bounty hunters, and the military.

A few hours later, those riders split up. Captain O'Connor led half the men, including three galvanized Yankees, after the two riders who veered off to the west. O'Connor let Hickok pick the men he wanted to ride with him. "Metairie, Crook, you, you, and you," the scout said, selecting Private Sebastian Slater, late of the 55th Tennessee Infantry, and two Kansas cavalrymen. He picked Gil and Crook because he had shared a few drinks with them at the saloon the night before. The other three were the closest to him, and hadn't talked a whole lot.

"That all you want?" O'Connor asked.

"Mor'n I need, Capt'n," Hickok replied.

That had been four hours ago. Hickok, Slater, Crook, and the two Kansans, troopers Arnold and Jameson galloped to Metairie, whose bay gelding danced nervously at the smell of blood. "First thing you need to do when you get back to Zarah," Hickok said, "is get yourself a real hat. That li'l cap of yours is hard to see." The scout eased out of his saddle, handing the reins to Crook, and walked to the dead buffalo. Shaking his head, Hickok reached behind his back and withdrew a long Bowie knife.

"Your boys got hungry, Metairie," he said evenly as he squatted by the buffalo's head. "Carved 'em a few steaks. Didn't do a good job, though. They is pilgrims for sure. Left the best part."

Gil couldn't see what the scout, hidden by the carcass, was doing. Finally Hickok rose, Bowie in his left hand and buffalo tongue in his right. "You boys might as well sit a spell, rest them hosses, and get some tongue. We'll catch up with them deserters soon enough."

The Kansan named Jameson dismounted immediately. "Good. I'm a-starvin'. I'll get a fire started, and we'll roast that tongue."

Ben Crook cleared his throat. "Somebody else must have the same idea." He pointed toward the horizon. Gil looked. So did the others. A thin trail of thick black smoke snaked its way upward into the blue sky, maybe five miles away, perhaps farther. Metairie found it hard to judge distances out here in the open.

"Sumbitch," Hickok said, tossing the tongue on the ground and sheathing his knife. "That ain't nobody's supper fire. Mount up."

The wagon collapsed, sending a shower of sparks into the air, as soon as they rode into camp. Metairie's heart had told him they would find a burning wagon, maybe a homestead, but he hadn't expected to see this. Clothes, pots, and pans littered the prairie, and a chest of drawers had been splintered into oblivion just a few feet from the ruins of the Conestoga. Four oxen lay dead in their yokes, and a woman sprawled on the ground, arrows protruding from just about every part of her body. A boy, barely in his teens, rested beside her, hacked to pieces. Both had been scalped. The corpse of a man, his head and torso burned beyond recognition, had been pulled away from the burning wagon. Apparently he had been tied to the front wheel and roasted alive.

Nor had Gil expected to find the deserters here.

Privates Sean Burke and Charley Scott, a couple of Georgians who had served in Gibson's Battery with Gil at Stones River, fought the spreading grass fire around the wagon with blankets. Corporal G. W. Hardee, one of the so-called orphans of the 9th Kentucky and no relation to the famous Confederate general, sat in a rocking chair amid the débris, cradling a doll while he rocked back and forth. At least Gil thought it was a doll.

"Mary, mother of Jesus," Hickok said. "Arnold! Jameson! Help them Rebs put out that fire. Reb" — he indicated Slater — "gather up them hosses. Metairie and Crook, y'all best keep your eyes peeled. I'll take a look-see." He spurred his stallion and loped out of the field of slaughter.

Numbly Gil pulled the Spencer from the scabbard, dismounted, and gave the reins to Sebastian Slater. He walked to the rocking chair and stood over Hardee. The Kentuckian's blood-stained hands held no doll. It was an infant, whose head was caved in. Metairie tried to swallow down the bile in his throat, tried not to lose his breakfast.

G. W. Hardee stopped rocking and looked up with pale blue eyes. Tears streaked down his dirty face. The lips under his thick brown mustache trembled. Metairie wasn't sure the corporal recognized him, even saw him, but after a few long seconds Hardee sniffed, cleared his throat, and said: "Hello, Sergeant."

"Corporal."

"We come across 'em. Musta been right after the Indians hit 'em. Me and Burke, we cut the daddy loose and pulled him from the fire." Hardee held up a raw left hand. "Burned myself a bit. Damn, Sarge, even the Yanks never done nothin' like this."

Gil remembered the Federal major back at Leavenworth, and his warning that this is not civilized warfare. But he also saw the body of his sister again, and his father's. Maybe . . . He chanced a glance at the dead woman and boy. No, even Jim Lane had never done anything like this, or, if he had, Gil had never witnessed it. He looked around. The grass fire had been put out, and the wagon had been reduced to smoldering ash.

Hoofs sounded, and Metairie raised the carbine and eared back the hammer. He exhaled with relief. It was Hickok, who reined in the stallion hard. His voice boomed, all friendliness gone and hatred in those cold eyes. "Pawnees, sure as hell, and them uppity sons-a-bitches left a trail a blind man could follow. We'll bury these poor folks when we come back. You Rebs, you got a choice. Ride with us or move on. I ain't wastin' no time with the likes of you when there's a pack of murderin' red bastards that need to be sent to hell."

G. W. Hardee rose. He wrapped the dead baby in his coat and eased the body onto the chair, rocking it gently. "I reckon we'll go with you boys," he said.

CHAPTER
TWELVE

Hickok swore and slapped his hat against the stallion's neck. A bright orange ball had just begun to sink below the western horizon, and the wind turned colder. Ben Crook also mumbled an oath underneath his breath. "They scattered," the Kansas cavalryman said. Metairie could tell that, and he was no tracker. Hickok had been right. Anyone could have followed the trail of the Indians, but now there were a dozen trails leading through the tall grass in every direction. Gil figured they would camp tonight and pick one trail to follow the next morning, but he wasn't an Indian fighter.

"What now?" he asked the trooper nearest him, Arnold.

"Turn back, I expect," he said.

G. W. Hardee heard the answer and bellowed: "Turn back? After what them bucks done to them po' folks back yonder? That the way you Yankees fight out here?"

Hickok reined his horse around and kicked it forward until he faced Hardee. Metairie expected the scout to rake the corporal, maybe even challenge him to a duel out here in the open, but Hickok's voice was even, calm. "Where you from, mister?" he asked.

"Kentucky."

"Cain-tuck. Y'all ain't seen Injuns since Dan'l Boone's day. So what do you know about fightin' out here, buster?" When Hardee failed to reply, Hickok gestured behind him with his hat. "I got a dozen trails to follow. I ain't got a dozen men. Trackin' 'em's easy in this grassy country, but, pretty soon, they'll be out of it, and we'd more'n likely loose 'em. I don't like this no better than you do, Cain-tuck, but that's life in Kansas. We'll go back, give them settlers a Christian burial, and head back to Zarah."

Hickok pulled his hat on his head angrily and spurred the stallion. Metairie followed. He was surprised when Hardee, Burke, and Scott turned their stolen mounts around and took the rear. They could have galloped away, headed for Texas or parts unknown, and Hickok wouldn't have cared.

The next morning, they buried the family beside the burned wagon. Charley Scott fashioned crosses from the destroyed chest of drawers, while Gil searched the scattered belongings for a letter or something that would tell them who they were burying, perhaps an address so friends or family could be notified. He found nothing, though. Whoever they were, husband and wife, son, and baby girl, they would soon be forgotten.

Hickok's Christian funeral had been a simple — "Rest in peace." Scott, Burke, and Crook crossed themselves. Metairie simply mouthed an "Amen." They left the graves of the unknown settlers, leaving the oxen for the buzzards and wolves. Gil tried not to think about it, but he had to wonder if the wolves would dig up the bodies, too.

No one spoke the rest of the morning.

In fact, few words were exchanged during the entire trip back to Fort Zarah.

"I see you caught the vermin," Lieutenant Russell greeted the party at the corrals. "Good job, Hickok, Corporal Crook." He looked at the three deserters, and smiled. "You boys should have put up a fight. Wild Bill would have made it quick on you. Now you'll face a court-martial and firing squad."

"We didn't bring them back, Lieutenant," Ben Crook said.

Russell looked dumbfounded. "What do you mean?"

"Well, sir, they simply come along on their own accord."

"Huh?"

"With the lieutenant's permission, sir, I'll make my report to the major."

Still, Russell had an escort lead Hardee, Burke, and Scott to the guardhouse while the rest of the patrol groomed their horses. All except Hickok, that is. He rode to the saloon.

If Lieutenant Henry Russell longed to see the deserters shot, he got no satisfaction. The three men weren't even whipped. After hearing Crook's report, Major Rankin decided to reduce the charge to absent without leave. They were fined two months' salary and sentenced to one week at hard labor. Gil didn't think the major was being charitable. More than likely, he didn't want to shoot any men he had or send them to Leavenworth. John J. Rankin had enough problems.

102

While Metairie had been gone, three other men had deserted. The night he came back, two more went over the wall. Of the five who deserted, three were former Confederates.

That afternoon, Captain Bernard O'Connor led his detail back to Fort Zarah. He brought Privates Abbott and Melvin with him, strapped face down, on a horse led by a dismounted cavalryman.

"They put up a fight?" an officer asked.

O'Connor replied stiffly: "Not against us."

The captain made his report at headquarters. Almost immediately Rankin ordered a full assembly at the parade grounds. Even the prisoners digging the latrines and building new quarters had to fall in. Gil Metairie stood at attention, staring at the two bodies, bedrolls draped over them, on the horse near the flagpole. He knew the men must be Abbott and Melvin. Some 2nd Colorado boys stood by the bodies, but they weren't what Gil would call an honor guard.

"Gentleman," Rankin finally began. "I have pleaded with you as soldiers over the past couple of days to fulfill your duty as soldiers, as honorable men. What that has netted me is fifteen desertions. You men of the Second Volunteers as well as those of the Second Colorado, Eleventh Kansas, and Seventh Iowa seem to believe that because General Lee surrendered to General Grant in Virginia, more than a thousand miles from here, that your duty is over with.

"That is far from the truth. We need soldiers more than ever on the Great Bend. Corporal Crook reported that the Pawnees struck a lone family traveling by wagon. Massacred them all. The wife ravaged. An infant girl brained."

That wasn't totally accurate. The dead woman had been fully clothed. Hickok had said that the Indians probably would have raped her, but she likely had put up a hard fight and forced them to kill her.

Rankin went on. "I have said that any man deserting will be shot on sight. Three men returned on their own accord. If any deserter is caught from now on, I will have them shot. But it's not just me that you have to fear." He nodded at the troopers standing beside the horse.

The bodies were lifted and carried in front of Rankin, unceremoniously dumped on the ground between the major and the entire post. Rawhide thongs were cut with Barlow knives and the bedrolls pulled off the corpses, followed by a collective gasp. A private near Peadar Flann dropped to his knees and vomited. The post chaplain began reciting the Lord's Prayer.

Metairie remained at ease. He had known what to expect. He had seen the family at the burning wagon. Abbott and Melvin were naked, hacked worse than if they had been caught in an enfilade of Yankee grapeshot and canister. Abbott had been scalped, his ears sawed off as trophies. Melvin would have been scalped, but he was balder than Arthur Bealer. His eyeballs had been plucked out, by vultures or Pawnees, Metairie didn't know. He wondered, though, if John Rankin enjoyed this.

Rankin was a hard one to figure. He had been fair, probably more than fair, with Metairie, and maybe even with Scott, Hardee, and Burke. But not always. And was this ghastly display necessary? Gil wasn't sure. He was glad he wasn't an officer, glad he didn't want to pursue the Army as a career.

"Dear God."

Metairie recognized the faint voice. He couldn't help himself, and turned toward the headquarters. Becky Rankin stood in front of the gunny-sack door, with a clear view at the bodies of what once had been two Texas horse soldiers from McCown's Division. For some bizarre reason, the old Rebel joke played in his mind again: Ever seen a dead cavalryman? Well, the officer at Leavenworth had been right. This was a different kind of war. Gil recovered, looked back at the major. Rankin had also heard his daughter. With a curt nod from the commanding officer, the Colorado cavalrymen quickly covered the corpses.

John J. Rankin stepped forward, hands behind his back, and looked down the long row of soldiers. "The War of the Rebellion is over, gentleman," he said after a long while. "But there is still a war in Kansas to be fought . . . and won."

"You think I was wrong yesterday," Rankin told his daughter over supper the following evening. They hadn't spoken since before his mandatory assembly, hadn't even seen each other since the incident on the parade ground.

"I did not say that," she said.

Rankin nodded. "That display yesterday . . . I did not intend for you to see those dead Rebs. That was merely a show for the soldiers I command. I apologize if it frightened you."

"I wasn't frightened, Father." She wanted to add — *But I was disgusted and ashamed.* — but decided to hold her tongue.

"Well, good." He struggled for words, sipped his coffee, and began. "It worked, you know, Rebecca. No one tried to desert last night. Not even those traitorous Rebs."

She started, faltered, decided it wasn't worth a fight. Rankin seemed pleased at this. He smiled, picked at his stewed cabbage, and said: "I have heeded your advice." He let it stand at that, waiting.

"What?" she asked quickly.

"To trust your Rebels. I'm having several squads sent out at first light tomorrow, with orders to guard the way stations in our jurisdiction. Actually, the Pawnees convinced me to do it. I'll let your secessionist friends fend for themselves. Oh, I'll send some loyalists with them, just to make sure. If they run, they'll be shot, by us or the savages. What do you think your Sergeant Metairie will do, Becky?"

She didn't answer. She was already heading for the door.

"Come on, Metairie," Hickok said. "Let's get drunk."

Gil smiled. "I don't have a pass . . ."

The scout grabbed him by his arm and yanked him off the corral post. "You do now," Hickok said. "It's best you learn the way things work in this man's army." He didn't let go until they stood by the sentries. "The sergeant's got my permission to leave the post," Hickok told the two Iowans. "Y'all savvy?"

"Yes, sir," one answered timidly.

"Good. We won't be gone long. Just to wet our windpipes."

Hickok didn't speak again until they sat at a table in the saloon with two glasses and a bottle of rye, or what the label said was rye. Gil wasn't so sure after the first drink. Hickok bit the end off a cigar and fired it up with a lucifer, puffed for several seconds, then spit, handed Metairie a cigar, and said: "Corporal Crook tells me you're bein' sent to guard a station between here and Fort Larned."

"I haven't heard . . ."

" 'Course, you ain't. Rankin probably figures if he tells y'all Rebs you're bein' sent to fight, you'll likely hightail it out of here. The major ain't never fought you boys. He don't know y'all like I do. I saw a good many men die at Pea Ridge, Elkhorn Tavern, whatever you wanna call it. Anyway, I'll tell you the way it's gonna be, 'cause you won't have me to protect your Rebel ass out there."

"Where . . . ?"

"I gotta lead a train back to Leavenworth. So I got to teach you about Injun fightin' in an hour. It's easy. First, make two camps at night. If you're on a scout, camp early and cook your grub. Small fires. Less smoke the better. Then put them fires out and move out a couple more miles. Sleep with your guns cocked, horses picketed right beside you. If you're trailin' them red bastards, Pawnees, Sioux, Kiowas, Cheyennes, it don't

107

matter, when they scatter, give up the chase. Don't split your men. Don't think that Injuns won't attack at night. For some tribes, it goes ag'in' their religion, but most'll hit you any time, any place. Savvy this . . . Injuns are people, individuals. That means what one does don't mean another'll do the same thing. Some of them boys is whiter than you or me. Others have a heart blacker than that sorry sumbitch Henry Russell. If you happen to find an encampment, hit hard and fast. Don't take time to pick your target. An eight-year-old snot-nose or eighty-year-old bitch is just as likely to blow your head off as a Cheyenne dog soldier. And if you run 'em off, first thing you need to do is kill the pony herd. Every last one of them. It ain't a job I like, but if you try to bring them hosses back, them bucks will steal 'em back from under your noses, sure as I'm sittin' here. Likely steal some of your own hosses, too. Oh, and buy yourself a real hat before you take off in the mornin'. That kepi ain't worth a spit out here. You'll be burned blacker than that pilgrim we buried the other day. Now that's all I gotta say. Let's get drunk."

Metairie only shared a couple of drinks with Hickok before leaving. He didn't want to be in his cups if he was leaving the fort tomorrow for who knew how long, and he didn't want to stagger back to Zarah and find that the two sentries Hickok had bullied had been replaced. Wild Bill didn't mind. He had spotted a game of five-card draw going at the neighboring table.

After stepping outside and filling his lungs with fresh air, Gil tugged on his goatee, pitched the half-smoked cigar into the street, and was about to head back to the post when he heard the man behind him. He turned on instinct and stared into the smiling face of a man he immediately recognized. The voice hadn't changed over the past few years either. Gil Metairie had hoped he would never hear the voice, never see the face again.

"Hello, Louisiana," Toby Greer said.

CHAPTER
THIRTEEN

Greer had changed. A jagged scar stretched from his right eyebrow to his curly hair, disappearing somewhere underneath his black porkpie hat, and a thick brown beard now replaced the thin mustache and ragged goatee, but there was no mistaking those big ears and a killer's smile. He wore a collarless blue flannel shirt and yellow bandanna instead of the shoddily made woolen guerrilla shirt and red kerchief that identified him as a Blackwater River Guard during raids, and two holsters protected the Navy Colts that had once been stuck in a wide belt. Gil glanced at Toby's scuffed boots. The knife and boot pistol were also gone.

Grinning widely, the guerrilla reached out casually and fingered the brass buttons on Metairie's blouse. "The Yankee Army must not feed you much, Gil," he said amicably. "You're a lot thinner than you used to be." He lowered his hand, stuck his thumbs in his gun belt, and shook his head, although the smile and friendly voice never wavered. "The colonel will be mighty disappointed in you, Gil. It broke his heart, you know, when you deserted us. I told him you was goin' to join a real army. It'd hurt him mighty bad now to see you decided the Yanks was a real army."

110

Metairie remained silent. He didn't have to explain anything to Toby Greer. Hell, Greer knew he had joined Cleburne's outfit, and he knew Metairie had volunteered in the Union Army for the sole purpose of saving his life. And what was with this colonel? Had Montulé promoted himself from captain during the past three years? No one else recognized Montulé's rank, certainly not men like Patrick Cleburne and Robert E. Lee, and only the most venomous fire-breathing secessionists would call the Blackwater River Guards part of the Confederate Army. Just then something Greer had said struck Metairie. *The colonel will be mighty disappointed in you. Will be. Was Montulé here?*

"You're a long way from Missouri, Toby," Gil said at last.

Greer laughed. "Well," he said, "Missouri isn't such a safe place for me, old friend. Did you hear about Billy Quantrill?"

Metairie shook his head.

"Yanks caught him in Kentucky this month. Shot him pretty bad. They said he fell into a pile of horseshit, couldn't move nothin' but his head. Anyway, with Bloody Bill dead and Captain Quantrill caught, likely dying, the colonel decided we'd best scatter. Figured I'd light a shuck west. Colorado maybe. Try my hand at minin' for gold."

Maybe Montulé wasn't here, Gil thought, if they had scattered like the Pawnees after a raid. "So you're just passing through?"

He laughed again. "Curious, ain't you. Actually, I got me a job freightin'. Needed a road stake. I was more than fair to middlin' with a jerkline, you see. Had me a job with an outfit in Sedalia. 'Least, I did before the Red Legs butchered my wife and baby boy." The smile had vanished. "You see, Gil, I ain't forgotten what them bluebellies done to my family."

Gil's eyes hardened. He stared at Greer waiting to see if he made a play. No, he finally decided, Toby wasn't going to try to kill him. Not here. Not now. "You'd best move on, Toby," he said. "With all the Federals around, Fort Zarah isn't safe."

Toby laughed. "Safer than Missouri, Gil. They'd hang me in Missouri. They'd hang you, too. Be seein' you." He started for the saloon, but stopped when Metairie said: "No, you won't."

Greer turned back, his eyes dancing with humor. "That's what you said back in Missouri, ol' pardner. Remember? But you was wrong then, too." He disappeared inside the saloon.

Metairie dodged a staggering drunk and moved away from the saloon, not really knowing where he was going. He should have been heading back to the post, but he found himself leaning against a corral beside the adobe way station, staring at the horses in the moonlight. On the ground by the gate, he spotted a light saddle, one of those made especially for the short-lived Pony Express riders, only this one lacked the leather mail pouch Missouri saddle maker Israel Landis had designed. No bridle, but he found a hackamore wrapped around a fencepost, and there was

112

sure to be a blanket around. He picked out a sorrel gelding that looked strong and fast. Metairie had never been the best horseman around, but the sorrel looked like it could take him far from Fort Zarah, far from Toby Greer. Yet he had no firearm. His Spencer waited back at the post. Head back, grab the carbine and a handful of loading tubes, tell the sentries Hickok wanted to do some night shooting. Risky, that was for certain. What if he met Hickok on the way back? What if the guards had been relieved? What if Lieutenant Russell saw him? Or Toby Greer? He was thinking too much. He should saddle up the gelding and ride out now, consequences be damned. Guns were easy enough to come by on the frontier. If he stayed here with Greer, he was sure to hang or be shot.

"What are you thinking?"

He jumped, spun around, and almost tripped into a pile of horse apples. Becky Rankin stood by a water trough off to the side of the adobe station. "Sorry," she said, "didn't mean to startle you."

Metairie's heart began to slow. He walked away from the corral, stood across from Becky in front of the trough. He tried to think of something to say, couldn't, and reached with his right hand into the cold water, made a few waves, listened to the soothing sound of the water sloshing against the cottonwood sides. He looked up at her. "Nice night," he said.

"Yes."

Another long, awkward pause. "I reckon I should be getting back to the fort."

"I suppose so. We wouldn't want you shot for desertion."

She knew. He figured he should make some sort of explanation. "Hickok's doing," he said. "Wanted to give me a few pointers on Indian fighting. I left him in the saloon. Figured I'd walk a spell before turning in. I guess the major ... your father ... wouldn't understand."

"Nor would Lieutenant Russell."

"You're right. I'd best get back before I wind up in the guardhouse and out another month's pay."

She started to say something, stopped, and looked past him at the corral. "You could go," she said softly, not looking at him. "No one would stop you. You could be in the Nations in a couple of days maybe, then in Texas. Go home. Where was it you told me you were from?"

"I don't believe I did. I enlisted in Arkansas. Was born in Louisiana." Should he continue? Part of him said no, but he added: "My home was on a farm in Osceola."

Their eyes met. An ox in a neighboring corral kicked a feed pail, but neither flinched. He wasn't sure Becky even heard it. After another silent minute, Becky reached into the trough and watched the ripples. "Why don't you go home now?"

"No home to go to," he said. "No family. I didn't ..." He waited, trying to think about what he wanted to say, what he should and shouldn't say. Finally she looked up from the trough. Her eyes were soft. He thought she might have been crying tonight, but it was hard to tell in the moonlight. He let out a long breath, inhaled deeply, let the air out slowly and continued: "When the war broke out, I guess I never really thought of what I would do when it ended, no matter which side won."

"You're not interested in the Army as a career?"

"Not hardly. No offense, ma'am. I know your father must be a military man."

"Militia," she corrected. "Volunteers. He went to West Point before I was born, but he failed philosophy and was dismissed from the academy. I think he hoped the war would give him a chance to redeem himself, but, instead of fighting the Rebels, he's stuck out in the middle of Kansas."

Maybe they both needed to talk. Metairie said: "Now that the war's over, maybe he'll get a commission in the regular army."

"Perhaps. I think what hurts him most is the fact that my mother was killed, and he never got a chance to mourn her, never got a chance to avenge her death."

The wind picked up, almost took off Metairie's kepi, and she changed the subject. Gil was glad of that. "We were in Denver before the war broke out. Have you ever seen the Rocky Mountains, Mister Metairie?"

"No, ma'am."

"We loved Colorado, but Father thought it unsafe to leave us there when the war broke out. Denver can be pretty wild. We stayed with him for a while at Fort Scott, but when he was sent to Fort Riley, he wanted us to stay with his sister in Baxter Springs."

Baxter Springs. Moon Montulé again. Gil decided to steer her away from that topic. "Did your father ask you to come here?"

She let out a mirthless laugh. "Not hardly. We've done nothing but fight since I arrived. I wanted to come. Maybe I shouldn't have." Becky smiled. "Do you know what . . . may I call you Gil?" He nodded. "Do you know what we have fought about, Gil?"

He said he didn't. "You," she continued.

Metairie stepped back. He hadn't expected the conversation to turn in this direction. Rebecca Rankin laughed, and she had a musical laugh. "Don't be afraid, Gil." She splashed water at him. "No, he thinks I am infatuated . . . his word, not mine . . . with you. I told him I hardly know you."

You don't know me at all, Metairie thought. *If you did, you certainly wouldn't be standing here talking to me.*

"I don't know, Gil. When I first talked to you, I think it was more out of curiosity than anything else. I don't know why I'm talking to you now. I'm sure my father would be furious if he found us together. He probably would think we planned this clandestine meeting. To be truthful, I just wanted to go for a walk."

"We'd best get back," he said. He stepped around the water trough and, to his surprise, offered her his right arm. She looked at it curiously for a second, then accepted. That stunned Gil even more.

"Are you sure you want to go back to the post?" she whispered, glancing at the corral.

"I'm sure," he answered.

She probably thought he meant that he was staying because of her, but that wasn't the case. At least, he didn't think that's why he was leaving the sorrel gelding behind. Everyone in Company B had a reason for staying. Peadar Flann would honor his commitment because he knew nothing else. He had always served in one army or another, and this one offered plenty of whisky. G. W. Hardee? He'd stay because of the atrocities he had seen committed by the Pawnees. Sean Burke, Charley Scott, and Sebastian Slater would likely remain for the same reasons. Arthur Bealer might stay. Gil wasn't sure about the Mississippian. Van Boskirk had nowhere to go, and, like Flann, he was a professional soldier. And Gil's reasons?

It certainly wasn't because of the oath of allegiance. He had sworn on a Bible to fight for the Confederate States of America, yet here he stood in a Federal uniform. Before that, he had made a blood oath with Moon Montulé, Toby Greer, and other Missourians to see Jim Lane and as many Kansas Red Legs dead as possible, but he had left them in January of 1862. He had seen what the Pawnees were capable of, and maybe that played a part in his decision. The horror of the fight on the plains, the sight of the butchered family, those visions would stay with him until he died. But he held no hatred for the Pawnees. In some ways, they were like the Blackwater River Guards, fighting for what they believed a just cause, giving no quarter and asking for none. So that wasn't it. Like Van Boskirk and many other Confederates, Metairie knew he had no place to call home any more. Osceola held too many

117

bad memories. His mother, if she still lived, had made it clear that she never wanted to see him again, and Gil knew in his heart she hadn't changed her mind. She could not, would not, ever forgive him. Yet Gil had come to terms with that.

No, Sergeant Gil Metairie had decided to stay because he was sick and tired of running. He had run from Missouri and men like Greer and Montulé, afraid of what he would become if he stayed, and he had run from wretched Rock Island, afraid that he would waste away and die like a sick rat in that God-forsaken prison. His father had run, too, fled his creditors in Alexandria, Louisiana, to start over on a Missouri farm, and rather than stay, Gil, then nineteen, ran back then, also. Ran because he was afraid to be alone. Well, he had grown up a lot since Alexandria. War will do that. This time, Gil wouldn't run. He'd stay, consequences — and Toby Greer — be damned.

Or maybe he was fooling himself again. Perhaps he wasn't running because of Rebecca Rankin.

CHAPTER
FOURTEEN

They didn't leave Fort Zarah the next morning, after all. Instead, Company B was ordered to take part in the rock detail, carving stones from the bluff and hauling them to the fort where new buildings were being thrown up. At least the stone quarters would be more permanent than the dug-outs and adobe huts. Soldiers from the Iowa, Kansas, and Colorado regiments were relieved of all daily duty, and the flag was lowered halfway down the pole while a trumpeter from the 7th Iowa played "Taps." One day the Yankees were celebrating their biggest victory, and now they were mourning their greatest loss.

Abraham Lincoln was dead.

Shot, the courier said, by a man named John Wilkes Booth while attending a performance of *Our American Cousin* at Ford's Theater in Washington. Lincoln had died the following morning, April 15th, and Booth had been killed ten days later. Someone had even tried to kill Secretary of State William Seward but had failed. It was a damned Rebel conspiracy, the courier said, and a bunch of those traitors were being rounded up now.

Gil didn't know what to think about that. He had never cared much for Old Abe, but he surely never wanted to see the President dead now that the war had ended. It just didn't make sense. And this fellow Booth had made things difficult for Company B. What little respect they had earned from the Federals at Fort Zarah had died with the galloper's message. What was it that Major Rankin had said? Once a Rebel, always a Rebel. Once a traitor, always a traitor. The Yanks definitely thought that was true today. Henry Russell looked over his charges with hate-filled eyes, as if he thought these former Confederates were partly responsible for Lincoln's assassination.

What also struck him was how far he was from civilization. Old Abe had been dead more than a month, yet word had just reached Fort Zarah. You would think that news of the commander-in-chief's assassination would reach an Army post quicker than that. There were no telegraph lines to Zarah, but still . . . Becky Rankin had been right. Her father had been forgotten out here. Major John J. Rankin would never earn a commission in the regular Army out here. Gil wondered if Greer had known about Lincoln's death last night. Probably. He had to if he had been in Missouri when he learned that William Quantrill had been captured — almost a month after Lincoln's death. Just didn't find the need to mention it.

"You Rebs quit your lollygaggin'!" Russell barked.

Metairie strained as he and Hardee lifted a heavy square into a wagon. "I'd like to drop a block on that arse," Hardee said.

Things became more routine the following day, and yet Company B remained at Fort Zarah. Peadar Flann finally dismissed the rumors that the volunteers were to be sent out on patrol and escort duty. "You see, laddies," he explained at the mess hall, "I figure the Yankee officers run their army the same way the Confederates did. You boys haven't forgotten about our camps in Tennessee and points south, have you? Remember? We're moving out tomorrow, they'd say, and tomorrow would come and we'd still be swatting mosquitoes. No, it's tomorrow for certain, they'd say, but a week later, we'd still be sitting on our backsides. Then, when we finally didn't believe them, the word turned out to be gospel and we'd be marching north."

Flann was right. Hickok was long gone with a pack train to Leavenworth, and a few patrols of the Colorado and Kansas went out, but Company B drilled. And drilled. And drilled.

Soldiers without arms. Eyes right. Eyes left. Eyes front. Heels on the same line, soldier. Knees straight, not stiff. Squad forward, common time. March! Halt! About face. Squad forward, double-quick step. March! Halt!

All day. All week.

Attention! Right shoulder arms. — Front rank, stand fast. Sergeant Van Boskirk, your men have missed their mark. Start over and get it right. Fall in. — Attention! Right shoulder arms.

Gil Metairie could say one thing about Lieutenant Henry Russell. He could have written RIFLE AND LIGHT INFANTRY TACTICS himself. On and on they drilled. The Union Army wasn't any different than the Army of the Tennessee in that regard, also. Gil remembered drill and drill after drill, the repetitive monotony often so frustrating the troops would pray for a battle just for a change of pace. Russell had the makeshift company practice everything, but he wondered if these maneuvers would be any good fighting Indians. The only practice Company B did not participate in was on the rifle range. That didn't bother Gil. He had served with many of these men since Shiloh. Every one of them knew how to shoot.

Pay day came and went, and Metairie didn't mind so much being fined a month's pay — because no one else got paid, either. The paymaster was late again, a common occurrence at Zarah. Still the post sutler and town merchants gave credit freely, and, while Peadar Flann sampled the latest barrels of whisky freighted in from Kentucky, Gil picked up a pair of high-topped boots and a wide-brimmed black slouch hat. He hadn't seen much of Becky Rankin since he had walked her home, nor had he seen Toby Greer. He hoped Greer had taken his advice and left, but somehow he knew that hadn't happened. More than likely, Greer was off freighting and would be back soon.

The next morning, instead of drilling on the advance of line in battle, Lieutenant Russell told Metairie to have the first squad report in front of headquarters. Metairie, Corporal Hardee, and privates Goldy Michaels, Warren Fry, Phineas Jones, Luke Murrah and Theophilus Hartranft stood at attention in front of the dug-out. Twenty minutes later, Russell held the gunnysack open for Major Rankin. The major listened as Russell issued the command.

"Sergeant, you will have your squad report at the corrals in one hour. Each man is to be issued one hundred and fifty rounds for the Spencer carbines and three days' rations. We will be marchin' to the Sweet's stagecoach station on the Arkansas, escorted by a squad of cavalry from the Eleventh Kansas. There we will remain until further notice, providing escort duty and other protection. Any questions?"

"No, sir."

"Very good, Sergeant. Carry out your orders."

Gil couldn't believe it. They were moving out.

Kurt Sweet's stagecoach station sat on the bank of the Arkansas about halfway between Forts Zarah and Larned. The living quarters were wretched; you had to look hard to find the dug-out that served as a bunkhouse for the station hands and, now, 1st Squad, Company B, Second Regiment, U.S. Volunteers. Although made of stone blocks, the main house wasn't built much better than the dug-out, but it suited a skinflint like Kurt Sweet fine. Cheap and lazy as he was, Sweet did an admirable job on the corrals and barn. A man took care of his livestock in this part of the country, even if he didn't take care of himself or his hired help.

A tall, fat man with close-cropped blond hair and usually bloodshot, blue eyes, Kurt Sweet hailed from Wisconsin, although it was hard to place his accent considering most of his sentences consisted of "uhn-huh," "uh," "er," and other grunts. Most of the stable hands were teenage boys, runaways most likely, from eastern Kansas, Nebraska, and Missouri, and the cook was a Russian named Gleb whose English appeared limited to "yes," "no," "come eat," "sumbitch" and "Dirty dishes in wreck pan, damn it."

Gil didn't think 1st Squad would get to know the people at the station. The soldiers usually ate separately from the station hands, dining on Warren Fry's grub rather than sampling the Russian's mess. Fry, a gunner with the Helena Artillery, had become a decent hand with the skillet, Dutch oven, and his coffee was strong, but, unlike Peadar Flann's, a body didn't have to carve it with a Bowie knife. Metairie had served with Fry as long as he could remember, but he hadn't learned the Arkansas teen could cook until now.

Like G. W. Hardee, Phineas Jones was another "orphan," once a sergeant in the 2nd Kentucky Infantry who had "seen the elephant" at Fort Donelson, Shiloh, and Baton Rouge before being captured at Vicksburg. Jones had no problems taking orders as a private. He had never cared much for a sergeant's job in the Confederacy anyway.

Gil knew little about Theophilus Hartranft, only that he had fallen in Tennessee while fighting with the 1st Alabama under Brigadier General William A. Quarles's Brigade. Fair-skinned, unsmiling with a receding hairline, Hartranft appeared to be in his early forties. The story going around Rock Island had been that Hartranft had been a substitute soldier. A rich cotton planter from Dale County had paid Hartranft three hundred dollars in Confederate script to serve in place of the planter's son. True or false, Hartranft had shown

124

he was no coward when the Pawnees attacked, and others remarked that he fought like a demon during the senseless slaughter at Franklin, Tennessee.

Easily the most likable of the squad, Goldy Michaels stood tall with curly brown hair and a constant smile. He had been captured in Georgia while serving as a corporal in the 19th South Carolina, part of Manigault's Brigade. He had a rich baritone, a much better voice than Metairie had, and would break out in song at any moment, bringing strong complaints from Lieutenant Russell. "Goldy," Gil had told him, "you might want to cut down on your serenades until after the lieutenant has gone to his tent."

"Can't help it," the Carolinian replied. "Sometimes the music just takes a-hold of me." And he quickly launched into "Sweet Betsy from Pike."

Luke Murrah had lost two fingers on his right hand and his right eye to shrapnel while serving with the 10th Texas Cavalry at Stones River. He recovered, refused a convalescence leave, and continued to fight for the Cause until he found himself surrounded at Missionary Ridge, and took a bullet in the thigh and a bayonet through the left shoulder before being subdued and shipped off to Rock Island. Murrah was stiff from the wounds, but Metairie was glad to have him in 1st Squad. The only thing the Texan complained about was the marching. "I'm a cavalry boy, Sergeant," he'd say. "Give me a horse and a Spencer and I'll ride through the Pawnee nation."

Lieutenant Russell, however, believed that if Luke Murrah, or anyone else under his command, got a horse, he would ride off to Texas. The officer didn't seem to understand that if anyone wanted to steal a horse and desert, all he had to do was walk to the corral while Kurt Sweet was in his cups and his hired hands were snoring like an old hound, pick a keeper, and ride.

So 1st Squad remained an infantry unit. The soldiers would climb aboard freight wagons and ride to Fort Larned, then march back on their own or ride with an eastbound train. The stagecoaches usually had a cavalry escort, and the only time Gil or his men saw other ex-Confederates was when the 2nd or 4th Squads would be riding escort on a wagon train to Sweet's station. Reunions never lasted longer than it took for the oxen or mules to drink, eat, and rest while the freighters sampled Kurt Sweet's forty-rod rotgut.

When they weren't on guard detail, the soldiers spent time drilling, policing the station grounds, or digging cisterns and a drainage ditch. That got to be such an awful duty that they enjoyed the monotony of riding in some slow-moving wagon and watching the dreary Kansas countryside creep by.

The summer sun turned into a furnace. Gil's beard filled in again. He tried washing the stink out of his uniform, but the smell always quickly returned. On one Sunday, a wagon train pulled in with an escort led by Corporal Crook and his 11th Cavalry boys and Sergeant Peadar Flann and 3rd Squad.

Metairie greeted his old friend warmly.

"I was beginning to think they weren't letting you out of Fort Zarah's sight," Gil told the Irishman after the two had embraced.

126

"Aye, but I told the dear major darling that it might be in the post's best interest if he were to let me sample the whisky at Fort Larned, and he, as well as the sutlers, readily agreed." Flann wet his lips. "Would there happen to be any John Barleycorn at this glorious part of civilization?"

Gil laughed. "I'm not sure I'd call it whisky." He nodded at Crook and the Kansans tending to their horses. "What's with the cavalry detail? The only escorts have been us old Rebels."

"Some settlers were massacred along Walnut Creek last week. And a troop of those Iowa Yanks had some fisticuffs, well, not really fisticuffs, with a band of Cheyenne dog soldiers just the other day. The major thinks the tribes might be getting a wee bit too bold for his liking, so he's sending cavalry squads as added protection. That's also why you're not relieving us. Your First Squad boys might need to protect this lovely station, while the lads and I get to see the country."

"I've seen it, Flann. You're welcome to it."

"Well, I'm mighty dry, Gil. Don't loose your manners."

"All right. Should we ask Corporal Crook to join us?"

"Certainly. With any luck, he'll buy. I sure can't. I haven't seen a bit of pay since I joined this man's army."

CHAPTER
FIFTEEN

A full moon lit up the Kansas prairie that evening long after Crook, Flann, and the freight train had pulled out of Sweet's station on their way to Fort Larned. At Corporal Crook's suggestion, Lieutenant Russell had doubled the guards. Michaels and Hardee had taken the first watch, and now Metairie and Murrah were relieving them. Gil sent the Texan toward the cistern to spell Goldy Michaels while he walked, Spencer in the crook of his arm, to the corrals to find Corporal Hardee.

"Quiet?" Gil asked, hoping for an affirmative answer.

"Like a cemetery," Hardee answered. The look on the corporal's face showed he immediately rejected his choice of words.

"Well, get some grub and turn in. Fry should have left you some stew and coffee. I told Hartranft and Jones to relieve us in three hours." Gil smiled. "Make sure they don't forget."

Hardee turned to leave, paused, and commented: "If you ask me, Sergeant, these Yanks ain't takin' the right approach to exterminating those red devils."

"I don't think 'exterminating' is the policy."

"Well, it should be. No matter, though, you don't think Generals Johnston or Hanson would take such a yellow-backed approach to fightin', do you?"

"What do you mean, Corporal?"

Hardee splattered a fence rail with tobacco juice. "I mean, all we do is ride escort on wagons and guard this rawhide-lookin', bad-smellin' bit of hell while them Injuns is free to go around half of bleedin' Kansas, rapin', killin', and liftin' scalps. General Hanson would hit them Injuns hard, drive 'em out of the country. So would General Johnston, or any other Confederate general worth the braid on his coat sleeves. You mark my word, Sergeant, one of these days that's what we'll have to do."

"Maybe," was all Metairie said, and Hardee walked to the dug-out. He didn't really believe the Kentuckian's argument. Sure, 1st Squad and all of the Company B had been confined to guard duty, but the Federal cavalry boys were scouting the prairie and chasing the Indians. They weren't just sitting back, doing nothing. And Gil would never question the bravery and loyalty of Albert Sidney Johnston or Roger W. Hanson, but what had their gallantry accomplished? General Johnston bled to death at Shiloh — maybe the war had been lost right then near the Tennessee River — and General Hanson fell in a charge at Stones River that saw some four hundred of his men killed or wounded. Hanson died a few days later near the battlefield.

He heard the pounding of hoofs then, coming from the east, down the Santa Fé Trail. "G.W.!" he called out, and ducked underneath a fence rail and inside the corral. He stood beside an adobe wall, rested the Spencer on the top, and peered into the horizon. Hardee hadn't made it far. He sprinted back to the corral and leaped over the fence. He licked his lips, levered a fresh round into the carbine, and took a position a few yards from Metairie.

One horse whinnied. Others began to dance around the corral nervously.

"What you make of it?" Hardee asked.

Metairie shook his head. "Too soon for the stage. Next one isn't due till day after tomorrow."

Hardee put two fingers in his mouth and let out a shrill whistle. "Riders comin' in, boys!" he yelled. "Riders comin' in!"

The door to the main building opened. Someone sprinted outside and took a position beside the well. One of the stable boys, Gil figured, too young and stupid to realize he left the safest place in the whole damned compound. Men filed out of the bunkhouse, and, in less than a minute, Henry Russell's voice carried with the wind, barking out orders. Kurt Sweet hurried to the corrals and between gasps asked: "Er . . . what's . . . goin' on?" His face glowed with sweat, and his breath stank of whisky. The shotgun the man carried shook in his arms.

Hardee pointed toward the road. The sound grew louder. "Somebody's comin'," he said, stating the obvious.

"Um," Kurt Sweet added.

"Coming down the trail," Metairie added. "Don't think it's Indians, but you never know."

No clouds showed in the sky, and the moonlight made it easy to see anyone. Gil was thankful for that. Would Indians take advantage of a full moon for a raid? He wasn't sure. But he didn't believe Indians on a raid would travel down the Santa Fé Trail, even at night. Still, it could be renegades. Toby Greer came to mind.

"Um," Sweet said again.

Gil could make out the jingling of harness now, and a squeaking wheel. A wagon ruled out Indians, and outlaws for that matter. Four galloping mules rounded the corner, pulling a Yankee ambulance. Gil made out the figures of two men in the driver's boot. Six horses and riders followed the wagon, hard to make out through all the dust, but Metairie felt sure that the riders were cavalry.

"Army wagon coming in!" he yelled. "Hold your fire!"

His command was relayed down the line. Kurt Sweet grunted, lowered the shotgun, and barked out his own set of orders. "Army wagon! You boys see to them mules!" That seemed to tucker Sweet out, so he stumbled back from whence he came.

The ambulance turned a sharp corner and slid to a stop in front of the corrals, the dust blinding and choking Gil and Hardee. A couple of horses blew, the driver set the brake, and a few men mumbled curses. A man shouted: "Where is Lieutenant Russell?" Without waiting for an answer, the man continued: "I want these mules taken care of immediately, and a fresh team

131

ready to lead us out at first light. This is official Army business. Mister Sweet will be paid in United States script for the rental of his animals, and the mules will be returned. Now where is Lieutenant Russell?"

Metairie recognized the voice. Major Rankin.

When the dust finally settled, Hardee and Metairie stepped out of the corral. The riders and men on the ambulance's driver's bench were some of the Colorado cavalrymen, busy now tending to the stock. Russell had hurried to the major, and the two men stood in front of the main building talking hurriedly as Kurt Sweet mumbled and nodded his head.

"What's up?" Hardee asked the ambulance driver.

"Major's got orders to report to Fort Larned. Word is we're getting ready for a major campaign against the Kiowas and Comanches. I guess the major don't want to miss out on the glory."

Metairie swung the gate open as two soldiers led the lathered mules inside the corral. Hardee mumbled: "You keep runnin' them mules like that, you and Rankin's gonna be walkin' to Larned."

The Coloradan jumped off the ambulance, landing with a grunt. "Yep," he said. "I just follow orders, Reb." He shouted toward the soldiers in charge of the team of mules. "You boys don't let them mules drink a-fore they've cooled down!"

Gil closed the gate and started to follow Hardee and the ambulance driver toward Russell and Rankin. Another voice stopped him.

"Hello, Gil Metairie."

He turned. Becky Rankin stepped out of the dusty transport. Gil tipped his slouch hat. He tried to think of something to say, couldn't, glanced over his shoulder, wanting to stay but knowing he should join the officers.

Becky smiled. "You'd better go, Sergeant. I don't want you to get reduced to the ranks on my account. How's that well water?"

"Drinkable."

"I might be thirsty, say in a couple of hours."

He couldn't help but smile. "That's a pretty good way to get me reduced to the ranks, Becky," he said, and hurried to join the major, lieutenant, Hardee, and Sweet. Of course, he knew he would find a way to meet her at the well.

Major Rankin turned when Metairie approached but didn't acknowledge his presence. He continued speaking to Russell. "Company H let a war party run off about sixty horses at Fort Larned on June Eighth. The following day, a wagon train under Company K's protection lost some one hundred mules and a herd of cattle totaling seventy-five head. Captain Molony took G Company out after them, Kiowas it's believed. Anyway, Lieutenant Colonel King has asked me to join Major Armstrong at Fort Larned to help prepare a campaign against the southern tribes."

Russell beamed. "Excellent, Major. What are my orders?"

"You'll stay here at present, Lieutenant. If Armstrong wishes you to report to Larned, you'll receive your orders. Until then, you shall carry on as you have been."

The smile vanished. Russell's response was barely audible, but Gil didn't have to hear it. Rankin turned abruptly. Metairie and Hardee snapped salutes, but the major didn't answer and marched toward the building, addressing Kurt Sweet. "Mister Sweet, I have the authority to rent a team of mules from you. Let's get down to business, sir, and perhaps you can find accommodations, food, and drink for myself and my daughter."

"Er, yeah, reckon so." Sweet followed the officer inside.

Metairie faced Russell. "Do we carry on, sir?" he asked. The lieutenant stared at him blankly. Gil repeated the question. Russell merely nodded and walked tiredly, defeated, to his quarters. "Go on, G. W.," Metairie told Hardee, patting the corporal on the shoulder. Gil walked back toward the corral. He would still be on guard duty in two hours, and he decided he would walk by the well around that time.

Becky arrived early, but Gil was waiting. He held out a dipper of water, and watched as she drank. The moon had set by now, but the campfires of the Colorado cavalry detail and 1st Squad, now too tired to sleep, provided enough light.

"How have you been?" she asked, returning the dipper to Metairie. He offered her more, but she declined. Gil dropped the piece of pewter into the oaken bucket before answering.

"Not much to report."

"You should shave that beard."

Gil smiled. "You're pretty forward, Miss . . . Becky."

"I'm the daughter of a militia officer."

With a nod, he said: "He must be pleased. A chance to go against the Indians." He stopped, realizing he had struck a nerve. He stopped, waited for her to speak, but it took a while.

"He's changed," she said. "I don't know why I'm telling you this, but . . . All we've done is bicker at each other since I arrived. Basically, he's ordered me off Fort Zarah. He had arranged my escort to Fort Larned, then he got his orders . . . 'request,' he calls it. Josias King is the commander at Fort Larned, and he outranks Father, but Father refuses to believe an officer in the volunteers can outrank him."

"Your father doesn't seem to understand that he's a volunteer himself."

Becky nodded slightly. "Yes, but he never served in the Confederacy."

Gil changed the subject. "Fort Zarah won't be the same without you, Becky. Where do you plan on going?"

She shrugged. "Denver, I think. A friend of mine, Julianne Moore, owns a bakery there, and she wrote that I could easily land a job as a schoolteacher there or some other town. Julianne Moore," she repeated. "Moore's Bakery, Denver."

This time Metairie laughed. "Becky," he said after he had recovered, "you aren't subtle, are you?"

She laughed, too. "You can remember that, can't you, Gil? If I'm not in Denver, Julianne will know where you can find me. After your enlistment is up."

Gil leaned the Spencer against the well. He placed his arms on Becky's shoulders and pulled her forward. They kissed lightly at first, then he drew back slowly. "You'd be a lot better off if I don't go looking for you," he said. Damn, he thought, he could never escape Moon Montulé. The shouts of "Osceola!" rang hard in his ears. He saw the carnage again, relived the horror of watching Montulé kill the Baptist deacon at the Olathe church, and heard the stories of the raid at Baxter Springs once more, the raid that had left Becky Rankin's mother dead.

"I know," she whispered, "more than you think I do."

You don't know that, he thought. He wanted to kiss her again, despite it all, but he put his arm around her shoulder and walked her back to Sweet's poor accommodations. She turned in the doorway, said good night, and kissed him on the cheek.

"When you feel like talking, I'm here," she said, and went inside.

CHAPTER
SIXTEEN

Morning dawned already warm, a bad omen for the rest of the summer day. Major Rankin's Colorado yellow-legs had a fresh team hitched to the ambulance and their own mounts saddled and ready to ride shortly after daybreak. Sipping his coffee, Gil stood by the cook fire and watched from a distance as Becky Rankin climbed into the dusty ambulance. She didn't wave, didn't even glance his way. Maybe she was mad. Gil didn't know if he had done anything to make her angry. More than likely, she knew it wouldn't be proper for a Federal officer's daughter to be social, let alone flirtatious, with an enlisted man — especially a former Johnny Reb. The major stepped out of the building, followed by Kurt Sweet, and began barking orders at Lieutenant Russell, a Colorado sergeant, and anyone else around. Russell would be in a foul mood, left behind again, and he'd take out his wrath on 1st Squad. Already scowling, the lieutenant snapped a salute, spun on his heels, and marched toward Metairie. "First Squad!" Russell called out. "Fall in." Gil sighed. The least those Yanks could have done was let them finish their morning coffee.

Metairie dumped out the rest of his coffee and tossed the tin cup into the wreck pan. He swung around, repeated Russell's command, and watched as the soldiers, quietly grumbling, formed a line behind the fire pit and snapped to attention.

Then they heard the screams.

Gil spun around. Russell froze in mid-stride, his jaw agape. The driver of the ambulance shrieked, clutched his chest, and toppled over the front, spooking the mules, which began to pull the wagon forward. Another soldier slid quietly from his horse, which galloped away, scaring the wagon team even more. The Federal sergeant shouted something, ran, and grabbed the lead mule's harness, cursing, yelling, straining to stop the team from becoming a runaway. Then it didn't matter. The far-side mule fell dead, stopping the wagon.

Somebody yelled. Horses snorted, stamped nervously, kicking up clouds of dirt. Something whipped past Metairie's ear, thumped into the adobe wall. The ear-splitting wails continued, eerie, sounding remarkably like a Rebel yell. By then Gil realized what was happening. He grabbed his Spencer, ducked, and saw the Indians on horseback, yipping, sending a downpour of arrows into the yard. They'd be after the horses.

"To the corrals!" Metairie yelled. He ducked, ran the action in the Spencer, aimed, fired, knowing he had missed. Rising, he jacked a fresh shell into the chamber and took off, Hardee and Murrah right behind him. Another arrow whistled over Gil's head. The Indians, Pawnees he was certain, charged. Then came a deafening volley from the corrals. Two Indian ponies

138

reared and crashed to the ground. Another Pawnee somersaulted off his horse. The charge faltered, veered. He already smelled and tasted the black powder smoke, the sulphur burning his eyes. Shiloh — Stones River — Missionary Ridge all over again, only these weren't Yankees they were fighting.

Lieutenant Henry Russell stood in front of the well, his face ashen, babbling nonsensical orders. "Fire and load lyin', Sergeant! Fire and load lyin'! Left shoulder arms! Front face! Report!"

Metairie swore. He spotted a Pawnee on foot, running hard, war club or tomahawk raised over his head. What Gil wanted more than anything was to get to that ambulance, make sure Becky Rankin was safe. Instead, he turned hard toward Russell, slammed his left shoulder into the lieutenant's chest, knocking him backward toward the well, and swung his carbine like a club. The stock caught the Pawnee under the chin, and the man fell as if he had been cut down by grapeshot, the tomahawk spinning to the ground. Hardee and Murrah ran forward. Neither looked back.

The Indian rose. Gil, shocked the man was still alive, swung the Spencer around, the barrel inches from the Pawnee's head, and pulled the trigger. Without looking at the Indian again, Metairie cocked the carbine and dived behind the well as a bullet ricocheted off the wall. Another slug smashed the oaken bucket. Gil wet his lips. Some of the Indians had rifles or muskets. It would get hot here in a few seconds. The Pawnees would sweep down on them quickly for the kill.

"Lieutenant?"

Russell looked up uncertainly. Blood seeped from the corner of his mouth. His lip was busted, probably from the fall. The officer's chest heaved. He said nothing.

"Lieutenant," Gil continued, "we need to get out of here in a hurry. You think you can run to Sweet's place? I'll cover you from here."

The officer nodded slightly. Good. For a moment Metairie thought Russell might still be in shock. But he seemed to have snapped out of it for now. There was nothing to be ashamed of. Gil had seen many soldiers act the same way in the early stages of battle. Russell clawed at his revolver, thumbed back the hammer, and looked at the main building and corrals. Three of the Colorado cavalrymen had taken positions in front of the ambulance, two of them firing from kneeling positions and the third lying prone to their left. Phineas Jones leaned against the rear of the wagon, resting his carbine against the ambulance as he fired, and Goldy Michaels stood next to him.

The sergeant helped Becky out of the transport and practically shoved her inside Sweet's main house, while her father stood in front of the doorway, firing his Colt revolver and directing orders to cavalrymen, galvanized Yankees, and Kurt Sweet's stable hands. The cook, Gleb, stepped outside in his apron, fired a double-barrel shotgun, thundered something in Russian, and went back inside.

Metairie peered over the top of the well. The Pawnees had fallen back to regroup, firing occasionally. Gil turned around, nodded at Russell, and yelled:

140

"Major!" Rankin looked his way. "We're coming in! Give us some cover!"

"Go," he told Russell, and the lieutenant scrambled to his feet and weaved his way toward the soldiers. Gil spun around, fired once, twice, three times. The weapons of 1st Squad and the Coloradans echoed. Metairie rose, cocked the Spencer again, and walked slowly, deliberately toward the wagon. He stopped, knelt, fired, ran the Spencer's action, and took a few more steps, then stopped, knelt, and fired again. He rose and continued, taking his time, not showing any trace of fear although his heart pounded and he found it hard to breathe.

"Run, you damned fool!" the sergeant shouted.

Not a chance, Gil thought. He turned again to fire, although now he remained standing, cocked the Spencer, and then headed toward the soldiers, turning, firing, continuing. *Rear-guard action,* he told himself. He had done this many times. He remembered Daniel Chevilette Govan's calmness under fire, and recalled the general's orders: "Fall back slowly, men! We are not retreating. We are not running. We'll never run!" That stubborn Arkansas planter had instilled a lot of pride in his men, and Gil Metairie wasn't about to disappoint him now. He hadn't run from any Yanks, and he certainly wouldn't run from these Pawnees. He turned one final time, pulled the trigger, and heard the loud metallic snap as the hammer fell on an empty chamber. Out of ammunition. Metairie swore and ducked behind the wagon.

Goldy Michaels handed Gil a loading tube. Smart man, that Michaels. He had had the brains to pick up extra ammunition before taking off for the corrals. Gil hadn't. He began to load the tube into the stock of the Spencer. Rifle fire ceased, except for an occasional pot shot, but the Indians began singing in the distance.

"That how you Rebs always retreated?" the sergeant said, shaking his head.

"We never retreated," Michaels answered with a laugh. "No Yanks ever seen our backs. Ain't no Pawnees gonna, either."

The Yankee smiled. "You'll get your head blowed off, Metairie, lollygaggin' like that. But I'm proud to know you. Jed Curry's the name."

Major John Rankin cleared his throat as he capped the nipples of his revolver. The major stood tall against the adobe wall, concentrating on reloading the Colt. "Don't recommend the sergeant for a Medal of Honor just yet," he said without looking up. "Those savages couldn't hit this wall from that range."

They never heard the shot, but as soon as Rankin had finished his rebuke, he howled, gripped his right thigh with both hands, dropping the Colt, and crashed to the ground. A cavalryman cursed, and Becky Rankin yelled: "Father!" Gil and Curry were at the major's side in an instant. Blood stained the officer's trousers and began to pool underneath his hip. His face quickly began to lose all color. Metairie looked up, saw Becky standing in the doorway.

"Let's get him inside," Curry said.

142

Metairie nodded, but the major shook his head. "No," he said through a clenched mouth. "I must command . . ."

"You ain't gonna command anything, Major," Curry said. "You'll bleed to death if we don't get a tourniquet on that leg."

A breath of hot air exploded from Rankin's lungs. "Damn it all to hell," he said. "Lieutenant Russell . . . I put you . . . command."

As soon as Curry and Metairie lifted Rankin, he screamed and passed out. The two men quickly brought him inside Sweet's house, leaving a trail of blood across the sod floor, and eased him onto a cot. Gil untied his bandanna and wrapped it tightly over the major's wounded leg. Becky knelt by her father and began cutting away his trousers with a small knife.

"Sweet!" Metairie yelled. "Fetch us some clean sheets, hot water, and whisky. Now!"

Curry stood. "You need anything, ma'am?" he asked Becky. She shook her head, and the sergeant hurried outside. Gil remained at her side, however. She worked hurriedly. Tears flowed down both cheeks, and her hands trembled. Slowly Metairie put his right hand on top of her hands. Becky's lips quivered, and she turned slowly toward him, sniffling.

"Here," Gil said softly. "I'll do this. You help Sweet."

When she was gone, Metairie slashed away at the blue trousers and looked at the wound, just below the major's hip. The slug was still in there. It would have to come out, or Rankin would die slowly of lead poison — if he didn't bleed to death first. Gil looked at

143

the ugly hole, saw the bits of bone, and knew the wound was bad. He had seen wounds like this in the war and knew the usual outcome. Amputation. And death.

This would require a better hand than his. He looked up and yelled: "I need Hartranft in here now!" The substitute soldier was the closest thing to a surgeon in 1st Squad. He may have taken a bounty to join the Confederacy, but he had proved his worth in battle and, afterward, doctored the less serious wounds suffered by the soldiers of the 1st Alabama. Back in Rock Island, one of the Alabama prisoners had told Gil that many Rebs in Quarles's Brigade would rather have Private Hartranft cut on them than some overworked sawbones they didn't know.

G. W. Hardee, not Theophilus Hartranft, stuck his head through the doorway.

"I need Hartranft, G. W.," Gil said.

Hardee blinked. "Theo's dead, Gil."

Metairie swore underneath his breath. Suddenly, outside, Russell began shrieking. "You craven coward!" he shouted. "Come back, you secesh bastard!" A pistol shot rang out. Hoofs rang. "Shoot that son-of-a-bitch!" A rifle fired, then another.

Hardee raced outside. Gil wanted to join him, but dared not leave the major like this, not with his daughter so close. Hardee appeared again. "It's Luke Murrah, Gil," he said. "He jumped on a horse and . . ."

The corporal spun around as a fuming Henry Russell shoved him aside, waving his revolver and howling at the top of his lungs. The lieutenant had

144

certainly recovered from his earlier shock. "One of your cowards ran, Sergeant! Do you hear me? He stole an Army horse and ran. That's cowardice, and I'll have him shot. Do you understand? When we get out of this, I . . ."

"Shut up!"

Russell turned slowly. Becky Rankin, trembling with rage, had dropped the sheets she had been ripping into bandages. "Get out of here, Henry," she said. "Get out of my sight. That's my father lying there, you dumb bastard, probably dying. You're in command outside. So command. But get out of here."

Russell stammered, tried to say something, couldn't, and quickly left. Hardee followed, and Gil looked at the bullet hole in the major's leg again. He became aware of Becky beside him now, and he looked up. She swallowed, wiped the tears from her face, and knelt beside him.

"I need that whisky and water," Gil told Sweet. "And bring me a knife."

CHAPTER
SEVENTEEN

By late afternoon, the dead animals and men were beginning to bloat in the unrelenting sun. The fight had turned into a siege, marked by only the isolated pot shot as both soldiers and Pawnees conserved ammunition. Wearily Gil Metairie found a wash basin and soaked his blood-covered hands before scrubbing them furiously and drying them on a dirty bar rag. Kurt Sweet offered him a drink, and Gil accepted, barely tasting the lightning as it burned his throat. He had opened Rankin's wound to let it drain, then probed for half an hour until he finally pried the flattened lead ball out. Gil tucked the bullet — .50 caliber or maybe something bigger, he guessed — into Rankin's trouser pocket in case the major wanted it for a souvenir. If he lived, that is. Metairie wouldn't give even odds right now. Afterward, he picked out all of the bone fragments he could find before cleansing the wound with Sweet's abominable whisky, heating the blade of a Bowie knife, and cauterizing the wound. He could still smell the burning flesh.

"What do you think?" Becky asked.

She had been with him the whole time, even holding her father down — with the Russian cook's help — as

146

he screamed and fought, while Gil dug into his leg with the knife, until he finally succumbed to unconsciousness. From then on, Becky helped dispose of the pieces of bone, wiped Gil's sweaty forehead, squeezed her father's hand, and whispered to him gently, telling him everything would be all right. Or perhaps she had been talking to Gil.

He motioned Sweet for another drink, but spotted his Spencer resting on the bar and reconsidered. Drunk on duty? That would be a first. "I don't know," he finally told Becky. "If we can keep infection out and get him to Fort Zarah in time, he might have a chance."

"Fort Larned," Becky said. "It's closer, and they probably have a better surgeon."

"Larned, then." Either way, Gil seemed sure of one thing: even if John Rankin survived the trip to Fort Larned, the post surgeon would saw off that leg. General John Bell Hood had lost his right leg at Chickamauga, fighting on Longstreet's left wing, yet he had continued to command, eventually taking over the Army of the Tennessee long after Gil had been captured. Hood had even suffered a bad wound in his left shoulder at Gettysburg, but fought on. Men could survive the worst war had to offer, but John Rankin was no John Bell Hood. He didn't have that unbending will, that refusal to surrender. Rankin would be lost without his leg, without his career as a soldier. His chance at finding glory or a brevet in the upcoming Indian campaign had ended at this filthy outpost. His life might end here as well.

The major let out a faint groan, and Becky turned to his side. Gil grabbed his carbine and walked outside.

"You good at fighting Indians, Sergeant?" Gil asked Jed Curry. The Yankee was squatting behind the dead mule and drinking from his canteen. Somehow, the Coloradans had unharnessed the other animals during the fight and gotten them into the corrals. Two other cavalry mounts lay dead, and several Indian ponies littered the ground. Flies buzzed around the carcasses, and the smell turned Gil's stomach.

Curry passed the canteen to Metairie with a shrug. "I've taken me a scalp or two," Curry answered. "Why?"

Metairie took a sip and corked the canteen. "If we don't get the major to a doctor in a hurry, he'll die. I'm wondering how long you think we'll be pinned down here."

The sergeant took his canteen and leaned it against the mule's swollen belly. "Losin' proposition for them Injuns," Curry said. "Probably didn't expect a bunch of bluecoats when they hit us, just you Rebs. Most likely they'll fall back in the middle of the night. You can take the major to Fort Larned if you wanna. Me? I'm takin' my boys after them bastards until they scatter. And iffen I catch them, they'll be many a Pawnee buck singin' his death song. You'd be mighty welcome to join us, Sergeant, lessen the lieutenant says no. That is, if you ain't yellow like your boy who stole my horse."

There was no need to reply. A few hours ago, Jed Curry had been ready to shake Gil's hand, to proclaim him a hero. Now, because of Luke Murrah's desertion, Gil and the rest of Company B had been reduced to the ranks, back to being shunned as Rebels, as traitors, as cowards.

Gil left the Yankee sergeant and ducked inside the corral. Four bodies were covered with saddle blankets. Three wore cavalry boots, but the fourth had a pair of worn brogans issued back at Leavenworth. Metairie peeled back the blanket and uncovered the calm, expressionless face of Theophilus Hartranft. The man looked to be asleep, but Metairie saw the broken arrow shaft protruding from the Alabaman's blouse. He covered the corpse's body and walked to the far side of the corral where Corporal Hardee sat, Spencer cradled in his arm.

"What happened with Murrah?" Gil asked.

Hardee spit out tobacco juice and shifted the plug from cheek to cheek. "Don't know," he said. "Didn't say nothin' to nobody, just did a flyin' leap into a Yank's saddle and lit a shuck west. Phineas says he run pretty damned good for a shot-up old man. Couple of Pawnees taken off after him."

It wasn't like the one-eyed Texan to run from anything. Gil would never believe Murrah a coward, no matter what Lieutenant Russell or anyone else said.

He changed the subject. "How many wounded?"

"None of us. Them Yanks got a couple flesh wounds, nothin' bad. And a couple of Sweet's boys got killed, too far away for us to bring 'em in. Don't think no more is wounded. Then there's the major? How is he, anyway?"

Gil shook his head. "Bullet busted the bone pretty bad. Got the bleeding stopped, the slug out, but . . ."

"Pawnee snake-in-the-grass picked the wrong target."

"Huh?" Snake-in-the-grass was the old Rebel phrase for sharpshooter, but Gil wasn't sure what Hardee meant. The corporal was staring past Metairie. He turned, and the Kentuckian's statement made sense.

"Sergeant," Henry Russell snapped, "I'm holdin' you responsible for Private Murphy's desertion under fire."

"Murrah," Hardee corrected.

The lieutenant continued as if he hadn't heard. "I am placin' you under arrest. Hand over your carbine, soldier, and you will be confined to quarters until your court-martial."

"Russell!" G. W. Hardee jumped up. "You ain't makin' a lick of sense. We're surrounded by savages, and'll need every gun and man who can pull a trigger."

"Silence, Corporal! I am in charge. You heard my order, Sergeant. Now get inside before I have you shot."

There was no need in pressing his luck. Gil leaned the Spencer against the wall, close to Hardee, and walked back inside Sweet's house. One officer half dead, the other half out of his mind. At times, the Yankee Army seemed a lot like the Army of the Tennessee.

The drums beat all night, ending Sergeant Curry's prediction that the Pawnees would withdraw. Somewhere outside, Goldy Michaels began singing "Lorena," and a Coloradan joined him on harmonica. The song lacked

150

the rhythm of the Pawnee drums, Gil thought, as he drifted off to sleep.

He jumped awake with a start, when Hardee knelt at his side.

"What time is it?" Gil asked, trying unsuccessfully to stifle a yawn.

"Just about dawn. Drums stopped 'bout an hour ago, and them bucks ain't pullin' out. Looks like they're gettin' ready for one more charge."

Gil pulled himself up, then remembered. "I'm under arrest."

Hardee handed him his carbine. "Yeah, and if you step outside, that fool of a lieutenant is apt to shoot you. But you'd best keep this . . . to protect Miss Rankin. You take care, Gil."

"You, too, G.W."

The Indians began to sing. Metairie jacked a shell into the chamber, found a good spot beside the open doorway, and waited. He chanced a glance at Becky, who busied herself putting a fresh bandage around her father's leg. Behind the bar, Kurt Sweet's mumbling prayers were punctuated by pulls on a whisky jug. A young stable boy took a position beside the only window in the building and thumbed back the hammer on his musket, the long gun a foot taller than the boy.

The singing stopped.

A bird began to chirp.

They would be coming now, Gil thought, all out. Hold out this time, and the Indians would call it a day. At least, he hoped they would. But could they hold out?

"Listen."

The word was spoken softly, but in the deathly quiet, Becky's voice had been unmistakable. Metairie looked at her. Her head was up, alert, listening. Gil lowered the Spencer. "Do you hear it?" Becky asked him.

He strained to hear, although he thought her imagination at work. But there it was. Faint, yes, but he could hear. Outside, someone else recognized the distant trumpet. "Hey!" an excited and relieved voice shouted. "Cavalry! Cavalry coming!"

The Pawnees heard the trumpeter, also. Gil stepped outside as the Indians galloped away. Soldiers, Coloradans, and galvanized Yanks rose from their positions. The trumpet sounded closer. Phineas Jones was the first to spot the dust. Two cavalry troopers broke into an Irish jig, and Goldy Michaels started singing "Bonnie Blue Flag." Gil slowly exhaled and leaned his Spencer against Sweet's house. He smiled at G. W. Hardee. The charging bluecoats grew closer. A guidon snapped in the wind.

"You're still under arrest, mister!"

Gil faced Lieutenant Russell. The officer held his revolver, but the barrel pointed at the ground and the hammer wasn't cocked. Gil decided against a fight. He simply said — "Yes, sir." — and watched the rescuers. But Russell wasn't finished. "I said get back in that buildin', Sergeant. Now."

"I don't think so." This came from G. W. Hardee. Gil and the lieutenant stared at the smiling Kentuckian. The corporal pointed to the galloping horses. "That's Luke Murrah with 'em, Lieutenant."

At last Gil understood. Murrah hadn't deserted. He had gone for help, riding as hard and as fast as he could to catch up with the freight train escorted by Ben Crook's cavalry boys and Peadar Flann's squad. Flann wasn't with them, but those Kansas yellow-legs certainly looked good. What was it Murrah had said? I'm a cavalry boy, Sergeant. Give me a horse and a Spencer and I'll ride through the Pawnee nation. Well, now he was getting the chance.

Most of the soldiers, Murrah included, continued their pursuit of the fleeing Pawnees, but Crook reined in hard in front of the ambulance. Gil let a curtain of dust sail overhead before he looked at the corporal.

"How bad are y'all hurt?" The question was directed at Metairie — not Lieutenant Russell or Sergeant Curry.

"Major Rankin's pretty bad off," Gil answered. "Six dead, four of them soldiers. A few minor wounds."

Crook nodded. "Sergeant," he told Curry. "If any of your men want to join us, mount up and follow me." He raked his spurs over his horse and galloped away. Curry and the Coloradans quickly began throwing saddles on their horses. Russell stood blankly, revolver still hanging at his side.

"Lieutenant," Gil said calmly, "should we hitch a team to the ambulance? Try to get Major Rankin to the surgeon at Fort Larned on the double?" Russell looked as if he hadn't heard. "Lieutenant?" Gil repeated.

At last, Russell nodded and holstered his Colt. "Do as you wish," he said, and went inside the building.

By the time the team was hitched to the transport and Metairie had stepped inside, Lieutenant Henry Russell was drunk. He leaned against the makeshift bar while Kurt Sweet refilled his tumbler with whisky. Gil ignored the officer and directed Jones and Michaels to bring the major gently outside. Becky followed them. Henry Russell ignored them, but not Kurt Sweet.

"What the Sam Hill you think you're doin', Sergeant?" the stationmaster blabbered.

"We're taking the major and Miss Rankin to Fort Larned," Gil snapped.

"Oh, no. You boys is paid to protect this station. Now what'll happen to us if them Pawnees double back and hit us? Damn it, Rebs, you ain't runnin' off and leavin' us to fend for ourselves against the whole Pawnee tribe."

Gil swore. Kurt Sweet hadn't talked so much since 1st Squad arrived. "All right," he said. "Michaels, you and Jones take Miss Rankin and the major. The rest of us will stay behind." The rest would be Gil, Russell, Hardee, and Warren Fry, but that seemed to pacify Sweet.

"We ain't never been to Larned," Jones began.

"Just follow the trail," Gil said. "How hard can it be?"

Becky, sitting on the litter next to her father, looked at him and mouthed: "Good luck."

CHAPTER
EIGHTEEN

He wondered if he would ever see Becky Rankin again. It didn't seem likely. She would see to her father at Fort Larned, and probably continue on to Denver. If the major died . . . ? Gil shook his head. It didn't matter one way or the other. Becky would stay at Fort Larned or go west, but either way Gil would be stuck at Sweet's station. Besides, he kept telling himself that he wasn't fit for Rebecca Rankin.

Corporal Ben Crook returned the following day, disgusted and tired. The Pawnees had scattered, so the Army had nothing to show for the fight. Even the dead Indians had been scooped up by the fleeing braves, denying Sergeant Jed Curry his chance at adding to his scalp collection. By the time the Army patrol returned, Metairie had buried the dead men and had the dead livestock hauled away and burned. Gil found himself in command. Henry Russell did nothing except sleep, eat, and drink Kurt Sweet's whisky. That suited Metairie and his men just fine.

The Colorado and Kansas cavalry troopers rode out toward Fort Larned, leaving Luke Murrah behind, and 1st Squad fell into the same dreary routine. Three days

155

later, Goldy Michaels and Phineas Jones returned in the Army ambulance.

"How's the major?" Gil asked.

Michaels shrugged. "He was still breathing when we got him to the post. The Officer of the Day said we'd best get back here, so we didn't stick around none. That fort's something else, though, Sergeant. I ain't seen so many bluebellies since Jonesborough. They weren't fooling when they said they'd get a campaign going against the Indians. Looks like we'll miss out on all the fun."

"Seems we've had enough fun, Goldy."

"Maybe."

The following week, a train of half a dozen wagons pulled in, escorted by Peadar Flann and 3rd Squad — only this time the soldiers were mounted, and they were driving a remuda of ten geldings branded **U.S.** Two of Flann's soldiers drove the horses into the corral, while the Irishman barked orders at one of the teamsters to bring his wagon around and unload the McClellan saddles. Flann tried to smile at Metairie as he walked up, but the sergeant looked uncomfortable in the saddle. Gil had never seen his friend on a horse before. It took all of his will power to keep from laughing.

"Aye, I know what you're thinking," Flann said, "so be a saint and hold your tongue."

"You getting down?"

"Well, I appreciate your concern for my backside . . ."

Metairie couldn't help himself. He quickly fired off: "I was thinking about your horse, Flann."

The Irishman let out a mocking laugh. "If I get off, Gil, I'm not sure I can get back on." He looked past Gil and saw Lieutenant Russell step out of the main building, whisky bottle in his right hand. Flann licked his lips. "But I guess it's for the best." With a groan, he practically fell to the ground, chastising the horse as it stutter-stepped and pawed nervously.

The two soldiers shook hands, then hugged.

"Since when did you become cavalry, Flann?" Gil asked.

"Mounted infantry," Peadar corrected. "It was Major Armstrong's idea. He's not a bad lad for a Yank, this Armstrong, and unlike most of the officers in this man's army he's treating us like men, like soldiers. Let's cut the dust, old friend, and I'll tell you all about it."

Metairie was on duty, but it didn't seem to matter. Russell wouldn't say anything if they sampled Sweet's stock, providing the lieutenant hadn't drained the last keg. Gil and Flann walked into the building and found a crude table. The Russian cook, Gleb, brought over a clay jug and two dirty shot glasses. Peadar Flann quickly filled both glasses and drained his quickly. Almost immediately he jammed his right fist against his sternum.

"Well," he said, "it isn't exactly Irish whisky, is it?"

Gil smiled. "You were saying . . . ?"

After refilling his glass, he explained: "Well, you know about the big campaign being organized at Larned. These Yanks finally came to the brilliant conclusion that it's mighty hard for infantry to guard places such as this station and freighters, like the one outside. Those horses in the corral are for you and your boys, Gil. Saddles, bridles, blankets, and all . . . compliments of the War Department. I guess they don't think we plan on deserting now. Quite a few of our boys are to take an active part in this campaign, Gil."

"But not you and me."

Flann shook his head sadly. "First Squad is to remain here. Third Squad is to continue escort duty. But it looks like Bealer and Van Boskirk will get to see the elephant. They were at Larned when we pulled out."

Larned. Gil tested his drink. Flann was right; it was a long way from Irish whisky. He pushed up his hat brim and asked Peadar about the major. But Flann hadn't known Rankin had been brought to the fort. He wasn't even aware of the fight at Sweet's station until Gil told him.

"Gosh, Gil, I'm sorry. Did any of your boys get hurt?"

"Hartranft got killed."

"Mother of Mary, here I am carrying on like a poor drunkard while one of the bravest men to ever wear the gray is lying in a grave just a few rods away." He raised his glass. "To Theophilus Hartranft."

After a few drinks, Peadar Flann could be a tad overly dramatic. Theo Hartranft had been a good soldier in the Confederacy and then in the Union Army, but Gil never would have called him "one of the bravest men to ever wear the gray." Still, Metairie accepted the toast. Their glasses clinked. Gil set his empty one on the table and shook his head when Flann offered to refill it. "You didn't see Miss Rankin, the major's daughter, while you were at Larned, did you?"

"No. I certainly would have remembered that *aingeal*, Gil. But there was so much activity going on at the fort, she could have been there. I didn't see much of anything, Gil. Well, I'd best get going." He stood, pulled his hat down tight, and hesitated. Metairie waited, smiling.

Flann wiped his lips with the back of a brawny hand, took a deep breath, exhaled slowly, and asked timidly: "Gil, *mo cara*, would it be possible for you to help me back in the saddle? I don't want the boys to be laughing at me, you know. Maybe we can take my horse around the back of the building. Perhaps there's a rock or something I can climb on to give me a little more height."

"I think we can find something, Flann," Gil said, and followed the Irishman outside.

After helping Flann mount his horse, Gil walked past the corrals, where G. W. Hardee and the rest of 1st Squad were examining the horses and equipment. Luke Murrah, who had been practically born in a saddle, was showing Warren Fry how to use the brush and curry comb on a horse before saddling. Metairie scanned the grounds for Lieutenant Russell, but didn't see him. He should tell Russell what he had learned from Flann — explain about the horses, determine if the lieutenant wanted to begin mounted training — but what was the point? Henry Russell was probably passed out on his

159

cot by now. The man didn't give a damn about anything since the Pawnees hit.

Still, Gil was the sergeant, and Russell was his commanding officer. He started toward the crude huts, passing the freight wagons when he heard Toby Greer's cold voice.

"Hello again, Louisiana."

Metairie spun around. Toby pushed up his porkpie hat and tugged on his beard. He leaned against the center of a canvas-covered wagon, holding a long whip in his left hand while his right thumb hooked the wide belt close to one of his Navy Colts.

"I thought that was you when we pulled up here," Greer continued. He laughed. "You always act surprised to see me, Gil. I told you I got hired on with this freightin' crew. How you been?"

Gil didn't answer.

Greer shook his head, smiling. "You sure have changed, Louisiana."

Now Metairie spoke. "You ought to light a shuck out of here, Toby. If those Federals catch up with you, you'll likely hang."

"Heard that argument before, Gil. No, sir, the way I see things is that them bluebellies is got their hands full trying to fight the Injuns . . . Pawnee, Comanche, Kiowa, Cheyenne. I don't think they're gonna pay me no never mind. But if they do, you just remember that they can make the gallows pretty big, wide enough to hang me and you. Yes, sir, I was looking at a poster back in Leavenworth before I headed this way. It was a listing of all the known men with the Blackwater River

160

Guards. You ain't on that list, but I am. Toby Greer. They got my name right. Guess I was too popular in Sedalia, and it seems somebody recognized me when we raided Baxter Springs."

Greer paused long enough to scratch his brown hair. "Anyhows, there's a reward offered for any information that leads to the apprehension of any of Colonel Montulé's men, so I reckon if the Yanks were to catch me, I could turn you in. That fifty dollars would buy me a pretty handsome coffin and tombstone, I warrant." He laughed then. "Oh, Louisiana, don't look so scared. It ain't like I would go about turnin' in one of my pards. Besides, I've got me an honest job these days. Half of Missouri is now lookin' for Colonel Montulé. He's the last of the Confederacy's gray ghosts. I heard that in Jefferson City, shortly before I rode out. Gray ghosts. I kinda like that. Funny thing, though. Them Yanks want to hang the colonel and me . . . and you, for that matter . . . yet they is willin' to make Bobby Lee and Stonewall Jackson into heroes. That don't seem fair to me. We were all wearin' the gray, all of us was fightin' the Yanks. How do you explain that?"

"Robert E. Lee and Stonewall Jackson commanded armies, Toby. You and Moon Montulé were nothing more than cold-blooded killers."

Toby wet his lips. The wagon master yelled for the freighters to get moving. "You rode with us, Louisiana. What does that make you?"

Metairie spun around and left, breathing heavily. He stopped by the cook fire and stared blankly at the coffee pot. He wasn't thirsty, yet he filled a tin mug and

161

watched the wagons as they pulled onto the Santa Fé Trail. Flann, bouncing up and down like a rag doll, and 3rd Squad's corporal, an Arkansas farmer named Paye, rode in front of the wagons. The rest of the squad pulled up the rear. Metairie scanned the wagons until he picked out Toby Greer's. He never let Greer out of his sight until the train had disappeared. Gil stared at the coffee and poured it onto the ground, untouched.

Greer was gone. Again. But Metairie knew he would be back all too soon. He wondered if Greer would turn him in if captured. Probably. The Missourian had always held a vindictive streak, but few Blackwater River Guards had ever been captured. "Die game, boys!" Moon Montulé had often shouted before and during scrapes with the Red Legs or Federal patrols. "It beats swinging from a Yankee rope!"

Tossing the empty cup into the pan of dirty dishes, Gil tried to put Greer and Montulé out of his mind. He found Henry Russell asleep on top of his cot, drenched in a stinking sweat that smelled of bad whisky. So much for duty, Gil thought, and returned to the corrals.

"How many of you are experienced horsemen?" Metairie asked. It was an honest question. Most of these men — with the exception of Murrah — had been marching across the South with the Army of the Tennessee, often without shoes and socks.

Luke smiled and raised his hand, but Metairie cut him off. "Not you," he said in jest. "We know you Texicans couple with horses."

That brought an eruption of laughter from the soldiers and nearby stable boys. Goldy Michaels said

162

his family had owned a couple of mules back in Camden, South Carolina, and he often rode one double with his sister on the way to Sunday preaching. Warren Fry had never been on a horse, mule, or donkey, and Phineas Jones had been bucked off once. G. W. Hardee was a pretty good rider. Gil knew that. They had pursued the Pawnees together with Hickok, and Metairie would call himself a pretty good horseman.

"All right," Gil said, "it looks like we're mounted infantry now, so we'd best get some training. Let's saddle up."

He busied himself preparing for mounted drills, and didn't think about Toby Greer again until the next morning when he saw the smoke rising into the cloudless Kansas sky.

CHAPTER
NINETEEN

"Damn."

It came out more as a sigh than a curse. Metairie's gut told him it was the wagon train. Kurt Sweet and Gleb had noticed the thick trail of black smoke, too. Gil turned around, but stopped. He had been about to inform Russell, but there was no point. The lieutenant would be too hung over to be of any use to anyone right now, so Metairie took charge. He ordered Fry and Jones, the least capable horsemen, to stay put. Michaels, Murrah, and Hardee would ride out with Gil to investigate.

"How many rounds per man?" Hardee asked.

"As much as you can carry," Gil answered, and hurried to the corrals to saddle the zebra dun he had issued to himself.

When Sweet realized most of the soldiers were riding out, he protested, panting and sweating from more activity than he was used to. Gil had heard tales of bravery about the soldiers from Wisconsin, the 26th and 36th, and those black-hat boys of the 2nd, 6th, and 7th, nicknamed the Iron Brigade of the West. Commanded by John Gibbon, they had quickly earned the respect of the Confederate soldiers in the thick of the fighting at

South Mountain, Sharpsburg, and Gettysburg. Gil had never fought against the Iron Brigade, and, from what he had heard, he was glad to have missed that opportunity. For a while he thought all men from Wisconsin were savage fighters. Now that he had met Kurt Sweet, he knew better.

"Sergeant, you can't just leave me and my boys with your two greenest soldiers and that drunken lout of a lieutenant," Sweet pleaded. "That smoke could be a Pawnee trick. Or worser, it could be Kiowas or Cheyennes. You taken them soldiers with you, and what'll we do if the Injuns hit us while you're gone."

"Four more guns won't do you much good, Sweet," he said.

"Sure they will, Sergeant. Your boys can shoot. I seen that. It just ain't right for you . . ."

Metairie had heard enough. "Are you willing to investigate that smoke?"

Sweet fell back to his stammering and incoherent mumbling. He shuffled his feet and refused to meet Gil's icy glare. The conversation was over, so Gil turned back to the gelding and slipped on the bridle. Kurt Sweet slowly turned around, said something Gil didn't catch, and walked away.

They held the horses to a canter, not the most comfortable gait for a rider but one that would keep the horses from becoming too winded. Two hours later, they slowed after spotting a man staggering down the trail like someone blind drunk. He wore the blue trousers of a soldier, but no blouse or hat, just his summer underwear, and kept falling to his knees. He would moan, pull himself up, and walk a few uneven paces before falling again.

"Jesus," Goldy Michaels said. "That's Corporal Paye."

Spurring their horses, they quickly covered the distance. Luke Murrah quickly dismounted and caught 3rd Squad's corporal before he collapsed again. The Texan eased the soldier to the ground, and Metairie handed him a canteen before Murrah could ask.

Gil knelt beside the Arkansan. Blood poured from a bullet hole in Paye's left shoulder, and another that had shattered the man's jaw. Most of the water Murrah gave him spilled out of his mouth, mixed with blood, and onto his muslin undershirt.

"What happened, Corporal?" Murrah asked, handing the canteen back to Metairie. "Where's Sergeant Flann?"

Tears streamed down the soldier's bloody face. He said something, flinching at the pain, but Gil couldn't understand. He leaned closer.

"Hit us," Paye whispered. "Didn't expect . . ."

"Who hit you?"

"Water," the man pleaded. Gil returned the canteen to Murrah and rose.

"Michaels," he said, "I want you to take Corporal Paye back to the station. We'll get him on your horse, and you'll have to lead him back. Then I want you to ride as fast as you can to Fort Larned, tell them something happened to the wagon train, and that we are investigating. Ask them to send a cavalry patrol pronto. Think you can handle that?"

"Sure, Sarge. But do you think the corporal can stay in the saddle?"

Luke Murrah answered the question. "He'll be face down," he said.

Gil looked back. The Texan closed the dead man's eyes. William C. Paye, the little farmer of the 1st Arkansas who had earned a handshake from Brigadier General Leonidas E. Polk at Stones River, had died a long way from his Arkansas post. Murrah stiffly stood, eyes on the dead soldier, and shook his head.

"You still want me to go?" Michaels asked.

"No," Metairie answered after a long moment. "We'll need you with us." He glanced at Paye briefly, then told Murrah: "Drag him to the side of the road. No time to bury him now. We'll do that later. Let's ride."

The smoldering ruins of four freight wagons lay on a campsite just off the Santa Fé Trail, and vultures and ravens were already feasting on the dead oxen, mules, and horses that littered the landscape. Hardee's and Michaels's horses became too skittish at the smell of blood, so Metairie ordered everyone to dismount. Goldy Michaels would hold the horses, while Murrah, Hardee, and Metairie went into the battleground on foot. Two teamsters and the wagon master had been shot while they drank their coffee. One of them lay face down in the ashes of the fire, and the wagon master, tin cup still in his hand and a purple hole in his forehead, stared blankly at the morning sun. Another freighter

167

apparently had tried to run, but had been cut down by a fusillade of bullets, and then trampled by charging horses. A lance pinned another teamster to the seat of his wagon, which hadn't burned completely, and Hardee found another man, his body filled with bullet holes and three arrows, in the shrubs.

None of the dead freighters was Toby Greer.

"Flann!" Gil called out. "Flann!"

No answer.

Most of the soldiers had been staked to wagon wheels and burned beyond recognition, but Private Sean Burke's head had been chopped off and placed on a stump. Near the place where the horses had been picketed — and most of them killed — Gil found Sergeant Peadar Flann, a lance through his beer gut, hands and face blackened by powder, and bullet holes in his left thigh and back. An army of ants surrounded the blood that had pooled around the Irishman's body. Gil knelt beside his old friend. He felt a tear on his cheek and quickly brushed it away.

"Bunch of tracks take off south!" Hardee called out. "But some more headed north, took a couple of wagons with 'em, those red sons-of-bitches."

Luke Murrah swore, too, and added: "First time I ever seen an Indian steal a wagon. Two wagons at that."

Peadar Flann's eyes jerked open, and Gil fell backward in fear. His heart raced, but Metairie quickly realized Flann still lived. "Hardee! Murrah!" he shouted. "Get over here quick!"

"Gil?" Flann's voice was barely a whisper. "Is that you, Gil, me lad?"

Metairie moved as close to Flann as he could. He wanted to ease Peadar's head into his lap but dared not move him, afraid that any movement would torture the Irishman. He glanced at the savage wound the lance had made, choked down bile, and forced a smile.

"It's me, Peadar. You're going to be fine."

Flann started to laugh, but mostly what he did was cough and spit a bloody froth onto the ground. "You and me both know better than that, Gil," he said hoarsely. "Hope one of your boys brought a flask of good whisky with him."

Metairie looked up. Both Hardee and Murrah shook their heads. Whisky wouldn't do Flann any good, especially with that lance rammed into his stomach, but it didn't matter. Gil knew his friend was right. Peadar Flann was dying. Metairie had seen enough men gut shot to know he wouldn't live much longer.

"Did Billy Paye make it?" Flann asked, and licked a spot of blood off his lips.

"We rode up to him on the trail," Gil answered. "He . . ." Metairie stopped. He considered lying to his old friend, but decided against it. Flann wouldn't like that one bit. "Paye didn't make it, Peadar," he said. "I'm sorry."

Flann closed his eyes. "He was a good lad, Billy Paye was. You know that, don't you, Gil? So was all me laddies. I used to think no soldier could ever match the boys of the British Forty-First Regiment of Foot, but the Fifteenth Arkansas sure proved me wrong, didn't they, Gil?"

169

Metairie nodded. The tears were flowing freely now, and he didn't bother trying to hide them or wipe them off his cheeks.

"We sure seen the elephant, ain't we, lads?" He was staring at Murrah and Hardee now. Both men smiled.

Hardee said: "Don't you worry, Sergeant. We'll kill as many of those red bastards as we can. I promise you that."

Flann waved his statement off with a weak flick of his wrist. "Indians my arse, Corporal. White men done this to me."

"White!" Hardee and Murrah shouted at the same time. Gil looked down. He had expected this. Toby Greer. The son-of-a-bitch would pay for this. Gil would see to that.

"White, sure as I'm Irish. Oh, they dressed up like Injuns, but they was white. Hit us at dawn while we was having breakfast. My fault. Should have known better."

He lapsed into a coughing spell and breathed heavily, his face a mask of pain. Gil wished he had some whisky, even Kurt Sweet's rotgut, anything to ease the Irishman's pain.

I should have warned Flann, Gil thought. *Should have told him about Greer, told him he was no good, to be careful.* Metairie knew what had happened. Toby Greer had helped lead the wagon train into an ambush. Dress like Indians, leave a few lances and arrows in the bodies, and make the fight look like an Indian massacre, have everything blamed on the Pawnees or Kiowas. But who had been with Greer? This whole damned thing smelled of Moon Montulé and the

170

Blackwater River Guards. The teamsters had been simply shot down, but the soldiers had been burned with the wagons, and Sean Burke had been chopped to pieces. The burning . . . the mutilation . . . these were the kind of atrocities Montulé and Greer would enjoy, making the soldiers of 3ʳᵈ Squad pay for what the Blackwater River Guards would consider treason to the Cause.

I'll see you in Hell, Toby Greer.

"How many men?" Hardee asked. "And did you recognize any of 'em?"

Peadar shook his head slightly. "Maybe a dozen. Hard to tell." He coughed again. Blood began to seep from the corners of Flann's mouth. "Didn't know none. Think one of . . . no, two . . . two were working for Mister Driskill."

Driskill had been the wagon master.

"The man who drove the spear in me, I saw him good." Another coughing fit stopped Flann. He gasped and cried out something in old Irish. "Man looked pale as a ghost. Long black hair, greasy. Mustache and goatee. He wasn't dressed like no Pawnee. Had a brace of revolvers on his hips and a couple of shoulder holsters. White hat and black ostrich plume. And the coldest blue eyes I ever seen."

Moon Montulé. It had to be. Metairie swallowed. His stomach churned uneasily. So the leader of the Blackwater River Guards was here in the middle of the Kansas frontier. Gil suddenly felt warm. He should have killed Toby Greer and Moon Montulé back in Missouri, before he quit the guards to join Cleburne's army. None of this would have happened if he had done what he should have. Gil's face flushed. The rage began to boil.

"We'll find him, Sergeant Flann," Hardee said.

"Aye, but you lads watch out for yourselves. I'm done for." Flann began mumbling something Gil couldn't catch, something about the old country, then he was crying for his mother, lost in the streets of New York City. Flann began shivering, although by now it was blazing hot. G. W. Hardee left to find a couple of bedrolls to help keep the dying man warm. He returned quickly and gently spread the blankets over the Irishman's overweight frame.

Flann's eyes moistened. Lucidity had returned. "Is one of you lads a good Irish Catholic?"

"Don't know how good I am, Sergeant," Luke Murrah said lightly, although his tone was forced. "But that's how I was raised."

"Would you do me a wee favor?"

"Name it."

"I'd like to give you my confession. Tell it to a priest, see if he'll give me absolution . . ." Flann coughed again. Gil put his right hand on Peadar's shoulder, squeezing it gently. "Take care of yourself, Gil," Flann said weakly.

Metairie nodded. "You're a top soldier, Peadar Flann," he said, and left with Hardee so the sergeant could make his confession in private. Gil and Hardee walked back to where Goldy Michaels held the horses.

"Michaels," he said, "I want you to follow the trail of horses as far as you can."

172

"What if they scatter like those Indians always do?" Michaels asked.

"Weren't Indians that done this," Hardee said.

Goldy Michaels stared at them blankly.

After Hardee explained what had happened, Metairie continued: "Just follow the trail as best you can. I don't want it to grow cold. G. W., ride as fast as you can to Fort Zarah and get a cavalry patrol back here. Catch up with Michaels and continue pursuit. Have some of the soldiers follow Luke and me."

"Where will y'all be?" Hardee asked.

"We're following the two wagons to the north."

Murrah walked slowly to them. "Sergeant Flann's gone," he said tiredly. "I'm sorry."

Metairie blinked. "We'll bury the dead before we take off," he said. He couldn't leave Flann as supper for the scavengers. Peadar deserved better than that.

"Did you get his confession?" Hardee asked.

The Texan shook his head sadly. "He started speakin' Gaelic," he said. "Couldn't understand him at all."

CHAPTER
TWENTY

Less than an hour after Metairie saw smoke snaking its way into the sky, Luke Murrah spotted the wagons, parked in the open plains. Both soldiers reined up, confused at first. Two men stood over the campfire while a third sat at a camp table, working on something. Neither man could tell exactly what he was doing from the distance. Two others stood at the front left wheel of the first wagon, one smoking a cigar, the other fanning himself with his porkpie hat. A sixth man, a sentry, waited at the edge of the camp, an Enfield musket cradled in his arms. Livestock grazed, not picketed, just beyond them.

"Right sure of themselves," Murrah said dryly.

"Ambush?" Gil asked.

"Don't think so. It's a poor place for it, and I count just enough saddle horses for six men."

Gil nodded. The one-eyed Texan had read the trail as soon as they left the massacre site. Two wagons, four outriders, and two horses tethered to the trailing wagon. Six men. But why were they waiting? Certainly these marauders had to realize a company of cavalry would be storming after them. Metairie stopped himself. *Company? Two men.*

If the odds frightened Murrah, Gil couldn't see it. Luke eared back the hammer on his Spencer, hooked out the chaw of tobacco from his mouth with his thumb, and spat. "Should we pay 'em a friendly visit, Sarge?" the Texan asked.

Gil hesitated.

"Either that or shoot 'em, from here, where they stand." Actually, to his surprise, Gil found that idea more to his liking. After all, what kind of chance had these men given Peadar Flann and those teamsters?

But Murrah added: "Like them Missouri border trash would, and I ain't like them." Kicking his mount into a walk, he rode straight into camp, bold as Bedford Forrest.

Metairie checked his own carbine and slowly followed. He saw what had forced them to stop as they neared the camp. The metal rim on the lead wagon's front wheel had overheated and come off, forcing the robbers either to abandon the vehicle and its plunder or repair the wheel. Most outlaws would have left the crippled wagon behind, but these men seemed sure of themselves, or maybe they were just plain crazy.

The guard shifted as Gil and Luke approached, brought his musket forward, but kept the barrel pointed at the ground. The hammer was already set a full cock. All he had to do was lift, aim, and fire. He didn't seem to care too much about the approaching riders. Instead, he stared past them. *Looking to see if we have more men*, Gil thought. The sentry whistled. The five others turned their attention toward the two soldiers, but none seemed threatened or concerned. The guard, a husky,

175

pockmarked man with a thick gray mustache and pale eyes, grinned, revealing rotten teeth, and said two words that took Gil aback.

"Hello, Louisiana."

Metairie recovered, tried to place the man's face but couldn't. Gil felt Murrah's questioning stare, burning. He knew Luke would hold some suspicion now, wondering if Gil himself were part of this scheme. A sharp *click* sounded, bringing Metairie's attention back to the sentry, but he found the man simply lowering the hammer on the musket before he turned and walked to the wagons. "This way, Yanks," he said. "Been expectin' y'all."

They followed on horseback, not speaking. Gil's mouth went dry, and the Spencer felt cold in his clammy hands. Once more he tried to remember the man, put a name to that ugly face, but . . . nothing. He hadn't really known many of the Blackwater River Guards personally — nor had he wanted to — except Toby Greer. All of them, himself included, had been aloof and cold, loners mostly, held together by Moon Montulé's unbending will and a common desire to kill as many Yankees as they could before they themselves were cut down by Federal musketry or a hemp rope.

"It's Gil Smith, boys!" the guard called out. "Come to join us."

He understood then, or at least he thought he did. The guards were pretending to befriend him, turning Murrah's attention from the killers to himself. But how had they known he would be coming after them? He looked at the horses, still saddled, and spotted one

176

well-lathered. They had sent a rider out on the back trail, Metairie reasoned, who had spotted only two men following them and, after recognizing Gil, had ridden hard to form this plan.

"Keep your guard up," Gil said in a hoarse whisper to Murrah. "Don't take your eye off them."

Murrah grunted something, and the two men reined up in front of the man at the table. He wore a sweat-stained white hat and the brown woolen shirt that had come to be recognized by Federals as the uniform of the Blackwater killers. Two Remington revolvers rested on his folding pine table, while he busied himself loading an Army Colt, pouring a measure of powder from a copper flask into a chamber, then placing a patch and round lead ball on top and ramming them home with the loading lever underneath the barrel of the .44. The man ignored the two riders and concentrated on his chore.

Shuffling his feet, the sentry turned to face the visitors. "Ran into a bit of a setback, you see, Smith," he said in a slow Missouri drawl. "Figured we was done for till we seen it was you a-trailin' us." He looked at Murrah. "Jones is my name. You lose that eye of yourn to Yanks?"

Murrah nodded slightly.

"Then maybe you'd like to join us. We be with the Blackwater River Guards from Missouri way."

"War's over," Luke replied.

"Not for us, it ain't."

Murrah didn't answer. His horse snorted.

The two men near the first wagon stepped away, hands resting on the butts of their revolvers. The other two, shirtless and drenched in sweat, left the fire and began moving toward the rifles stacked beside the wagon tongue.

"That's far enough," Gil called out, and they stopped.

The man at the table began capping the nipples on the Colt. "You can stop that, too," Murrah said.

He looked up, unsmiling, face shadowed by the wide-brimmed hat, pulled the hammer to full cock, and waited. The tension seemed to lessen, however, when Metairie's horse picked this moment to empty its bladder. The man smoking the cigar near the wagon laughed.

"Smith," Jones said easily. "You might want to talk some sense into that trooper of yourn, tell him how we fights when we gets riled. There's only two of you, and you'll be bitin' off a chaw too big against the eigh . . ."

Metairie realized the mistake immediately. They hadn't been trailing six men as Luke guessed. There were eight. How could he have forgotten about Greer? Toby had been working one of the wagons, and it stood to reason that at least one more man had been in on the ambush. Everything flashed through his mind. After the ambush, Toby Greer and another guard had driven the wagons, and two other bush-whackers tied their horses behind the second wagon to ride shotgun. Greer and another man had to be hiding in the tall grass, rifles trained on Metairie and Luke. *Stupid!* He should have known.

Hell, only his dead father and Toby Greer ever called him Louisiana.

Jones had stopped in mid-sentence, catching himself before he spoke the word eight. By then, though, it was too late. Metairie shouted something — he wasn't exactly sure of what himself — and leaped from the saddle, his horse taking off in a panic and overturning the desk, spilling the Remingtons and knocking the sitting man onto his backside. In the corner of his eye, Gil saw Luke Murrah raising his Spencer slightly and pulling the trigger, then leaping off his horse. Another gun boomed. The Texan's horse squealed and crumpled.

The man knocked down next to the table tried to stand up, fumbling with the Colt. Gil shot him in the face at point-blank range and dropped to a knee. Jones was dead, too, staring blankly at the Kansas sky. Murrah's first shot had hit him dead center in the chest. Gil's neck burned. Blood trickled. He understood a bullet had creased him. Everything was happening so fast. Metairie seemed aware of the bullets thumping the ground beside him, smacking Murrah's dead horse. White smoke burned his eyes. Yet, he heard nothing, not even his own carbine when it bucked in his arms.

The cigar-smoking man grabbed his chest and dropped, while the guard nearest him fired a Henry rifle rapidly, not aiming at Gil, but at Murrah. Metairie pulled the trigger, knew he missed, shot again, and the Henry and its owner fell silent. Two men reached the stacked rifles. Gil's Spencer fired. One man spun around and disappeared. The second seemed to

179

hesitate, glancing at his partner, then toward Metairie. Next he staggered back, sank to his knees, and fell sideways. Metairie wasn't even sure if he had pulled the trigger.

He could hear now, the pounding of heavy fire to his left. He took a deep breath, recognized the shrill yell of a charging guerrilla, and turned as a heavy-set, red-bearded man lunged at him. Something flashed in the giant's right hand. An Arkansas toothpick. Gil cried out as the blade sank deep into his right thigh. The big man withdrew the knife, twisting as he pulled out the blade, and straddled Gil, crushing the breath and almost the life out of him. He tried to grip the carbine, realized he had somehow lost it, saw the glint of the bloody blade once more as the red-headed man raised it over his head.

Gil held his breath, waiting for death, but the man seemed to pause as if he were in deep thought. His fist relaxed, and the long knife fell heavily to the dirt. Blood began to seep from both corners of his mouth, disappearing into the thick red hair, and the man stood up, wobbled, and crashed on top of Jones's body.

Crying out in pain, Metairie rolled over and found the Spencer. His leg burned as if on fire, and he saw his trousers already covered with blood. The knife had nicked an artery. He thought back to Shiloh, his first real battle, and remembered General Johnston shot in the leg and bleeding to death because he had sent his surgeon off to help the wounded. He'd die, too, but that eighth man — it had to be Greer — might kill him first before he bled to death.

180

"Murrah?" His voice sounded weak, faraway, as if someone else were speaking to him.

No answer. Gil turned slowly.

Luke Murrah, hero at Stones River, Missionary Ridge, and too many other battlefields, the Texas cavalryman who said he could ride through the Pawnee nation with one Spencer and a sturdy mount, sat leaning against his dead horse, eye patch slightly askew, smoke still drifting from the barrel of the carbine he gripped tightly. He looked to be sleeping, but Gil had seen too many corpses to know that Luke Murrah would never wake up. Damned fool Texan had saved Metairie's life, too, shooting that red-headed bastard with his final shot.

Footsteps. Someone running. Groaning, Gil tried to raise his Spencer and fire. He could vaguely make out Toby Greer dashing for the horses, but he had no clear shot. Metairie fired once anyway, cocked the carbine, and pulled the trigger again. The hammer clicked empty. Greer had swung into a saddle by then. Gil rose slightly, saw the Missourian galloping north, pulling another horse behind him, fleeing. He'd ride one horse to death and then another to escape.

He swore, and suddenly laughed. "Greer, you're one brave son-of-a-bitch," he said. "Running away from a dead man."

Metairie pulled himself up, gasping at the pain, and looked again at his blood-drenched leg. The Kansas plains began to spin. Lightheaded, he knew, from the loss of blood. No way to stop the bleeding, either. Not now. Too late. He'd be joining Luke Murrah soon at those Pearly Gates, where St. Peter would hold him accountable for everything he had done — from the atrocities he hadn't prevented in Missouri to letting good men like Luke Murrah and Peadar Flann die today — and send him straight to Hades.

Still, he found himself reaching for the bloody Arkansas toothpick. He gripped the rosewood handle, dragged the knife — it felt more like a cavalry saber — to him, and somehow cut back the trouser leg so he could see the gaping wound. Gil sighed heavily, dropped the knife, and fell forward. His eyes slowly opened, and he saw something else glittering in the sunlight beside the overturned table and the man he had killed.

A powder flask.

He filled his lungs, and he crawled like a dying dog, reached out, grasped the flask as he rolled over and sat up. It took both thumbs to force back the brass latch he was so weak, but he turned the container over and small black grains poured out until emptied. He packed the powder into the knife wound, and stared at the smoke, dragging himself and bloody leg again. Although the campfire burned no more than twenty yards away, it might as well have been twenty miles. Metairie knew he'd never make it. He'd pass out first, and never wake up. He stopped, saw another dead man in front of him.

Metairie's eyes closed again, tightly, and he let out another faint cry. Then he forced himself to look at the campfire again, watching the smoke, tormenting himself. He looked down at the dead Blackwater River Guard. His heart skipped.

He swept the cigar into his fist and jammed it into his mouth, pulling long drag after long drag, and spitting out mouthfuls of juice. Nothing. He tried again, half crying, half praying, until he tasted a faint trace of smoke in his mouth. He sucked harder. The end of the cigar began to glow. Three more pulls, and the cigar tip turned red-hot. Metairie forced himself into a sitting position and lowered the burning cigar until it touched the black powder.

His thigh erupted in flame and pain. Gil Metairie felt sick, and then nothing.

CHAPTER
TWENTY-ONE

Someone had poured burning coals on his thigh. He woke up, blinded by the brilliant white sun overhead, and waited until the world stopped spinning. Senses of sight and taste had left him, but he could smell. The stench of death, of burned flesh and gunpowder, disemboweled bodies, excrement, and sweat. Shiloh and the cry of the wounded and dying, the men crawling to Bloody Pond to bathe their wounds. Or was it Stones River, where Rosecrans and Bragg pounded their armies against each other for control of the corridor from Nashville to Atlanta? He remembered it all, could still feel the ground shaking from the horses, eyes wide in terror, charging across the fields, pulling cannon and caisson, the grapeshot cutting down elm and pine trees like Paul Bunyon's axe. No, his mind seemed to tell him, not Shiloh, not anywhere in Tennessee. He fought for breath, hot, stale, and saw the black smoke as Osceola burned from the torches wielded by Jim Lane's jayhawkers, saw his father's dead body, and his sister . . . the specter faded away to the butchery at the Olathe Baptist Church, Moon Montulé gunning down the deacon named Lincoln, and then one of the Guards unsheathing his knife and doing that

184

unfathomable atrocity to the dead man's body, something he had tried to block out for years.

Maybe this was the beginning of death . . . like the preachers said, your life passing before you. He closed his eyes.

The sun hadn't moved when he woke, but he knew he had been asleep for an eternity. A sharp throbbing replaced the intense blistering in his thigh, and someone had filled his mouth with cotton balls. "Murrah," he said in a waterless voice. Just speaking two syllables hurt. No one answered, and he couldn't say more. Not now. Where was Luke? What had happened? He turned his head away from the sun, but the world remained a blur. A mound of dark flesh came into half focus, and he saw the one-eyed Texan leaning against his horse. Something moved. He could hear the air popping, two *whumps*, and more movement, and then he saw it clearly: the vulture, perched on the bloated horse, plucking out a beakful of Luke Murrah's face.

"Oh, Jesus!" Metairie cried as he rolled over and vomited, spraying his hands with bile and slime, heaving until he thought he would choke out his own intestines. Still gagging, tears streaming, he fell into the pool he had purged from his stomach, filled his lungs with hot, foul air, and, staring at the ground, forced himself to crawl away from Murrah.

The gunfight came to him slowly, like pieces in a puzzle. When he stopped crawling, he looked up and realized he rested beside one of the wagons. Gripping the spokes of a wheel, he pulled himself into a sitting

185

position. The knot on his bandanna took forever to loosen, but he finally wiped his face with the piece of calico. Next he examined his leg, but the sight sickened him more, and he thought he would choke. Water. He needed water. His eyes turned toward the vulture and the dead horse. There might be canteens around the camp — had to be — but he knew where he could find Luke's.

Gil Metairie began dragging himself back to the Texan's body. The vulture cried out, and he became aware that other carrion filled the campsite, feasting on the bodies of what once had been men. He touched something foreign, saw the Yankee-made Smith carbine, hammer cocked, nipple capped, ready to fire. Gil struggled with the weapon before resting the stock against the ground, barrel pointed at the sun, and pulled the trigger. The .50 — caliber weapon detonated, and the air seemed alive with flapping wings.

Two minutes later, Metairie uncorked the canteen on Luke's McClellan saddle and drank greedily.

How long had he been here? A day? Week? It didn't matter, but he had to leave now. The smell had become an abomination, and the vultures would return, along with coyotes and wolves. Gil found three more canteens and stuck the loaded Remington .44s in his deep mule-ear trouser pockets. Walking was out of the question, and by now he felt too weak even to crawl. Yet somehow he did.

His right hand gripped the lethal knife the Missourian had stabbed him with, and Gil stretched his

186

long arm forward and sank the blade into the soil. That left him exhausted. A minute, maybe more, passed before he could continue. Still gripping the knife's handle with his right hand, he reached out with his left hand, found the knife, and, grunting, pulled himself forward. As he filled his lungs, he worked the blade loose and extended his arm, Arkansas toothpick in hand again, he stabbed the earth, dragging his body, heading southwest, toward Kurt Sweet's place, a million miles from nowhere.

Stab and drag. Stab and drag. Stab and drag.

He did this until the sky blackened, and he slept.

When dawn came, he slaked his thirst and picked up the long knife.

Stab and drag.

Stab and drag.

Stab and drag.

The point of the blade had broken off a long time ago. Two of the canteens, now empty, littered the plains miles — or maybe only yards — behind him, along with his boots and strips from his Federal uniform, even the two Remington revolvers. Both hands felt raw, and his trousers and long johns were shredded beyond recognition. Filth covered what remained of his clothes. As he sat up, he looked at the maggots in his thigh. Let them eat his decaying flesh. That was good, healthy, but soon they'd be eating . . .

It didn't matter. He would die here. Collapsing, he watched the darkening clouds blot out the broiling sun. A lifetime later, he felt the cooling rain. He should take advantage of the cool, he told himself, but no muscles co-operated, so he napped. When his eyes opened, he decided to die.

"Heavenly Father, forgive me. End this agony. Take me."

The voice that answered came not from God, or Christ. Nor Lucifer.

"Louisiana?"

No, he thought, *it couldn't be*. Gil rubbed his eyes, but the kindly face still smiled down on him. The last time Gil had seen the old Cajun, Baptiste Metairie's face was purple, eyes bulging, and he had bitten through his tongue after Jim Lane's men had murdered him, strung him up in front of his own home while other jayhawkers raped and killed poor Arianne and forced Gil's mother to watch.

"Pa?" Gil said.

"You ain't giving up, are you, Louisiana?" The thick accent sounded musical. "Letting your papa down?"

Gil said softly: "I'm dying, Pa. It's over."

Baptiste laughed. "Why didn't you die back with them others?" He couldn't answer. "Or at that Yankee hell they call a prison? You reckon that girl you fancy will rest easier if they never find your body?"

"No, sir." He hadn't thought of Becky Rankin until now.

"You've made me right proud, son," his father said. "Mighty proud. I was always a coward, running out of Alexandria . . . never should have done that, that was my grandfather's country and his grandfather's as well.

Never taking a stand during the unpleasantness, letting your sister . . ."

"Wasn't your fault, Pa."

The rail-thin farmer ignored him. "But you took a stand, learned from them mistakes." The Cajun laughed. "My son wearing the Yankee blue. Odette would raise Cain over that. But I think you're doing the right thing."

"Mother loathes me," Gil said sadly. "She wanted me to stay with Montulé."

Baptiste waved him off. "Odette was one hard woman. Hate ran through her veins, just as it runs through Moon Montulé, Toby Greer, Major Rankin, and that fool lieutenant, Russell. But you ain't like them, Gil. What's more, you're a survivor. Them other fellas, they are far from that."

He soaked the words up sluggishly. *Odette was one hard woman. Was.* "Mother?" he asked.

His father's rectangular head shook slowly. "Odette's dead, Gil. She died while you were at Rock Island. Stroke, they say. Mouth full of snuff and a belly filled with hate. Bass Leigh wrote you, but you never got the letter."

An apparition. Baptiste Luc Metairie was a ghost. This was some sort of dream, or nightmare, but Gil couldn't wake up. "You're dead, too."

"*Oui.*" The word came out as a faint whisper.

"I have no family left."

They remained silent for a while. Finally, Baptiste Metairie leaned forward to brush a lock of hair off his son's forehead. He straightened, smiling, and said softly: "Son, make your own family. Follow your own path. You want to know why you didn't stay back with those dead men, to join them and be picked over by buzzards and wolves? You want to survive. You want to live. Forget the past. Live for today, live for tomorrow. Follow me." He spoke something in bastard French, laughed, and waved as he walked past Gil. "*Adieu*," he said. "Stay here and die, or crawl and live."

"Papa!" Metairie turned in a panic, yet his father kept walking. Gil grabbed the dead Guard's knife and lunged forward, plunging the broken blade into the dirt, jerking himself hurriedly after the disappearing figure of Baptiste. "Pa!" he whined again, prying the Arkansas toothpick loose and slamming it an arm's length away. "Please wait," he said. "Papa, don't leave me."

Stab and drag.

Stab and drag.

Stab and drag.

Baptiste Luc Metairie, murdered outside of Osceola almost four years ago, had vanished. Exactly when, Gil wasn't certain. Chasing a vision from delirium or a ghost sent from God, the gaunt soldier, now almost completely naked, had pulled himself for the past two days. He had refilled his canteen at a small water hole, where he had waited until dusk when a jack rabbit came. Metairie killed it with his knife, crushing the animal's head with the knife's heavy handle — one hundred percent luck and zero percent skill — skinned the animal, and ate it raw.

190

That was all he had eaten during this hellish eternity except for the few pieces of jerky he had carried with him and something else he had found on the trail that had made him sick. He had forced himself to eat the jerky, but now, at the water hole, he discovered that he was hungry. He spent the night there.

A strange noise woke him shortly after sunrise. He listened. The jingle grew closer. At first, Gil thought it might be spurs. He started to cry out, but stopped himself. It might be the Army, but it could also be Toby Greer or some other killer from the Blackwater River Guards. Wait. By now he could make out the sound of a horse. No . . . horses.

He pushed himself up, peering through the high grass, and saw them. Metairie flattened himself, cursed silently at his mistake. He had dropped too fast. The horses had stopped. Someone had seen the rapid movement.

Their voices carried in the early morning air.

"*Tzena?*"

"*Tocusé.*"

"*Tábo?*"

The second man's guttural answer sang out, cut short when the first began to mock him. Gil couldn't understand the words, but the tone was unmistakable. They debated on horseback for a while — why they didn't just ride over to investigate Gil would never know or understand — before they must have shrugged the movement off and rode on, the silver bells woven into the mane of one rangy pinto singing lightly in the early morning.

Metairie forced himself to look up once more. The two men, black hair glistening, feathers dancing off the barrels of the muskets they carried, never looked back.

Indians. From the look of them not Pawnees, but Gil wouldn't risk his life to find out if they were friendly or hostile. He decided to wait here a while, suddenly exhausted, and welcome sleep.

A giant hand crushed his lips. Metairie's eyes shot open, frightened, as he squirmed and tried to sink teeth into his assailant's palm. The Indian's flowing hair waved in the wind, and he swore, shaking Gil's left shoulder violently, whispering, speaking English. Not an Indian, but a white man. The face, sporting a permanent mustache and week's growth of beard, became familiar, but the voice sounded far from friendly, hoarse and quiet, yet commanding.

"Damn it, Metairie. Quit your squirmin' and stop bitin' me, or you'll get us all killed. These plains are full of Comanch'."

Gil stilled himself. Comprehension came slowly.

"Hickok?" he asked at last.

CHAPTER
TWENTY-TWO

"You look like you've been skinned with a parin' knife and boiled for an hour," Hickok said. The scout had wrapped some sort of poultice made from chewing tobacco over the wicked thigh wound before slipping an Indian rubber poncho over Metairie's sunburned, scratched body, the only type of clothing Hickok could offer.

Night had fallen, and, after waiting by the water hole all day, Wild Bill began preparing to leave. He uncorked a canteen and gently lifted Metairie's head. Gil drank, expecting water, but coughed as the liquor burned his throat.

"What is that?" he asked.

"Brandy," Hickok said, and winked. "This is my good canteen. Keep water in t'other."

Gil was taking another long drink, when the tall plainsman pulled away the tin canteen wrapped in Union blue, saying: "That's enough." Hickok then asked: "What happened to your leg?"

"Got knifed. Bleeding real bad." He explained how he had cauterized the wound.

Hickok shook his head in amazement, and said: "That's a hell of a thing."

"Don't cut it off," Metairie pleaded. "Don't saw off my leg." He thought back to those hospital tents after the battles, recalled the terrifying screams, useless boots piled high beside blood-stained canvas, and scores of amputated legs and arms being hauled off by orderlies in wheelbarrows, all the while weary surgeons worked relentlessly like farmers butchering their hogs for winter lard and pork.

"Ain't likely, Metairie. I'm no sawbones."

Gil tried to reach out, grasp Hickok's buckskin sleeve, but the scout moved away to wrap the canvas strap of the canteen over his saddle horn. "Don't let them doctors take my leg off, either," he said.

Hickok turned, smiling. "We're not at Fort Larned yet, *amigo*. And with as many Comanches and Kiowas as I've seen the past two days, it's more than likely that we'll be dead long before we ever reach a real doctor."

Exhaustion overtook Metairie. He sank back, exhaling, bone-tired.

"Whoa!" the scout commanded. "Don't go to sleep on me, Metairie. We're gonna ride by night for a spell."

Metairie couldn't ride, as weak as he was, with that bum leg. He said as much to Hickok, who responded: "I'll get you in the saddle, and you just grab the horn and pull leather. You ride. I'll walk."

After being pulled to his feet, Gil leaned against the big man in buckskins for support. Hickok's black Morgan, a new horse, snorted and danced around as the strange two-headed, four-legged monster half-stumbled toward it, but the scout called out in a soothing voice, and the horse calmed down. Metairie gripped the saddle horn with both hands while Hickok patted the Morgan's neck, cooing, rubbing his hand across the stallion's dusty coat toward its belly. Whispering, now humming a tune — "Lorena" maybe, Gil wasn't sure — Wild Bill gently lifted Metairie's left leg and eased his bare left foot into the stirrup. Hickok rose, patted the Morgan's neck once more, and asked: "Ready?"

Gil nodded.

Hickok's powerful hands and long arms guided Metairie into the saddle, although the rapid movement and exertion left Gil reeling, dizzy, nauseated. The saddle horn felt cold in his sweaty hands, and the rubber poncho stuck to his clammy skin. Metairie vomited, and the Morgan snorted and tried to swing around.

"Easy," the scout told the horse.

A few moments passed. Gil straightened, sighed. Sickness and dizziness passed, but now his leg burned and throbbed, shooting pain down to his foot and all the way up his spine.

"Ready?" Hickok asked again.

It was morning, and Metairie had just been spooned a weak broth made from boiled jerky in water thickened with hot brandy. Now Hickok was eating his own breakfast — hardtack and jerky and coffee. The campfire had been small, practically smokeless, but the scout kicked it out as soon as the coffee and soup were ready, not wanting to risk being discovered by any

Kiowas, Comanches, Pawnees, or Cheyennes. "Thick as fleas on a cur dog," Hickok had said.

"Why did you leave that camp?" Hickok asked.

Metairie thought before answering. The smell of the corpses . . . the vultures picking at the dead . . . or simply the wanting to find help, to crawl away from the carnage all the way to Sweet's way station. What had he been thinking? An Army patrol would have followed the trail and eventually found Gil at the site. If he had stayed put, by now he would be lying on a hospital cot at Larned or Zarah.

"Shouldn't have," Gil said at last. "Must have been out of my head."

The scout merely shrugged. "Maybe. Then again, might have been lucky for you that you left. Indians found it before us. Hacked up those bodies to pieces, damned prairie niggers, dumped out just about everything the wagons were haulin', then burned them. If they had found you alive . . ." He let it trail off, dumped the dregs of his coffee onto the ground before continuing. "Anyway, the patrol I was scoutin' for come up less than an hour after those Indians took off. Fresh trail, so we went after them till they scattered couple of days later, then came back to bury the dead. That's when I saw your trail. I sent the soldiers back, took off after you. Got to admit, though, I expected to find you dead and bury you."

"I'm glad I disappointed you."

"Me, too. Get some sleep, Metairie. We'll wait here till nightfall."

196

★ ★ ★

After the following night, Hickok decided to risk traveling during the day. They had traveled less than two hours before stopping. Gil had been dozing in the saddle, and the stoppage of movement jerked him awake. Licking his lips, Hickok asked Metairie to make room, said his feet were beginning to hurt and he felt like riding. Gil kicked his feet free of the stirrups and slid back, and Hickok acrobatically swung into the saddle, somehow not knocking Gil off with his long legs.

"Wrap your arms around me, Metairie," he commanded, "and grab your wrists."

As soon as he obeyed, Gil felt the scout tying his arms together with a bandanna, snug against the buckskins. Something was wrong. Hickok kicked the Morgan and turned the horse around before drawing one of the Navy revolvers from his sash. Gil leaned to his right and looked. Six or seven Indians had spotted them. They weren't charging, just watching suspiciously. Maybe a quarter of a mile separated them. After a long minute, one of the Indians whooped, kicked his paint horse, and took off, raising a musket and firing. The others followed.

"Comanch'," Hickok said. "Best riders this side of the Mississip'. Hold on, Metairie."

The Morgan took off as Hickok's moccasins jabbed the stallion's ribs. Gil pulled himself tight against the scout as he bounced every which way on the cantle. A musket popped, and Metairie forced himself to look back. The Comanches had spread out, running their horses hard, but gaining no ground on the sleek

197

Morgan. White smoke rose over one horse's neck, and then the report of the gunshot carried over the distance. A bullet was no threat now. Not at that range, not with those Indians bouncing on their horses' backs, firing ancient weapons.

The question, however, was how long could the stallion carry them both before faltering. Metairie swallowed and turned back.

Hickok didn't lack intelligence. He knew horses and Indians. As soon as he had put a lot of ground between the Comanches and themselves, he reined in the Morgan and turned back to watch his pursuers, allowing the black stallion to rest and catch its wind. Gil looked back. One of the Comanches had fallen out of sight, and two other mounts were laboring. Hickok let them close in to about five hundred yards before turning the horse around, telling Metairie to hold on and stabbing the Morgan with his heels. The stallion took off like a cannonball. Gil held tight.

Twice more, Hickok let the black horse rest, allowing to Comanches to draw close. At last he swung the horse around and stopped. This time, though, his right hand swept down and drew a Bowie knife from its sheath. Almost instantly he cut loose the bandanna, and Gil felt himself toppling over the horse's rump. Panic struck him. Hickok was abandoning him, leaving him to be tortured and killed by those Comanches. Metairie hit the ground with a thud and soft cry, and the Morgan charged. Gil tried to choke out a shout, a prayer, to beg, but his voice wouldn't work. He lifted his head off the ground, heard a shot, then another, and saw the Morgan carrying Hickok not away from the Indians, but toward them, meeting their charge, firing his Navy Colts from both hands. The Comanches had thinned out to only three, the others in all likelihood having abandoned their pursuit because their horses had played out.

One Indian somersaulted over the back of his horse, and the other two spread a wide arc away from the brilliant plainsman. The Morgan slid to a hard stop, and Hickok turned to his right, firing once, twice. A dun horse screamed and fell hard, spilling its rider. Hickok whipped around to his left, pulling the trigger. Nothing. Misfire or out of bullets. He shoved the useless weapon into his sash, tossed the Navy in his left hand to his right, and fired again at the remaining Comanche. Horse and rider, however, were out of pistol range. Amazed, although he had seen the bravery of Indians before, Gil stared open-mouthed in disbelief as the Comanche circled around, keeping out of pistol range, until he loped toward his comrade hiding behind the dead horse. That brought him into the range of Hickok's .36, although it would take some shooting from the scout. Hickok fired twice, missing, and a lithe man leaped from behind the dun carcass and swung onto the horse of his rescuer. The Comanches galloped away, leaving behind their dead friend, and Hickok gave them a parting shot before turning around and riding back to Metairie.

"You all right?" he asked.

Gil's head bobbed slightly.

"Wait here." Hickok said, and Metairie didn't have the strength to say — "Just where the hell do you think I'm going?" — although he wanted to. "I'm gonna scalp that Comanch' buck and ride down his pony." Wild Bill's lips curved upward underneath his mustache. "Give me a horse to ride. Like I said, my feet are hurting from all that walkin'."

Gil's heart pounded against his ribs, and he suddenly felt cold. He fell against the grass, saw the world spinning, and tried to wet his cracked lips.

Suddenly Hickok was looking down at him, pale eyes showing concern. "Metairie," he said as he knelt. "You don't look so good."

Wild Bill's bronzed face had transformed into that of an older man, paler, with fat jowls, thick black mustache, and pointed beard. The eyes were now brown, enlarged by the spectacles pinching his nose. He scribbled something on a chart and sat down beside Metairie, who tensed at a squeaking noise and a feeling of sinking. Gil felt his hand being lifted, and then the stranger pressed a thick thumb against his wrist and drew a watch from his tunic with his other hand, watching the ticking watch and mumbling something in a harsh language. German. Gil became aware that no sky looked down on him, but a ceiling. Rafters. He could feel the linen sheet and navy wool blanket covering him. The man released his wrist, returned the pocket watch, and patted his shoulder with a meaty paw.

200

"*Guten Morgen, Herr* Sergeant. *Wie geht es Ihnen?*" he said. "I say good morning, how are you? I am Captain Albrecht, surgeon. Glad you could join us today."

Gil tried to speak, couldn't, tried again. The words croaked out. "Where . . . am . . . I?"

"Post hospital, Fort Larned."

Metairie looked down the bed hesitantly.

"Your leg is still there, Sergeant," the surgeon said. "Ve did not expect you to live, though."

"How . . . long?"

"Two veeks. That scout brought you in. You have been talking out of your head. Fever broke. I think you might live."

"Thank you, Doctor."

"You do better by thanking your nurse." The cot rose as the heavy-set doctor stood and left. "I bring you some soup. You eat, no?"

Gil nodded, and tried to piece together what had happened, but he couldn't remember anything after Hickok had knelt over him and felt his forehead with the back of his right hand. His head craned slowly now, and he saw three other men on cots across the room. Another, sitting in a rocking chair in the corner, smoked a cigarette and stared at the bandaged stump where his left hand should have been. Metairie shivered. Someone was coming, most likely the German doctor bringing his food, but when he turned back, he saw Becky Rankin holding a tray.

"Hello," she said softly.

He took the food slowly. Soup and hot tea, nothing solid yet. Becky spooned it to him, wiping his dribble off with a napkin. He felt like an invalid, too weak to feed himself. It embarrassed him, but Becky seemed to understand. "It's all right," she said softly. "You're already getting stronger. You'll be out of here in no time."

He wanted to cry on her shoulder, to wail and wail, but he couldn't move. Finished with the food, Becky moved the tray, leaned forward, and kissed him softly, first on the forehead, then on his lips. He felt the tears rolling down his cheeks now. She brushed them away.

"Get some sleep, Gil," she said.

Three days later, Metairie could feed himself, real food, even some coffee. He still stared in stunned silence at the deep scratches, now scabbed over, and bruises covering his body. Bandages covered both hands, although he managed to hold utensils and cups, and another bandage, changed daily, was wrapped around his right thigh.

"You're the talk of Kansas, Gil Metairie," Becky told him. "I wouldn't be surprised if a reporter from *Harper's Weekly* showed up to write a story about you." She laughed musically, and took his empty plate and cup.

"How's your father?" he unexpectedly blurted out, and the music died.

"He's all right," she said stiffly.

Gil quickly changed the subject. "I haven't thanked you for all you did. Captain Albrecht says you were my private nurse, staying with me, holding my hand . . ."

Her smile was forced now, apparently still thinking about the major. "I thought you were going to die," she said in a hollow voice. Gil couldn't think of a reply. She still held the tray of dishes, half wanting to take them away but pulled by a desire to stay with him. "You kept screaming, talking . . ." A long pause followed.

"I'm sorry about your sister," she said. Their eyes met. "I have to go. Be back soon." She left him there, dry-mouthed again, wondering exactly what all he had told her, or anyone else for that matter, during his ravings.

CHAPTER
TWENTY-THREE

"I told you I would be here if you ever wanted to talk," Becky Rankin told him the following morning. "Well, I'm here."

The implication, to Gil, was that it was time to talk, and he had better make it good. He guessed that he had mentioned more names than his sister's and undoubtedly had damned himself to the Leavenworth penitentiary or the gallows while tossing, mumbling and screaming during his feverish state. Yet maybe only Becky had heard him. The German doctor had yet to mention anything, nor had any of the patients sharing the hospital with him, and by now Metairie could walk on his own, slowly and awkwardly with the use of a crutch, but at least he could make it to the privy behind the building instead of using the chamber pot. If anyone wanted to arrest him, they certainly would have done so by now.

He cleared his throat, and looked into Becky's dark eyes. He couldn't read them, but, oddly enough, he felt like talking, coming clean, so there would be no secrets between them.

"My father was murdered by Jim Lane's killers in September of 'Sixty-One," he said. "So was my sister. I'm sure you've heard about the Osceola affair."

Becky nodded. "You told me you weren't slave owners. Why would . . . ?"

His laugh was mirthless. "They killed him because they didn't care . . . maybe it was because he wouldn't choose a side, I don't know . . . I wasn't there. But even if you think you can justify hanging my father, you surely can't defend what they did to Arianne."

"I am not defending Senator Lane." Her tone suddenly softened, and she took his right hand in her own. "I know there was injustice on both sides . . . Osceola, Baxter Springs, Lawrence, Olathe."

"I was at Olathe." The words came out as if someone had kicked him in the stomach, and Becky's reaction appeared the same. "I don't know why I joined the Blackwater River Guards," he said. "No one was thinking clearly in Missouri in the early years of the war. Lane's jayhawkers had wiped out most of my family, and the irregulars were the only ones doing something about it. An eye for an eye, that kind of thing. I really thought we were on the side of justice when I joined." He laughed again, hollowly. "Didn't take me long to realize the truth."

She looked away, suddenly pale. He could barely hear her whisper. "It's true. You rode with Moon Montulé, the butcher."

"Becky, I said I didn't know why I joined, but I know why I left." He waited for her to face him, and, when she didn't, he squeezed her hand softly, pleading. Her eyes met his at last. "I never fired a shot at Olathe, just stood and watched, sick at the whole damned thing. If I were a man, a real man, I would have spoken out, fought against Montulé, tried to stop them."

"They would have killed you."

Ignoring the truth of her statement, he went on. "Anyway, I couldn't take any more after Olathe, so I left, rode out." He told her about his mother's reaction, then about enlisting in the 15th Arkansas Infantry, serving with Govan and Cleburne, fighting at Shiloh, Stones River, and other places, nameless now and long forgotten, until captured. "You know the rest."

It felt good, he thought. At least it did right now. He couldn't say how it would feel if they led him to the wall to be executed by firing squad, or made him walk up those wooden steps and fixed a noose over his neck.

Becky sighed, shaking her head, and mumbled something about "the damned war." Then: "The things people do . . ." She paused. "You . . . Father." Another sigh. "War. You grow up with a soldier for a father, and that's all you seem to know, especially out here on the frontier. The abolitionists and the fire-eating slavers. Jim Lane and the Confederate gray ghosts like Bloody Bill and Montulé. And now the Indians. Gil, do you remember what I said about going to Denver?" She didn't wait on an answer. "I still am, as soon as Father is better. Do you remember the name of my friend?"

"Julianne Moore," he said. "Moore's Bakery." Funny, he thought, his memory for names was horrible, but this one was burned in his mind. He could forget it no more than he could his own, or Becky's. "You think you might . . . ?"

206

"Becky," he said firmly. "The Army might not be so inclined . . ."

She was suddenly smiling. "You've been incapacitated for a spell, Gil Metairie. I heard some officers talking about you volunteers just the other day. Your term of enlistment is just about up."

He hadn't really thought of that. Now he remembered the Yankee captain at Rock Island, administering the oath of allegiance. The words echoed: *Be stationed on the frontier for a period of not less than one year.* That year was about up. Yet that wasn't his biggest concern.

"I'm not talking about my enlistment, Becky," he said. His voice had a slight edge to it now. "There's the matter . . ."

She understood. Yet her eyes brightened after half a minute. "Gil," she said excitedly, although her voice was barely above a whisper. "There's a list of known Confederate irregulars wanted by the authorities. I saw it tacked up in headquarters. It lists mostly John Does, but a few names of killers who rode with Bloody Bill, Moon Montulé, and Quantrill. There's no Gil Metairie on that list."

He knew that. Greer had told him at Sweet's station. "I wasn't known as Metairie. I was . . ."

She pressed long fingers on his lips, silencing him. "Don't tell me," she said.

"But those John Doe descriptions . . ."

"I've read those descriptions, Gil, and you're not going to be arrested by anyone based on those things. In Colorado . . ."

He cut her off. "Are you proposing, Rebecca Rankin."

Her laugh was infectious, and she playfully slapped his hand. "No," she answered after catching her breath. "But if you play your cards right . . ."

It made sense, Gil reasoned over the next two days. He hadn't ridden long enough with the Guards to be recognized. Only two men could identify him, Toby Greer and Moon Montulé, and the chances of their being taken alive and fingering fellow Guards were practically nonexistent. Then again, Greer might just single out Gil for spite. He had promised as much the last time they had spoken.

Metairie had become something of a celebrity at Fort Larned. Becky's prediction that a *Harper's Weekly* correspondent might drop in never materialized, but as he grew stronger, Gil attracted a host of visitors.

"Hello, Bealer," Gil said one morning, and gripped the balding Mississippian's hand firmly.

"Lookin' fit for a man who should be dead," Arthur said. "I ain't never been sick, Metairie. How does it feel to be on your backside while the rest of us are riskin' our lives for damyankee God and damyankee country?"

"Figured everything's in good hands, Bealer, as long as you're out there."

The sharpshooter laughed. "You missed the big to-do. Your favorite bluebelly lieutenant, one Henry Turd-Head Russell, had charges preferred against him for a general court-martial. Conduct unbecoming an officer, drunkenness on duty, conduct prejudicial to

208

good order . . . I think I got that right . . . and a slew of other charges. But, Union Army being what it is, they let him resign rather than face the embarrassment of gettin' cashiered and maybe spendin' time bustin' rocks. Now, in the Rebel Army, we would 'a' shot him."

Gil blinked, disbelieving. "Russell's gone?"

"Lit out for parts unknown, lucky for him. I think half the fellas here still want to kill him."

Bealer kept the visit short, promising to bring Gil a bottle of whisky and maybe some good food the next time he could get away.

Perhaps the most important, the most meaningful visitor — with the exception of Becky — was Josiah King, the 2nd Regiment's lieutenant colonel and commanding officer at Fort Larned.

"My apologies, Sergeant," King said. "I meant to pay my respects sooner, but have been busy." He didn't have to explain why. With the campaign against the Indians in full swing by now, Gil was surprised to find the ranking officer still at the post. "I've always said enlisting volunteers was a capital idea, and you've proved me right. You proved the whole policy right, you and others of your ilk. Medals and handshakes are not enough for what you and Private Murrah accomplished against those marauders."

Guilt lay heavy on Metairie's chest. Luke Murrah had died. Gil had lived. Why? Two men had gone up against eight killers. It seemed unreal that he could have survived that shoot-out, that seven robbers and murderers could be dead at the hands of Murrah and himself. What had it been — luck, the hand of God?

Luke Murrah had been the braver of the two, Gil knew that, but the Texan had died, saving Gil's life in the process. Metairie had seen other brave men fall, charging all around him in Tennessee and Georgia, yet for some strange reason no Minié ball or Union grapeshot had taken his life.

"Luke Murrah was the brave one, Colonel," Gil said.

"I'm certain he was, but you've done your part, too, soldier, here on these verges of hell. General Grant and President Johnson may never hear your name, or Private Murrah's, but you have earned the thanks of me, sir, and of Kansas."

It sounded like a prepared speech, but Gil appreciated it. As long as someone knew about Luke Murrah.

"I'll be leaving the fort soon, Sergeant." King rose. "Just wanted to wish you a speedy recovery. I'll certainly make sure my replacement knows what you and Murrah have done."

Metairie straightened. "Replacement, sir?"

"I've been relieved of command here, Sergeant," he answered stiltedly. "I'm to report back to Fort Leavenworth. Colonel Cloud will take over shortly."

"I don't understand."

"Peace, Sergeant. I guess they don't bring you much news in the post hospital, although they should. Well, Colonel Sanborn is the new commander of this district. Colonel Caraher and I are warriors. Sanborn and Cloud are peacekeepers. It seems that Colonel Jesse Leavenworth has reached a peace agreement with the various tribes, so our campaign against them has been called off. The chiefs will meet for a peace council at Bluff Creek in October. It's good news, really, and I understand the changes. Warriors serve in war, and peacekeepers command in peacetime. Still . . ." A trace of regret entered his voice. "We saved the Union. Now perhaps we have saved Bloody Kansas. But what becomes of the warriors? Well, peace is always welcomed, Sergeant. Good bye. Good luck."

They exchanged salutes, and Gil's eyes followed King as he ducked out the front door. Peace. He thought of the colonel's words. King thought of Metairie as a fighting soldier, but Gil knew the truth. War sickened him. But he wondered what would become of warriors like Colonel King and, more importantly, Major John Rankin? Becky's father had hoped that the campaign would bring him glory, national recognition, but the leg wound he had received at Kurt Sweet's and now this stunning news of peace would end that chance.

He felt like walking, and not just to the two-seater out back. After finding his crutch, he headed toward the front door in his nightshirt and bare feet.

"Don't go out yonder, Sarge," one of the sick soldiers, an artilleryman with the Company F of the Mounted Howitzers, called out mockingly. "They'll bust you for being out of uniform."

Gil smiled and pushed open the door. A cavalry patrol from the 15th Missouri rode out, escorting a small wagon train, while other soldiers drilled and drilled. He spotted a scout, coming out of the sutler's, and started to wave, thinking it was Hickok, but stopped when he saw the man was too short, and his hair too dark. Metairie hobbled down the length of the covered porch, watching the hubbub of activity around the sprawling post. It occurred to him that he hadn't seen anything of Fort Larned except the hospital and the outhouse. Larned seemed huge compared to Fort Zarah, although few of the buildings, most of them built of adobe, looked permanent. A city of canvas tents stretched out across the plains, providing shelter for most of the fort's residents. He studied with longing the shade trees that sprang up along what he assumed were the banks of the Smoky Hill and Republican Rivers. Too far for him to walk for the time being, he decided. Lost in thought, he didn't hear the buckboard pull up in front of the hospital.

"Good afternoon, Sergeant," Becky Rankin called out.

She and her father remained seated, a colorful blanket covering the major's legs. Becky had driven the buggy, and now she set the brake and jumped down. The hospital door opened, and Captain Albrecht stepped out, saying something in his thick German accent to the major. Rankin stared ahead blankly, bitterly, his gaunt face covered with beard stubble, self-pity, and hatred. The surgeon spotted Metairie and grinned. "Ach, Sergeant. *Gut.* You valk. Good. Valking good. You keep improving." Metairie couldn't help but notice that the doctor's smile vanished as soon as he faced Rankin again.

Metairie watched, embarrassed, as an orderly and Becky tried to help her father down. He swore at them,

212

trying to shove them away, saying he could get down himself, but he almost fell. The blanket dropped into the dust. Gil tried not to gape as Becky handed her father his crutches. Both she and the orderly stepped back, and Major John J. Rankin moved by himself, onto the porch, as Metairie's eyes kept dropping to the empty, pinned up, right pants leg. Rankin stopped and stared angrily at Gil.

"What's the matter, you son-of-a-bitch? Never seen a one-legged man before?" He hobbled inside with another curse.

CHAPTER
TWENTY-FOUR

By the time William F. Cloud took command of Fort Larned, Gil had made a daily routine of walking to the Smoky Hill and back. In fact, he told Captain Albrecht that he felt fit for duty, but the German sawbones laughed and barked out something in his native language, ignoring the suggestion. Corporal Hardee, serving as a courier from Zarah to Larned, brought a cane carved from an ash tree, and Metairie made use of the gift, replacing the cumbersome crutch.

"You're a fast healer," Becky commented one morning after bringing Gil a new wardrobe: shiny black boots, for the post commissary was out of brogans, kersey blue trousers and canvas suspenders, a blouse a size too big, campaign hat, socks, a wool shirt, and even underwear. The shirt was gray, and he found a bit of humor in that — if a former Rebel sergeant now serving in the Union Army was being issued a shirt the color of his former uniform then the war was, indeed, over — but kept it to himself.

"It's like Christmas," Gil said with a laugh.

"Not if I know the Army," she answered. "This will come out of your pay over the next two months. You'll probably have to reënlist to pay off your debts."

"Not likely."

They hadn't talked about Becky's father. Gil hadn't wanted to bring it up, nor had she. So they avoided the subject of Major Rankin just as Gil had tried to avoid mathematics in school. Metairie had seen the hurt in Becky's eyes when her father snapped at her in front of the hospital, but the eyes he remembered the most were the major's. He could understand Rankin's bitterness. John J. Rankin had been a cavalryman almost as long as he had been able to ride, and the United States cavalry, volunteers as well as regulars, had no use for one-legged cavalrymen. John Rankin was finished as a soldier.

From his walks around Fort Larned, Gil could see no change between Cloud's command and King's, reminding him that the Federal Army was just like the Rebel Army in this regard. Commanders came and went, lived and died, bickered and bickered, but the armies never changed. The enlisted men, and maybe a lieutenant or captain here and there, did the same work over and over again, and they were the ones who did most of the dying.

Sergeant Arthur Bealer lived up to his promise. The next time he visited Gil, he brought a fried turkey drumstick and half a bottle of whisky. The label on the bottle read **Gilbert Muir from Liverpool,** but the liquid inside tasted like something from Kurt Sweet's undiluted kegs. Not that Metairie complained. Bealer brought Hardee and Hickok with him. Like a party. Gil enjoyed the food, whisky, and company. Even the perpetually sick private from the Mounted Howitzers crawled from his bed to sample the whisky.

"What's the latest on the peace treaty?" asked Gil, still starved for news despite his wanderings around the post. He passed the bottle to Hickok, who took a delicate swig and handed the whisky to Bealer.

"Word is Colonel Leavenworth's supposed to meet with a bunch of chiefs, Kiowa, Comanch', most of the South-western tribes, on the Fourth of October, have a bunch of speechifyin', and make a few marks on worthless paper, guaranteein' protection along the Santa Fé Trail and the settlements."

"You don't believe it?"

The scout shrugged. "Kit Carson thinks it's good. We'll see. I just think gettin' Bobby Lee's word that he'll quit fightin' is a whole lot different than gettin' some red nigger's."

Wild Bill's mood had soured considerably. Gil had never thought about it much, but perhaps Hickok was one of those warriors Colonel King had spoken of. If peace came to Kansas, maybe the Army wouldn't need the scout's services any longer.

The allegedly Liverpool whisky had gone from Bealer to the artilleryman and back to Metairie. Arthur Bealer added: "Merchants seem optimistic. And we haven't seen any signs of Indians between here and Zarah lately."

"Just wait," Hickok muttered.

"Well," Bealer said, "I'll be glad to see it. I don't know about you boys, but I've got me a hankerin' to get back to Mississippi, sip some muscadine wine, and stretch out under a magnolia tree. 'Sides, I think it'll be mighty interestin' to see one of them red savages up close when he's not tryin' to . . ."

"Lift your scalp?" Gil cut in, and couldn't control his laughter.

Even Hickok brightened, and rubbed the sharpshooter's bald head.

The artillery private drained the whisky.

Hickok grunted and pulled the makings for a cigarette from his vest. "Don't think you Rebs will be on hand for the peace agreement, if it ever gets signed." The scout had Metairie's and Bealer's attention, but the artilleryman, now that the whisky bottle had been emptied, begged his pardon and strode back to his cot.

"Brought in word yesterday from Colonel Sanborn. Orders are for you Second Regiment boys to start gettin' ready to march back to Fort Riley. I reckon you'll be headin' back to Riley and then Fort Leavenworth shortly, probably this week."

Arthur Bealer removed his glasses. "What on earth for?"

"Because," the scout replied, "in just more than a month you Johnny Rebs will be out of this man's army. Unless, of course, you're dumb enough to enlist in the regular army. Oh, I hear there's been some talk from General Pope and others to do some fast thinkin' and figure out a way to keep you boys in, give you a chance to serve another year . . . that says a lot about how you Rebs have handled yourself out here . . . but I don't think anything'll come of it. No, sir, Mister Bealer, if I were a bettin' man . . . and I've been told a time or two that I am . . . I'd lay odds that come October or November you'll find yourself under a magnolia, scratchin' your 'coon dog and dreamin' of your missus. And you, Mister Metairie . . ." Hickok laughed. "Nah, I've got no notion where I'll find you."

Grinning, Arthur Bealer said: "Denver, I'm thinkin'."

Gil sat up straight.

The Mississippi sharpshooter's smile widened, and he cleaned the lenses before putting on his glasses and saying: "You can't keep secrets in the army, Gil, Yankee or Reb."

The day after Sergeant Gil Metairie left the post hospital and reported for duty, orders came for Company B, 2^(nd) Regiment, to rendezvous at Fort Larned by no later than the 5^(th) of September and proceed at due haste to Fort Riley to await further orders. Those orders, however, were well-known. The galvanized Yankees would march on to Fort Leavenworth to be mustered out of the United States Army. Honorably discharged. Free to go home, or wherever. Gil looked west and thought of Denver.

But peace didn't come so quickly to Kansas.

Metairie stood in the blacksmith's shop, watching William Mackey shoe a team of mules. The smithy didn't appreciate the sergeant's presence. "I've been shoein' horses since a-fore you was born, soldier. You ain't gotta watch me." He sprayed the roaring fire with tobacco juice, which sizzled.

"Orders, Mister Mackey," Gil replied. "We don't want to have a sore-footed mule and have to abandon one of the Army's good wagons. Besides, maybe I'll want to become a blacksmith when I'm a civilian."

He wasn't lying about the orders, although they came from Captain Albrecht, who suggested that Gil not overdo anything for a while. But coming to the post livery had been his own idea. Sweating next to a forge, helping Mackey whenever he'd let him, would toughen Gil, prepare him for the long march across Kansas. Besides, Metairie was sergeant of Company B's 1st Squad, which these days included himself, Corporal Hardee, and privates Goldy Michaels, Warren Fry, and Phineas Jones, now all on detached service. Hardee was serving as a courier, Michaels and Fry were filling 3rd Squad vacancies, and, because of the impending peace agreement, Jones was now the lone Army guard at Kurt Sweet's station. Gil Metairie found himself the noncommissioned officer of a squad that no longer existed.

Sudden shouts interrupted Gil's thoughts and Mackey's work.

"Sergeant of the guard! Sergeant of the guard!"

Both men stepped out of the barn's work shed. Two soldiers half carried, half dragged another man toward the fort headquarters while the sentry screamed for the sergeant. Metairie found himself drawn toward the scene, and he picked up his pace, hurrying to the commanding officer's adobe shack. He recognized the wounded man as Private Charley Scott, eyes full of fright, an arrow sticking through his left arm.

Colonel Cloud himself, followed by a sergeant-major and freckle-faced lieutenant, stepped out of the headquarters building, obviously bothered by the intrusion. "Speak up," Cloud commanded Scott. "What happened?"

"Ambushed," Scott said feebly. "Indians."

"That's impossible!" Cloud roared.

"Colonel, it ain't likely this boy stabbed himself with that arrow." This came from William Mackey, who had followed Gil from the livery.

Shaking his head, the blacksmith turned and bellowed: "Somebody fetch Doc Albrecht! We got a wounded man here!"

Cloud stared at Charley in bewilderment, and Gil realized that neither the colonel nor his lieutenant or sergeant-major were about to do anything more than just stare at the bloody arrow and the 2nd Regiment soldier about to go into shock from loss of blood. Metairie knelt beside the Georgian.

"Charley," he said in a calming voice, "what happened?"

"Messenger detail to Zarah, Sergeant," Scott answered. He bit his lip to fight of a spasm of pain. "Made it as far as Ash Creek when they jumped us."

"How many with you?"

"Three. Kansans providing escort for me. Had orders . . ." He cried out in pain. "Sorry," he said.

Gil looked up, saw Captain Albrecht running as fast as he could carry his overweight frame across the parade grounds.

"Doesn't matter, Charley," he said. "How many Indians?"

"Couldn't tell. A lot. Weren't Pawnees, though. I'd recognize them."

220

Peace! Hickok had been right. Metairie rose and stepped back to make room for the surgeon. Albrecht wrapped a tourniquet around Scott's arm and detailed two men to carry him to the hospital. Gil stared at Colonel Cloud, waiting for an order.

The officer swore, rammed his right fist into his left palm, and said — "Take care of this, Mister Wilkinson." — and returned to his office.

I'll be glad to be rid of this army, Gil thought, and waited for the lieutenant to think of something. He had to give the junior officer credit, though.

Lieutenant Wilkinson looked Metairie in the eye, sternly, and barked out his command: "Sergeant, you will take a patrol of volunteers, no more than a dozen men, and proceed with due haste to Ash Creek. Take three extra horses with you, Sergeant. Bring the messenger's escorts, alive or dead, back to the fort as quickly as possible."

"And the Indians?" Gil asked.

"Bring the men back, Sergeant. Those are your orders. You are not to pursue the hostiles. We will do nothing to jeopardize the peace council at Bluff Creek. Carry on."

He didn't know the volunteers accompanying him. Most of them were with the 14th Missouri Cavalry, and a few from the 3rd Wisconsin. Not galvanized Yanks — just regular Union volunteers. They discovered the first mutilated body only three miles from the fort. William Mackey, who had insisted on coming along with the soldiers, recognized the boy as an 11th Kansas Cavalry trooper named Hill, although that had been difficult because the attackers had scalped him and bashed in the lad's face. Hill's body was strapped over one of the horses, and Metairie led the pursuers on. Two miles later, they discovered the second body, pinned to the ground with arrows, chopped to pieces.

Gil's leg was beginning to stiffen, but he rode on. Less than five hundred yards from the Ash Creek crossing, Metairie discovered the third body, scalped, hands and feet amputated and tossed aside like empty boxes, chest ripped apart. When he had ridden up, Gil had scared away a wolf that carried off one of the trooper's hands. Metairie dismounted gingerly and knelt over the mangled corpse. Oddly enough, he didn't feel sick, just sad.

"My God," one of the soldiers said, "what's that on his chest?"

"His heart," Mackey answered. "Bastards cut out his heart and stuck it there for us to see."

The soldier's eyes remained open, and Gil closed them, took a deep breath, and slowly let it out. He wanted to say a prayer, but couldn't find the words. "I'm sorry," he said, and walked away from the mess that had once been Corporal Ben Crook.

One of the troopers swore quickly, looking away from the carnage and toward Pawnee Rock. "Sergeant," he said, "it's them. It's those damned Indians."

Gil's face jerked up. He could make out the charging horses in the distance, not heading toward Metairie's patrol, but toward something else. A wagon train.

"Mount up!" he shouted. "Cock your carbines."

222

"But our orders . . . ," one of them began.

"To hell with orders," Gil said, and pulled himself into the saddle.

CHAPTER
TWENTY-FIVE

The wagon master had also spotted the attackers, and the wagons quickly formed into a circle. By now, Gil could make out the din of the coyote-yipping Indians and the popping of muskets, but no one, freighter or brave, had much talent as a marksman. Metairie held the Spencer at his side in his right hand, reins in his left, teeth grinding. The wind burned his face, and his stiff leg and backside felt raw. He wasn't used to being in a saddle, let alone galloping into battle. Not that he anticipated much of a fight.

Sure enough, one of the warriors reined up, pointed with his rifle at the charging soldiers, and, almost instantly, the Indians took off, circling the corralled wagons and dashing for safety. Metairie thought about his orders. Only the dumbest, most pompous martinet would prefer charges of disobedience for coming to the rescue of the wagon train. The soldier who had questioned Gil back at Ash Creek was raw, too green to realize that a soldier couldn't always follow orders given at headquarters when he was out in the field. What was he supposed to have done, let the warriors attack the freighters while he and his command just watched? But now that the attackers were fleeing, he faced a dilemma. Stop or give chase?

He didn't think about it for long. In fact, Sergeant Gil Metairie never slowed his horse. The troopers and the blacksmith followed without hesitation. A cheer erupted from the wagon train. Lieutenant Wilkinson and Colonel Cloud might thrash Gil's judgment, but the reaction from the freighters told Metairie he had made the right decision.

They would never catch the warriors. The Indians were better mounted, better horsemen for that matter, and were quickly outdistancing the soldiers. Gil's horse began to tire, and he reined to a halt on the banks of the Arkansas River, watching the last brave whip his paint horse across the sand hills on the far shore. A Wisconsin cavalryman splashed his mount into the shallow water and fired a fruitless shot.

"Hold your fire, trooper," Metairie said glumly.

"We just gonna let them go?" the pockmarked teenager blurted out angrily.

"We'll never catch them," Gil answered calmly. "They'll scatter, and our horses are playing out. Besides, we did our job. They won't be back."

"The sergeant's right," Mackey said. "He knows them bucks, that's for sure. Best thing we can do is escort that wagon train and our dead back to Larned."

Metairie smiled to himself. Less than a year in the Federal Army, and only a few months on the frontier, and he had become a veteran Indian fighter.

Metairie delivered his report to Lieutenant Wilkinson, who accepted it without comment. He slept soundly, and woke up before reveille, waiting for the bugler or trumpeter to shatter the peace of dawn. Gil had been chosen as part of the honor guard that would lay Corporal Ben Crook, Private Vernon Hill, and Private Sid Olivia to rest with full military honors in the post cemetery. The entire post, except for those on sick leave and one Major John Rankin, turned out for the funeral. He saw Becky there, though, standing among the laundresses, servants, and wives as the bodies of the soldiers, wrapped in blankets because wood was too scarce a commodity to waste on the dead, were lowered into freshly dug graves as a trumpeter from the 15th Kansas sounded "Taps."

After the ceremony, orders came for all sergeants and officers with the 2nd Regiment to report in front of headquarters. Colonel Cloud stepped out of the building, still in his dress uniform from the funeral, and placed his white-gloved hands behind his back.

"Gentlemen," he said, "I know you thought you would be going home soon, but this latest act of butchery has changed everything. The peace council is still on, but I, and Colonel Sanborn, believe it in the best interest if we postpone your marching orders until after Colonel Leavenworth's peace council. We must show the Comanches, Kiowas, and other savages that the United States Army is a powerful force, one they must not trifle with. That is all. Lieutenants, issue your orders to your sergeants, and carry on."

It sounded like war talk from a peacekeeper, Gil thought.

"Sergeant Metairie?"

Gil turned, saw a young second lieutenant with slicked brown hair and a drooping mustache, both reddened from the sun, holding a kepi at his side. The officer went on: "I'm Lieutenant Marion, Sergeant. Don't believe we've made each other's acquaintance."

"No, sir."

"Sergeant, I'm promoting Corporal G. W. Hardee to sergeant to take over Third Squad." Metairie nodded. It made sense. Goldy Michaels and Warren Fry had already been, for all intent and purpose, transferred to 3rd Squad, and Hardee deserved the brevet. The officer continued: "We're going to move a large force, including Companies F and H, to the Little Arkansas." He smiled. "Anyway, you don't have much of a squad left, Sergeant."

Metairie agreed, pointing out the assignments of Michaels and Fry and Phineas Jones being left at Kurt Sweet's station.

"Sweet will be screaming for more protection once he hears about what happened at Ash Creek and Pawnee Rock, and he might be right. Sergeant Van Boskirk's squad will be sent from Zarah to Sweet's, Private Jones will stay with them as I am detailing Private Anderson of Fourth Squad to replace Hardee as courier."

"Very good, sir. So where does that leave me?"

"Special assignment, Sergeant. I will fill you in on the details tomorrow, day after tomorrow at the latest."

To a degree, Colonel Jesse H. Leavenworth, 2nd Colorado, reminded Gil Metairie of the Confederacy's

General John Bell Hood. Leavenworth's dark, receding hair was disheveled, yet his thick mustache and beard were neatly trimmed. Powerfully built, wearing an open frock coat, buttoned vest, white shirt, and loose cravat, Leavenworth gripped Metairie's hand firmly. Like Hood, he didn't just earn respect, he immediately commanded it. Of course, the colonel still had the use of all of his limbs, unlike the unfortunate Hood, but Leavenworth had the same eyes as the former commander of the Army of the Tennessee, burning with an intensity matched by a strong voice.

"Sergeant Metairie," Leavenworth said, "it's good finally to put a face with the name I've heard so much about. Have a seat, Sergeant. I'm a volunteer, not much for the formality of military manners. Brandy?" Gil declined. "Cigar, then?" He accepted.

They exchanged the usual formalities — the weather, the Confederacy's surrender, the work of the 2nd Regiment — and finally reached a pause that told Gil the time for Leavenworth to make his point had arrived. Lieutenant Marion had escorted Gil to the Sibley tent near the corrals. Word had spread throughout Larned that Leavenworth had arrived the previous night, getting ready to make his way to Bluff Creek for the peace meeting, but until now Metairie had yet to see the famous colonel in person.

"I've worked hard to bring peace to the Santa Fé Trail," Leavenworth said, blowing a plume of blue smoke toward the top of the canvas tent. "Commanded this fort for a while in 'Sixty-Three. It took a lot of work, cost a lot of lives, to keep the Trail open during

228

the conflict back East. I think it's time to give peace a try, don't you?"

"I'm all for peace, sir."

Leavenworth placed his cigar on an ashtray resting between a Bible and a double-action Starr revolver. "Satanta of the Kiowas and Ten Bears of the Comanches, along with the leaders of the Arapahoes, Cheyennes, and Pawnees, are willing to try peace. That's why the council at Bluff Creek is so important. Do you know how you win over Indians, make them peaceful?"

Gil considered before answering, and deciding that Leavenworth wanted and respected honesty, Gil said: "Most men I've talked to believe that you kill them, sir."

The colonel returned the cigar and nodded. "You've been spending too much time with men like Hickok, Sergeant." He held up his hand to stop Metairie from commenting, although Gil had no intention of interrupting. "I understand those views. I've had to form enough burial details, but I don't favor extermination. Hell, back East a lot of Northern fire-eaters are screaming for the heads of Jefferson Davis and Robert E. Lee, but I say the War of the Rebellion is over, so let us return to our homes and live. Now in Kansas, and the entire Southwest, we have a chance for peace."

"Do you think the Indians will abide by any treaty, Colonel?" Gil asked. "Three men were killed the other day, an unprovoked attack, sir."

"I know, Sergeant. Let me put it this way . . . when Robert E. Lee surrendered, and then the other generals, Johnston, Stand Watie, the war ended. But you saw what those irregulars did to that wagon train. You and that other soldier . . ."

"Luke Murrah, sir."

". . . killed those bushwhackers, and with good reason, and for the good of all of the United States and her Territories. That's the handiwork of Moon Montulé, I swear. My point being, Sergeant, that even though the Confederacy is no longer, most Rebels having been paroled, there are still men like that butcher Montulé. That doesn't mean we should kill you and other former Rebels." An uneasiness began settling over Gil like ominous clouds before an electrical storm. Leavenworth went on: "Bad apples, I guess you would call them. The Cheyennes that attacked that detail are just bad apples. There will be more, of that I am certain, but on the whole, I think, we will have substantial peace, unlike the bleeding that has been going on for years. How long it lasts, I can't predict. But if we can have a year of peace, or even six months or six weeks, if we can go that long without having women ravaged, children kidnapped, and men slain, then I think it will have been worth it."

Leavenworth's cigar had gone out. He relit it, flicked the match into a spittoon, and smiled. "I've strayed, Sergeant. I asked you how we obtain peace from Indians. You don't win it by crushing them, as we have crushed the rebellion. You've seen enough by now to know it's impossible to overpower an enemy that scatters and disappears with the wind. You buy peace, Sergeant. You buy it with annuities, promised gifts.

Blankets, sugar, trinkets, bolts of calico, even silver and gold." Leavenworth smiled. "White culture has rubbed off on some of these Indians. They know the value of gold and silver. Some of them do, at least.

"Pardon my long-windedness, Sergeant. That scout, J. B. Hickok, spoke highly of your ability. So have others . . . Lieutenant Colonel King and Captain O'Connor. Kit Carson, a man I trust and respect, recommended you for the assignment I'm about to offer."

Metairie felt he had to interrupt this time. "Begging the colonel's pardon, sir, and no disrespect meant to Mister Carson, but I've never even met him."

"No, but he has heard of you."

Gil nodded, slightly embarrassed at his growing reputation, undeserved in his eyes.

Leavenworth went on. "I have twenty wagons, sir, filled with goods to be given to the Indians who attend the Bluff Creek council. I am asking you to take command of that train, pick your best men, and make sure it reaches Bluff Creek no later than the fifth of next month. I'm leaving with a handful of men and Indian agents in two days to begin preparations for peace. On Sunday, an armed force, in a show of strength for those bad apples I've mentioned, will converge on the Little Arkansas. One week later, you are to begin moving to Bluff Creek. Your escort will be small, no more than fifteen soldiers, from the Second Regiment. It's a dangerous assignment, Sergeant, because I've promised Ten Bears and the others these gifts."

Metairie didn't like this at all. The smoke in his mouth tasted bitter, and he removed the cigar, spit into the brass cuspidor, and couldn't hide his feelings in his face or voice. "Colonel," he said, "why not send the wagons with that large force? It'll offer much more protection."

Leavenworth shook his head.

"But, sir," Gil pleaded, "you're acting as if you want the wagon train to be attacked."

"I do, Sergeant. I fully expect those bushwhackers led by Montulé himself to hit the train. Hell, I don't expect it. I know he'll do it."

CHAPTER
TWENTY-SIX

Yes, Gil Metairie was sick of the military, the waste of lives, the orders, the whole damned army, Union and Confederate. He accepted Colonel Leavenworth's assignment, mainly because he felt he had no choice. I'm ordering you to volunteer, that kind of thing. Yet he understood Leavenworth's reasoning. Peace, tentative, perhaps, but peace nonetheless, would be secured from the Plains Indians. However, the only way to end Moon Montulé's grip was by luring him into a trap. Montulé and what was left of the Blackwater River Guards were like those Indians, scattering and disappearing, almost impossible to subdue. But Leavenworth was risking the lives of those freighters, and fifteen soldiers Gil had to pick, none of whom could know they were being used as bait.

"Your men and the civilians will be told they are taking the wagons to the peace council, after which they will continue on to Fort Riley for further orders," Leavenworth said. "Those orders" — the colonel smiled — "will be your marching orders to Fort Leavenworth where you'll be mustered out. This will be your last mission, Sergeant, in this man's army."

Last. Poor choice of words, Gil thought.

Was it worth risking the peace council and the lives of innocent men? Leavenworth seemed to be gambling everything. If Montulé attacked the train — and won — the goods would never reach Bluff Creek, and the chiefs might hit the warpath for vengeance. Gil had suggested that he escort an empty caravan while wagons filled with the trade items be sent with Leavenworth's troops. But the colonel shook his head. Too many spies near Fort Larned, he argued. The bushwhackers would learn of the trap. The colonel had spies, too, though, and they informed him that Montulé and his gang had remained in the area after the ambush and robbery that left Peadar Flann dead, and Montulé needed a stake before leaving Kansas.

Wagons filled with merchandise and twenty thousand dollars in silver and gold — that was too juicy a plum for a fiend like Montulé. Leavenworth promised to leave two patrols of the 2nd Colorado, men he would personally vouch for, behind at Pawnee Rock. "When you are attacked," he said, "send a galloper there, and my Coloradans will back your play, Sergeant. You'll just have to hold out until they get there." Jesse Leavenworth wanted Moon Montulé as much, maybe more, than he wanted a successful meeting with the Comanches, Kiowas, Cheyennes, Pawnees, and Arapahoes. "I had an uncle and aunt killed in that church in Olathe," he said, "by that black heart."

Maybe that was the real reason Gil Metairie took the assignment.

The following morning, he sent word for Brevet Sergeant G. W. Hardee and 3rd Squad and Sergeant

Arthur Bealer and 2nd Squad to report to Fort Larned. That wouldn't quite be fifteen men, but Gil didn't see any need in asking more men to die. He did, however, decide to ask Hickok to serve as scout, if he could find him.

Just before the wagons began moving out of Fort Larned, Gil told Hickok, Hardee, and Bealer to ride with him on the pretense of checking Ash Creek for signs of an ambush. Metairie knew the Guards wouldn't hit the train this close to the post, but he had to tell his three friends exactly what they were facing. He wasn't so concerned about secrecy any more, not with the wagons moving for Bluff Creek, not with men like Hickok, Hardee, and Bealer.

"Well," Bealer said after Metairie finished his speech at the crossing, "I reckon this means one thing . . . Yanks finally trust us. Don't think we'll run off with the wagons and join up with Montulé."

With a grunt, G. W. Hardee shook his head, unconvinced of the Mississippian's statement. "What it means to them Yanks is that we're expendable. Bait a trap for a killer with a bunch of old Rebs. Don't matter none if we gets killed."

Gil added: "We should pay attention to the freighters. When they hit Sergeant Flann's train, a couple of the teamsters were in on the attack. Keep your eye on any civilian who looks or acts suspicious."

"You mean like Henry Russell?" Bealer asked.

Bewilderment masked Gil's face. At first he thought the sharpshooter was funning him, but Arthur grinned and said lightly: "You been runnin' round like a chicken with its head cut off, gettin' us ready, but not lookin' at just who it is we're escortin'. Yessir, former Lieutenant Henry Russell is now drivin' a wagon."

Bealer was right. Metairie had spent too much time getting the two squads ready, making sure the horses were fast, strong animals, double-checking the supplies, and overseeing the placement of a heavy crate into one of the wagons. Henry Russell? Driving a wagon? Could he have joined up with Montulé? Or would the leader of the Blackwater River Guards simply have shot the former lieutenant on the spot? After all, Russell was a Yankee, and Montulé had never been known for his generosity or trust when it came to men who wore the blue. More than likely, Russell wanted to go back East, and driving a wagon with a military escort seemed the safest way.

Hickok, who had said nothing, shifted in his saddle and scanned the road behind him. Gil looked, too. He could make out the outline of the wagons, and the boys of 2nd and 3rd Squads riding escort. The vehicles weren't the cumbersome, heavy, ox-driven ones handled by jerk lines but smaller military-issue covered wagons, each pulled by a team of six mules. Better for speed, Metairie thought, in case the freighters had to make a run for their lives when the bushwhackers attacked.

Gil pushed up his slouch hat. "One other thing. If you three want to pull out now, I won't stop you."

Arthur Bealer colored a bunch of dead grass with tobacco juice. "Hell, Gil," he said, "we didn't get to see

236

the surrender at Appomattox Courthouse, so I'd like to see the big dance at Bluff Creek."

"Me, too," Hardee chimed in.

Hickok remained silent, eyes trained on the wagons. He reached into his saddlebags and pulled out a spyglass. Gil considered him for a moment, then told Bealer and Hardee: "There is one more thing."

"You just said that," Bealer spoke out of a large grin.

Gil shook his head at the joshing. "In that last wagon, you'll find a large crate stamped peaches. It's a present from Colonel Leavenworth. Pass them out to your men tonight."

"Peaches?" G. W. Hardee shook his head. "Is that our last supper? Mighty white of that bluebelly colonel."

"They're not peaches, G. W.," Gil said. Slowly he unbuttoned his blouse, reached inside, and pulled out the revolver he had jammed into his waistband. "They're just like this one." He held up Colt's .44-caliber Army model. "Plus percussion caps, full powder flasks, and thirty balls per man. Take one for yourselves, too."

Bealer shook his head and patted his saddle scabbard. The Army-issue Spencer carbine hung at his side suspended by a leather strap over his shoulder, cavalry-style. The scabbard held a sniper's rifle, a .50-caliber Sharps equipped with a telescope sight almost as long as the rifle barrel. "Never had the knack for shootin' short guns," he said.

"Thought there was only twenty wagons." This came from Hickok. The three former Confederates faced the scout, who had lowered his spyglass and pointed toward the wagon train. Gil couldn't make out the train clearly, so he moved his horse closer to Hickok, and the plainsman passed him the long brass telescope.

"Check the caboose," Hickok said.

Sure enough, a black wagon pulled by a team of four horses, bounced along the road behind the covered wagons, although the distance remained too great to make out the figures sitting in the driver's box even with the telescope. Frowning, Gil snapped the spyglass shut and returned it to Hickok. He didn't like surprises.

"Let's get back," Metairie said.

He slowed the roan's gait, when he reached the train, and studied each driver carefully as the covered wagons passed. Most were bearded men, sunburned, cheeks bulging with tobacco, dressed in muslin shirts, frayed coats, and canvas trousers, their heads topped with a variety of hats: bowlers, slouch hats, one bell crown hat, and a couple of caps. They held the long leather reins deftly in ungloved hands, and paid no heed to Gil Metairie despite his impolite staring. All but one driver, that is.

Gil almost didn't recognize Henry Russell. He had only seen the lieutenant in his officer's uniform, and now he looked grimy, his black beard unkept and dirty, and a dark campaign hat pulled down low over his eyes. The only clue that he had once been a soldier were the blue trousers, the officer's leg stripes ripped off. A buckskin jacket hung loosely, the bunched-up bottom protruding around his right hip. Revolver, Gil determined, but there wasn't anything suspicious about that.

"The hell you lookin' at, boy?" Russell growled.

238

Metairie didn't answer, and the wagon passed. He considered the other drivers, recognizing none, and took a sharp breath when he saw the last wagon: a shoddy, old, wooden prisoner transport with barred windows and a rear door, not the best traveling accommodations for a one-legged officer and his daughter, but probably the only wagon available. Major John J. Rankin tugged hard on the reins, stopping the vehicle, and studied Gil with those hard eyes. At his side sat Becky, the wooden crutches separating the two.

"What are you doing here?" Gil snapped.

Becky's eyes lit up with shock at Metairie's tone. Rankin wrapped the reins around the brake and leaned forward. "Sergeant, let me remind you that as of now I am still an officer in the Army and you are not. You will not address me or my daughter without proper respect. Is that understood?"

Metairie was taken aback. He recovered some of his military bearing and apologized. Becky seemed to relax. The major continued. "I have missed my opportunity, Sergeant, to subdue these red heathen, but I think that I, more than anyone, have earned the right to attend the peace council."

"Yes, sir, Major. But this is a dangerous assignment, and I think it would be best if your daughter returned to Fort Larned."

"Balderdash. You know my daughter. She demanded to be at my side. We're going to Bluff Creek, and after the treaties are signed, you and your men will escort the wagons to Fort Riley. Becky and I will proceed to Fort Leavenworth, then back home to Baxter Springs, and

239

you and your Rebs can go wherever you want, to Hades, for all I care. Now carry on, Sergeant."

He stared at the dust left by the wagons as Rankin whipped his team to catch up. Moon Montulé. Henry Russell. Now Becky Rankin and her father. Gil swore, and spurred his horse.

"I'm sorry about today," Becky said softly.

Gil looked up. He had been cleaning the roan's shoes with a pick, so occupied by his work that he hadn't heard her come up. Actually, he had been checking every saddle horse, making sure the animals had been properly groomed, fed, watered, picketed, and the shoes had been cleaned. Many hadn't, so Gil had done it himself. Sweat dampened his face and shirt despite the chill of evening. He finished with the hoof and lowered the horse's leg, patted its neck, and moved closer to Becky.

"I'd feel better if you could talk your father into returning to Fort Larned," he said. "I can give you an escort tomorrow morning."

"He won't listen."

"Will you?"

She paused, thinking about answering before deciding not to. "What's the matter, Gil?"

His shoulders slumped. "We're bait, Becky. Colonel Leavenworth thinks Moon Montulé will try to ambush us before we reach Bluff Creek."

"Montulé?" The three syllables came out softly, spread out. Her eyes gazed at the horses without seeing anything. After several seconds, she looked back at Gil.

240

"Colonel Leavenworth would do that, risk your lives, risk the treaty?"

This time Metairie didn't answer. "Go back to Larned, Becky."

"No," she said sharply. "My place is with Father. I won't abandon him, abandon you, for . . ." She started to tremble. Gil reached out, pulled her close. Her head fell on his shoulder, and Metairie brushed her hair, whispering that everything would work out. She pulled away from him.

"Gil," she said, looking up. "We were planning to go back to Leavenworth, get an escort maybe, or ride with another wagon train. I was to make sure Father got settled in at Baxter Springs, then I'd take a stage to Denver. But late yesterday afternoon, he asked Colonel Cloud for permission to take part in the Bluff Creek council before he resigned, or was forced to resign because of his leg. Cloud agreed."

Metairie nodded. "He's right, Becky. If anyone has earned a place at the Bluff Creek talks, it's your father."

Her head shook violently. "That's not it, Gil. The night before, Henry Russell dropped by our quarters. He was in his cups. I could smell it on his breath, and demanded to talk to Father. Father . . . he had been drinking, also . . . asked me to leave the house. I did, went for a walk, then stood across from our quarters and waited for Henry to leave. They must have talked for more than two hours. When Henry left, I asked Father what they had talked about, and he just said nothing. Henry came by again yesterday. You don't think . . . ?"

"No," Gil said. "Not your father. Russell, maybe, but not . . ."

"But, Gil. The silver and gold for the Indians . . . we're carrying it in the wagon. Twenty thousand dollars. Not much for thousands of Indians, but for two men, or a cutthroat like Moon Montulé. Gil, Father recommended that he carry the gold and silver. Colonel Cloud agreed. It was loaded into our wagon late last night, in secrecy. Then we packed a few of our belongings . . . that's why we got a late start. We left just after the other wagons pulled out. But we didn't take everything of ours. Father said we could have them sent along later."

"Your father's an honest man, Becky," Gil said, pulling her close, kissing her forehead, but inside he had his doubts.

CHAPTER
TWENTY-SEVEN

As far as Gil could tell, John Rankin and Henry Russell kept to themselves. No secret meetings, no acknowledgment of each other during breakfast or supper. A person could interpret that to mean they were conveniently avoiding each other to lessen suspicion or, more likely, they just didn't want anything to do with each other. Both men were bitter, almost loners. The military had been their lives, and now they were out or on their way out. But would they double-cross the United States government, risk the welfare of Kansas settlers and travelers along the Santa Fé Trail, for money? Twenty thousand dollars was a tidy sum, but it wasn't that much. And no matter how angry or greedy Russell and Rankin had become, Metairie just couldn't see them joining forces with a butcher like Montulé. If all this were not enough, the major's wife, Becky's mother, had been killed by Moon Montulé's men.

Gil observed the pair for two days and nights before giving up. Whatever happened happened. If they were part of the Blackwater River Guards, he would find out soon enough. Or maybe not. Nothing had happened yet. Maybe Colonel Leavenworth had guessed wrong. Perhaps Montulé had fled Kansas, making a dash for

Canada or Mexico. He sighed. A man could worry himself to death trying to figure out what might or might not happen. He was acting like a green soldier who had never seen the elephant. A veteran sergeant should know better than this. He recalled one of General Cleburne's admonitions to an overly excited lieutenant at Shiloh: "Don't think. React!"

Autumn had turned cooler now. Gil warmed his hands with a tin mug of coffee and watched. The canvas tarps over the wagons glowed warmly from the setting sun, and the freighters busied themselves frying salt pork and slurping coffee. Russell pulled a small flask from his boot top and sweetened his coffee, ignoring the wagon master as he barked out commands to other drivers. Across the camp, John Rankin stirred a pot while his daughter prepared two bedrolls underneath the prisoner transport. Bealer and Hardee assigned pickets and joined Gil at the campfire.

"When's the last time you slept, Gil?" Bealer asked as poured a cup of coffee for G. W., then himself.

Metairie answered with a shrug. He sipped his drink, stifled a yawn, and decided he should check on the horses.

"Horses can wait," Bealer said with a smile.

"Yeah," Hardee added. "Miss Rankin ain't finished her supper yet. She won't be sneakin' out from under her daddy's nose for a half hour or so."

Bealer shook his head and stretched out on the ground with a grunt. "G. W.," he said lightly, "in the Confederate Army, if I remember right, an enlisted man

244

such as Sergeant Metairie here was not allowed to socialize with the daughter of an officer."

Hardee nodded. "It ain't considered proper in the Yankee Army neither, Arthur." Both men were beaming now, and Gil took their ribbing with a smile himself. G. W. went on: "And back home in Georgia, a gentleman certainly didn't have clan . . . clan . . . what's the word I'm lookin' for, Arthur?"

"Clandestine."

"Yeah. Didn't have clandestine meetin's with a lady while her daddy slept."

"Mississippi was the same, G. W. Unless a body wanted to take a load of birdshot in his buttocks."

Gil finished his coffee. "You two finished?" he asked.

Neither answered. They both guffawed.

"Where's Hickok?" Gil asked, changing the subject.

"Ain't come back from his scout," Bealer replied, and Hardee added: "He said he might not be back till after dark. You worried?"

"Not about him," Metairie answered, placing his cup by the fire and turning to leave.

"Where you goin'?" Bealer called out.

"To check on the damned horses," Metairie said dryly, and his two friends' laughter trailed him as he walked away.

He heard Becky's footsteps and looked up, lowering the left hind leg of a dun remount and sliding the pick into his trouser pockets. "I was beginning to think you weren't coming," he told her. "About to get too dark to work on those horses."

He loved Becky's smile. She gestured toward the horse. "Did its hoofs really need cleaning?"

"No," he said. He had scolded the boys of both squads after the first night, telling them that they had to take care of their mounts, hoofs included, or they would find themselves walking to Bluff Creek, and then walking to Riley. That had done the job. The real reason, however, was that, if Montulé attacked, he would have to send a galloper to Pawnee Rock to fetch those 2nd Colorado troops, and a lame horse would be a sorry excuse for why he, Becky, and everyone else in this wagon train had been killed.

They talked for a few minutes about nothing, avoiding mention of her father, Russell, and Montulé like scarlet fever. Gil took her hand in his own.

"You still wish I had gone back to Fort Larned?" she asked.

"Right now, no," he said. "But tomorrow I might have a different answer."

The spell had been broken. Gil regretted his words, hated to hear Becky ask: "You still think Montulé will attack?"

"I don't know," he said after a moment's reflection. "I thought today would be most likely. If he waits another day, we'll be close to Bluff Creek, and Leavenworth has a lot of soldiers waiting at the Little Arkansas."

"So maybe . . ."

"Maybe," he said flatly.

The smile returned, and she released his hand and walked toward the cavalry mounts. With her back to him, she asked: "What would you do in Denver, Gil?"

246

"Find a job, I reckon." He moved toward her, closer, breathing in the aroma of her hair. It smelled of sage. He slipped his arm around her waist. "There are jobs to be had in Denver, other than schoolteaching, aren't there, Becky?"

"You're silly," she said, and leaned her head on his shoulder. He liked that, too.

"I never was much of a farmer back in Missouri," he said, surprised at his honesty. "Dad did most of the work, while I spent a good deal of time playing cards in town."

"Some people consider gambling an honest profession," she said.

"Honest I was, but the way I played I don't think I'd make it a profession. I suppose I could sweep out a store, swamp a saloon, find something to do to support a wife and family." Those words surprised him, and he started thinking. What could he do? He couldn't farm, if they had farms in Colorado. Yes, he had a strong back, and, yes, he was a quick learner. Find work on a ranch? In a mine? Fell trees or build houses? Maybe, but as he stood here, Becky Rankin in his arms, he realized that the only thing he knew how to do, and do well, was be a soldier. And he was sick of soldiering.

"We'll find a way," she said.

And Gil felt oddly reassured. He would marry this girl, go to Denver, start a life with her, and they would find a way . . .

The sudden sound spun him around, and he stepped in front of Becky and drew the revolver, thumbing back the hammer and stopped.

"Hickok!" he said, staring at the scout in the dimming light. Hickok, on foot, reins in his left hand, horse behind him, studied the Colt in the dim light.

"Touchy," he said. "You mind puttin' that thing away." It wasn't a question.

Apologizing, Metairie lowered the hammer and shoved the .44 inside his blouse. "Didn't hear you come up till now," he added in a way of further explanation.

"Obviously." Gil felt better when he thought he saw Hickok's smile.

The plainsman tipped his wide-brimmed hat and unsaddled his horse. Becky was about to leave when Hickok asked her to stay. They waited in silence as the scout rubbed down his mount and picketed it with the others, then placed a feedbag over the animal's head, and walked toward them, the horse's teeth noisily grinding the oats.

"Saw somethin' that might interest you both," Hickok said. "About four miles west of here."

"What?" Gil asked.

"Moon Montulé's camp." Metairie's mouth went dry. "Leastwise, I think it's him," Hickok continued. "Figured maybe you and me might ride out there at first light, let you take a look-see. You seem to know a lot about this Montulé bastard. You could identify him."

Gil nodded. There hadn't been any animosity in the scout's voice. He had just been stating facts, plain and simple. But a two-man scout against the Blackwater River Guards didn't seem smart. "Why not take most of my men?" he asked. "Better yet, we could see if any teamsters wanted to come. If it's Montulé, we'll attack rather than wait to be attacked."

"Nah," Hickok said. "Moon Montulé's no threat to us."

"What?"

"He's dead."

Metairie hesitated at the edge of camp, and he wasn't sure if it was because of his own nerves or the smell of blood that his horse spooked. Slowly he dismounted and handed the reins to Arthur Bealer. The sharpshooter had insisted on joining Gil and Hickok, and the scout had agreed. They left Sergeant Hardee in charge of the escort that morning, saying they would catch up with the train as soon as possible. Becky Rankin had wanted to go, but Hickok said there was no way in hell he'd take a woman there. Gil didn't blame him.

"Bad apples," Metairie muttered, and pulled an arrow out of the bloated corpse of one of the Guards.

"Huh?" Hickok asked.

"Nothing," he said dully.

The scout took the bloody arrow from Gil, studying the shaft and feathers before announcing: "Kiowa."

Bodies littered the camp. Dead horses, mules, men, most of them already picked over by vultures and ravens, coyotes and wolves. A ripped canvas tent fluttered in the wind next to a charred wagon. One Dutch oven remained suspended from a tripod over the ashes of a round fire, and three mutilated corpses surrounded the scene. Gil saw other groups of bodies near old fires, plates and cups scattered with coffee pots. Then he tried to picture what had happened. Montulé's men, preparing breakfast, were hit by the Kiowas fast, furiously, who killed most of them before they had time to react, the others trying to flee, but not making it far. *Like that first morning at Shiloh,* Gil thought.

Hickok pointed at the corpse. "You recognize him?"

Gil glanced again at the disfigured face, shook his head, then realized Hickok knew. His head jerked up. The scout tossed the arrow to the ground. "You ranted a lot before I got you to Fort Larned," Hickok said easily.

"You could have turned me in. I'm sure there's a reward."

"Hell, Metairie, don't you know me better than that by now?" His long arm stretched toward the ruined tent. "I think Montulé's in there."

Both men stepped over and around the carnage, leaving Bealer to hold the skittish animals. During the war, the Blackwater River Guards had survived years of being hunted by jayhawkers, lawmen, Unionist clans, and Federal soldiers. They had murdered, plundered, and pillaged in the name of the Confederacy. For months since the surrender, soldiers had combed most of Missouri and Kansas searching for Moon Montulé without luck. The Guards had killed Peadar Flann, and the United States Army hadn't come close to breaking Montulé's reign of terror. But a large band of Kiowas, on the way to a peace council at Bluff Creek, had come across the Guards and attacked, slaughtering the slaughterers. "Bad apples," Colonel Leavenworth would call those warriors. But Gil Metairie would have hugged and kissed every last one of them.

"How long?" Gil asked as they continued walking.

"Two, three days. Less'n twenty bodies, but I don't think any vamoosed. No sign of it, anyway. Bucks picked up all the weapons they could, some plunder, and made off with the horses. One last fling before tryin' peace, I reckon."

"Twenty men." Moon Montulé's command had once numbered more than three hundred.

"War's over, Metairie. I'm bettin' that's all he had left. Lot of 'em probably went home, and you took care of seven this past summer."

"You think he would have attacked the wagon train with only twenty men?"

"Yes. But you knew him better than me. What do you think?"

Metairie stopped. He looked down at the body in front of him, face down, just outside of the tent, and shoved his boot under the dead man's body. He kicked and felt his heart jump as the corpse rolled over. Toby Greer. Eyes burning with fear, not hate, in death, a purple hole in the center of his forehead, a chunk of hair ripped from his scalp, three more wounds in his dirty blue shirt, boots missing, fingers and toes chopped off. Toby Greer. Dead. Gil looked inside the tent, and he answered before stepping inside.

"Yeah, he would have tried to ambush us. Moon Montulé didn't give a damn. He just hated Yankees, wanted to kill as many as he could, hurt as many as possible, steal as much as possible. Yeah, he would have attacked with twenty men, or only ten. Die game, he always told us. He knew he would die sometime."

"Bet he didn't figure on goin' out this way."

Moon Montulé lay in a four-poster bed inside the tent, still wearing his nightshirt. A bed in a canvas tent in the middle of the Kansas plains. Gil shook his head. That blackhearted son-of-a-bitch had always been a strange one. His mouth hung open, filled with coagulated blood, and his blue eyes stared at a gaping hole in the top of the tent. The man was white in death, but he had always appeared pale, and his delicate hands still gripped his bed sheets tightly. The thick facial hair had turned grayer over the past four years, and his long black hair had been a grand trophy for some Kiowa brave. Strange, Gil thought, the despised demon of Olathe and Baxter Springs didn't look so frightful in death. He looked scared.

But it was, indeed, Moon Montulé, and he — and Toby Greer — were quite dead. The Blackwater River Guards were no more.

Gil Metairie was free.

Then he heard the faint report of gunfire.

CHAPTER
TWENTY-EIGHT

The wagons weren't moving. Nothing else appeared out of the ordinary. Civilians and soldiers milled about as if they were preparing to make camp, but a second later Gil felt as if he had been kicked by a buffalo bull. The prison wagon! It was gone. Swearing angrily, Metairie kicked his already lathered horse into a lope, the roan's hoofs tearing up the Kansas sod like a farmer's plow. Hickok and Bealer followed.

Gil's first reaction to the gunshots had been stomach-turning fear. Moon Montulé may have been dead, but perhaps some of his men had escaped the Kiowa attack and were now butchering Hardee and the others . . . and Becky. He soon ruled that out. Hickok had been right. The Blackwater River Guards were dead, but that quick succession of gunshots — he had heard only a half dozen or so, a solo round, then a handful more several minutes later — had told him something was going on at the wagon train, something deadly. Leaping over dead bodies, he had torn through the camp and swung into the saddle, whipping the horse into a hard gallop, Hickok and Bealer right behind him. Yet Metairie hadn't survived the war by being stupid. As soon as he saw the wagons, he reined up and studied everything. A good soldier never charged into a situation he didn't understand. Satisfied that whatever had happened was now over, he rode on.

He couldn't make out the jumbled statements being blurted out by soldiers and freighters all at the same time, but he saw three men hovering over the prone body of a soldier. Gil's heart ached as he leaped from the saddle and stumbled ahead. Two 3rd Squad boys saw him coming and backed away, giving him room. Another wrapped strips of homespun cloth over G. W. Hardee's left shoulder.

"G.W.," Gil said easily, kneeling beside his friend.

The Georgian's eyes opened. He was shirtless, pale, and blood-stained the length of his arm. His Adam's apple bobbed, and through a firmly set jaw he managed to say: "Sumbitch shot me, Gil."

"Who?"

"Henry Russell." He sank with a gasp, unconscious.

Gil spun around, hearing the wagon master, a Central Ohioan named Cannon, swear, spit, and comment: "Here I was, worryin' over you old Rebs, thinkin' if anyone waylaid us it would be you, and who done it . . . a damned man who once wore the blue."

"Where's Miss Rankin?" Gil said forcefully. "Where's their wagon?"

"Russell took 'em," someone said, and the myriad voices went off again, unintelligible, scattered, whining, scared.

"Shut up!" he boomed.

Everyone fell silent. Metairie stood, scanning the faces for someone he could trust. He nodded at Goldy

254

Michaels, and the South Carolina baritone from Manigault's Brigade took a quick breath, exhaled, and, began: "Rear axle busted in one of the wagons, Sergeant, forcing us to stop while some of Mister Cannon's boys got to work. Sergeant Hardee sent a couple of Second Squad boys, Petty and Gray, on up ahead as sentries, and Warren Fry to watch our back trail. The rest of us picketed our horses, and started boiling some coffee. Next thing we know, Major Rankin is pulling his wagon into the center of camp. We didn't think nothing of it, but then Lieutenant Russell comes over, whips out his revolver, and clobbers Pat Brock over the head and starts screaming."

Gil looked around, saw Brock, a Conway boy who had served with Metairie in the 15th Arkansas. A white bandage parted his curly black hair. He looked ashamed, although it could have happened to anyone.

Michaels continued: "He says we're . . . meaning him . . . taking the wagon, and, if we do what he says, nobody'll get hurt. First thing, he says, is for us to bring in those sentries Sergeant Hardee had posted.

"Sergeant Hardee, he tells me to go out and fetch the boys . . . maybe I should have told them what was going on . . . so when we get back, Russell tells us to start throwing our guns in the back of the prison wagon." For the first time, Gil noticed that no one in the camp was armed. "We start doing that, but Sergeant Hardee goes for his revolver, and Lieutenant Russell plugs him. All this time, Miss Rankin has been sitting with her father on the seat of that wagon. The shot spooks the horses, and, while her father's fighting for control, she jumps off. Heck, I'm guessing that she was trying to tackle the lieutenant, but she glanced off his shoulder and hit the ground. He moved fast, grabbed her, and pulled her up, said if anyone else tries something like that he'll blow her brains out."

Goldy paused to catch his breath. Gil waited anxiously.

"About then, Major Rankin, he shouts something to Russell, says Miss Rankin's got no part of this and for him to leave her alone. The lieutenant, he shakes his head, says Miss Rankin is good merchandise for bartering, says she'll help keep the soldiers back. Major Rankin says something like the hell you say . . . Becky's not part of the deal. Lieutenant Russell turns, and the major's drawing his revolver. Russell shoots him, three times. Miss Rankin's screaming, and her pa falls off the wagon. The horses are snorting up a storm now, but the major had set the brake. One of Mister Cannon's fellas starts to swing out with his whip, but Russell gut-shoots him, then makes Miss Rankin crawl up into the wagon seat. He grabs the major's revolver, gets up there with her, and says if anyone follows him, he'll kill her. They took off, and we figured it would be best to wait on you, Sergeant."

Gil rubbed his eyes. Michaels added: "That fella the lieutenant shot . . . he died."

"Where's Major Rankin?" Metairie asked.

"We put him in the back of one of the wagons, tried to make him as comfortable as possible, him being an officer and all. One of the wagon drivers is with him now." Michaels's eyes cut to G.W. "You think Sergeant Hardee will live?"

"I don't know," Gil answered, and followed Warren Fry to the wagon where Major John J. Rankin lay on top of bolts of calico cotton meant for the Kiowas, Comanches, Cheyennes, Arapahoes, and Pawnees. The wagon driver, a slim man with thinning white hair and a thick mustache, climbed out when he saw Metairie and slowly shook his head.

"Is he awake?" Gil asked.

"Barely," the driver answered. "But I don't know how he's lived this long."

Metairie pulled himself into the wagon and sat beside Rankin. The major's breaths were ragged, with a sickening sucking sound every time he inhaled or exhaled, bubbles of blood forming atop one of the bullet holes in his chest. His face was drained of all color, and a thin line of blood trickled from the corner of his mouth.

"Major Rankin, sir?"

The officer's eyes opened, but wouldn't focus. "Who's there?" the major cried out weakly.

"Sergeant Gil Metairie."

Rankin seemed to relax. "Metairie, of course." He coughed, turned his head to one side, and spit out a clot of blood. "Where's Becky?"

"I don't know, Major. I was hoping you could tell me."

"Becky wasn't to be harmed, Sergeant. I would do nothing to jeopardize my daughter's life. You believe me, don't you?"

"Yes, sir."

The major shuddered. He coughed again, shaking his head, and laughed hollowly. "We were to leave her behind with the others. No one was to be hurt. That's the way Russell explained it to me. I am a damned fool. Figured the Army owed me something for this." He jabbed a finger toward his missing leg. "Go to Mexico, I thought. Buy one of those *haciendas*, maybe help train soldiers for the emperor against those rebels."

He would ramble on like this, Gil thought, until he bled to death or choked on his own blood. "Becky, sir. Which way would Russell go? You had to have some sort of plan. You couldn't just outrun the Army with a wagon loaded down with silver and gold."

Rankin shook his head. His breathing stopped, and he stared emptily at the wagon tarp. For a moment, Gil thought he had died, but then the sucking noise resumed and the major coughed hideously.

"Russell," Gil said after the spell had passed. "Where is Russell going?"

"Kurt Sweet's station," Rankin finally answered. "Figured we could run the horses hard to there, then get a fresh team before anyone caught up with us. Were supposed to run off all the horses, leave everyone afoot. That would buy us time. When you and Hickok and the other man took off this morning, we decided to try it now. Didn't fancy trying to get Hickok to throw down his guns."

Sweet's station. That was all Gil needed. He stood up to leave, but Rankin grabbed his wrist, his grip strong for a dying man. "Don't . . ." The major gasped. "Don't let that bastard hurt Becky." He coughed again, and Gil sat down. Rankin was fading quickly now.

"Sweet was to help. Promised him . . . two thousand dollars. Reckon Russell had . . . been planning this . . . for a long time. We'd get to . . . the station, empty the money . . . then Sweet'd send . . . dumb Russian cook . . . raising dust for . . . Nations. Figured the troops would chase . . . after him, and . . . time they . . . caught up, found out . . . they'd been put on . . . wrong trail . . . we'd be riding hard . . . for the Territories, well as hard . . . as I could ride. Rich men."

"Nine thousand dollars?" Gil said harshly.

"More than . . . you'd make in fifty years . . . in the Army . . . Serg . . ."

So Rankin and Russell had planned this together, Gil thought, and hadn't joined up with Moon Montulé. That made more sense, as the Missouri cutthroat would have murdered them both. Metairie could understand Rankin to a degree. He had seen his last chance at glory, his dream of commanding in the Regular Army, severed along with his right leg. Yet he had put his daughter, Major John Rankin's greatest accomplishment, in harm's way, and Gil couldn't feel sorry for the dying man, not even pity.

Rankin released his hold, and Gil stood. He jumped out of the wagon and had taken a few steps when the major cried out his name. Metairie hesitated, and with a frown, looked back inside.

"I'm here, Major," he said.

"Sergeant . . . you promise me . . . you . . ." — another cough — "you make sure . . . Russell doesn't

259

. . . hurt . . . my Becky. You . . . take care . . . of her." He laughed. "Nine thousand dollars . . . you were right . . . doesn't sound . . . like . . . much . . . now." He cried out sharply. "Promise me, Sergeant!"

"You have my word, Major."

"Good. Henry Russell . . . what I . . . get . . . for supping with . . . the devil. Sergeant?"

"Yes, sir."

"You tell . . . Bec . . ."

The sharp breaths and ugly sucking noise ceased.

"How's the major?" the wagon master asked.

"Dead," Gil said. "We'll bury him with your man, Mister Cannon. How long until you have that axle fixed?"

"Two hours, I reckon."

"All right. Then you'll start moving toward Bluff Creek . . ."

"But, Sergeant, I don't have an armed escort unless you count three men. If you think I'm going to keep going where Indians are thick as fleas . . ."

"You'll keep going, Mister Cannon. Colonel Leavenworth needs these goods for that treaty. Michaels!"

"Yes, Sergeant."

"I want you to get a good horse and ride as hard as you can to the Little Arkansas. Find Colonel Leavenworth's assembly. It should be a bunch of our boys from Companies F and H. Tell them what happened. Have them send an escort to meet up with this train." He glanced at Cannon, who nodded silently, satisfied.

260

Gil sought out Warren Fry. "Fry," he said, "I want you to ride back to Fort Larned, report what has happened, tell them to send troops to Sweet's station. That's where Russell is heading. And tell them Russell has Becky Rankin as a hostage. I don't want her hurt. Also, have them arrest Kurt Sweet. He was in on this whole damned thing. Twist his arm hard, and I guarantee you he'll confess to everything. And Fry, you and Michaels both report that Moon Montulé is dead, his whole gang cut down by Indians."

He found Hickok. "I'd like you to stay close with the wagons," he said. "That should make Mister Cannon and his men feel better."

The scout nodded. "Maybe, but I figured I'd ride with you."

"I appreciate the offer. I truly do. But I'd feel better knowing you were here, just in case."

"All right, Metairie. You take care."

"You, too." Gil's own horse was too winded, so he saddled another. Russell had been in a panic when he took off, forgetting to run off the horses. That would cost him. Metairie saddled another horse as well, figuring to switch mounts when the first one tired. He looked up, saw Arthur Bealer throwing a McClellan saddle on the back of a bay gelding.

"Arthur," Gil said, "I need you to stay with the wagons. You'll be in command with G. W. out of action."

"Hickok can take care of things, Gil. I'm ridin' with you."

"Thanks, but . . ."

"Sergeant Metairie," — Bealer's eyes glowered through his spectacles — "don't try and give me any of your damyankee orders."

CHAPTER
TWENTY-NINE

He stopped on the top of a knoll, saw the black wagon in the distance, on its side, two horses down in the traces, the other two standing idly, no one moving. Gil swore, turned around his horse, and waved for Bealer to stop. The Mississippian had found it difficult keeping up with Metairie. Arthur Bealer could barely hide his happiness for resting his bay horse and his blistered backside.

"I thought you weren't much of a horseman," he said.

"I'm not," Gil answered. "The wagon's overturned, maybe a quarter mile away."

Bealer's eyes magnified beneath the glasses. "Miss Rankin?"

Gil shook his head. "Don't see her. Russell, either."

"Took off on foot," the sharpshooter said. "Must be desperate."

"Or he's waiting for us behind that wagon, or inside it. He had to figure we'd come after him."

"What do you think?"

"I'm riding down there. I want you to stay behind, stake your horse, and cover me from the top of that knoll with your Sharps."

Now Bealer grinned. "That I can do."

"If Russell raises his head, kill him."

"You're takin' a big risk. That yellow Yank might shoot you on the spot."

"He might. I'm counting on you killing him first . . . but only if you have a good shot. Don't shoot if he's got Becky near him."

Bealer nodded. "Now aren't you glad I came with you?"

Gil's horse snorted. He rode on, pulling the second mount behind him. He reined in about a hundred yards from the wagon and drew his Colt. Slowly he approached, reading the sign, looking for any movement. Russell had been pushing the team too hard, driving too fast. A wheel had hit a deep pit, and the wagon had flipped onto its side. The two downed horses cried out piteously, each with at least one broken leg. Russell could have at least put the animals out of the misery, slit their throats with a knife, if he didn't want to risk a gunshot.

Gil scanned the back of the transport, the door off its hinges, on the ground. He saw the protruding barrel of a Spencer and stopped before realizing the carbine was one Russell had taken with him. No one was holding it now. It had simply fallen part way out of the wagon from the wreck.

So where was Henry Russell?

And Becky Rankin?

He started to move around the wagon, heard something, and reined in. The Colt felt heavy in his right hand. He realized he was sweating although the weather remained chilly. He examined the grass surrounding the wrecked wagon. The tall blades danced gently in the wind. If Russell had run from here, he would have left a path. No, Henry Russell hadn't left, and that meant he could only be either behind the vehicle or hiding inside.

"Come on out, Russell," he said.

Nothing.

"It's all over."

This time, he heard grass rustling from behind the wagon. He pointed the Colt in that direction. "Russell."

"You haven't forgotten about my hole card, Sergeant Metairie." The voice was high-pitched, almost maniacal, except the last two words had been extremely bitter. Russell laughed. "You don't want me to have to kill Miss Becky, do you?"

"Gil . . ."

"Shut up!"

Metairie stretched in the saddle, thinking. "It's all right, Becky," he said. "It'll be over soon." Nothing came to mind. Stand-off. "What do you want, Russell?"

"Bring your horse around here," he ordered. "But first, toss that carbine over here . . . where I can see it."

Gil shifted the revolver to his left hand, pulled the Spencer out, and pitched it as far as he could. It crashed butt-first on the ground near the broken door, flipped over, and landed about fifteen feet behind the wagon, well out of Russell's reach — not that he needed another weapon. At least now, Gil thought, Bealer knows Russell is here. The sharpshooter will be ready.

"Now the revolver."

He eased down the hammer and flung the Colt away. It disappeared in the grass.

Russell laughed. "You're pretty good at takin' orders, Reb. You alone?"

"Yes."

"You're a damned liar."

"Come out and see for yourself."

"Where's Hickok?"

"I left him with the wagon train."

"And Sergeant Bealer?"

"Left him, too."

"And you expect me to believe that?"

"Believe what you want. I'm alone."

"All right, Sergeant. Now I want you to ride behind this wagon. Keep your hands where I can see them. If you try anything, I kill Becky. Then I kill you. Savvy."

"I understand."

"I understand, sir! Rebel trash. Say it."

"I understand, sir."

Gil kicked his horse into a walk. He thought about leaving the trailing horse, but decided against it. Russell would be excited at the prospect of getting two mounts. Metairie was right, for the lieutenant gleamed as Gil circled the wagon and turned around. About ten yards separated them. He looked first at Becky, saw her bruised forehead and busted lip, the sleeves of her dress ripped. Not from Russell, Gil figured, but from the wreck. Henry Russell held a Remington .44 in his right hand. His left arm hung loosely at his side, broken in all likelihood.

Metairie waited. Russell's revolver pointed at his chest.

"Two horses. You're prepared, Sergeant. I'll give you that."

Gil nodded toward Becky. "Let her go, Russell."

"Let her go, Mister Russell, sir." He was enjoying this.

Gil checked his temper. Russell straightened. "Say it, damn you!"

"Let her go, Mister Russell, sir."

The former lieutenant tried to stand, couldn't, and realized his disadvantage. "Hands high, Metairie," he said. Gil obeyed. With only one good arm, Russell stuck the Remington into his waistband and reached up, gripping a spoke in the wheel over his head and pulling himself up, grimacing, gasping, then jerking the revolver free and aiming at Metairie. Gil hadn't moved during the entire time. Russell caught his breath, more at ease now. Henry Russell was slouched, more from pain than expecting a trick, so Bealer wouldn't have had a shot, and probably wouldn't now that they were behind the wagon.

"Step down off that horse, Sergeant."

Again, Gil did as he was told.

"Over there, where I can see you."

Metairie took a few steps away from the horses.

"Farther!"

Gil obeyed.

"I'm leavin'," Russell said. "If you don't do nothin' stupid, you'll live. Try something, and I'll kill you.

Kinda hate to leave all that treasure in the wagon, but what the hell. I'd rather live."

He staggered toward the horses. Gil watched, waiting. Russell wouldn't leave them alive. As soon as he got on that horse, he'd kill Becky and him. Metairie saw that in the former officer's eyes. Once mounted, maybe Bealer would have a shot, but Gil wasn't sure. Gamble on Becky's life? His own? And Bealer's Sharps rifle was a single shot. If he missed that first shot, he'd not likely get another, and with two horses to Bealer's one, Henry Russell would get away.

Russell reached for the reins, but the horse shied away from him. He stumbled, cursed, and straightened, swinging his Remington toward Metairie. But by then, Gil was moving.

"Hiya! Hiya! Hiya!" Metairie screamed, and the horse whinnied and reared.

Russell turned his attention toward the panicked horse, dodging the vicious hoofs, and backed away, snapped a shot at Gil, missing, just before Metairie's left shoulder cut into Henry Russell's stomach. Both men crashed to the ground. The horses bolted. Gil rolled off and came up, kicking savagely at Russell's head. He heard the boom of Bealer's Sharps, but knew instantly that the marksman had missed.

Ignoring the searing pain in his broken arm, Russell still held the Remington. He fired. The bullet cut a furrow across Gil's left forearm. Metairie kicked again, this time hearing the solid thud as his boot connected with Russell's jaw. Both men fell backward. Gil arched his back, swung up, propelled himself to his feet. Too late. Henry Russell, broken arm and all, had beaten him. He saw the flash of black steel, felt the crushing blow as Russell slammed the revolver across his forehead, and dropped, stunned, trying to move, unable to get his muscles to work. Russell laughed, thumbed back the hammer.

A gunshot. Henry Russell staggered back as Metairie watched, perplexed. Gil pulled himself into a sitting position, tried to clear his head, as he slowly understood that it hadn't been a rifle shot. Bealer hadn't fired. Metairie looked, saw Becky Rankin holding Gil's Colt. Russell swore, backing away, as Becky pulled back the revolver's hammer, aimed, fired, missed, tried cocking the .44 again. But Russell, still backing away, cocked his own pistol.

"You bitch . . . ," he started.

Gil sat helplessly as Russell extended his arm and aimed, point-blank, at Becky Rankin.

Then Henry Russell's head exploded, and he was catapulted five yards away, landing in the sea of grass as the report of Arthur Bealer's Sharps echoed.

CHAPTER
THIRTY

Fort Leavenworth, Kansas

Gil walked Becky to the stagecoach station, and watched as a bald man in buckskins strapped her luggage behind the Concord. "You have your ticket?" he asked for the fourth time.

"Yes," she said, and they stood awkwardly on the boardwalk, trying not to shiver in the cold.

Satanta, Ten Bears, Jesse Leavenworth, and all of the other leaders, red and white, had made their marks on the treaty at Bluff Creek. The Indians had taken their "annuities," including several late-arriving sacks of silver and gold, and rode away, promising to leave travelers and settlers alone — for a while.

The Army had failed to catch up with Kurt Sweet. It seemed the stationmaster had got wind that the plan had fallen apart, and he had taken off for parts unknown. Brevet Sergeant G. W. Hardee kept both his arm and his life despite being transported first to Bluff Creek and then to Fort Riley before seeing a proper surgeon. There, the Georgian was given another field promotion, to Sergeant-Major, by Colonel Caraher himself.

Major John J. Rankin was reinterred at the post cemetery at Fort Zarah with full military honors. This

270

came after Gil Metairie reported to Colonel John Sanborn that Rankin had had no part in Russell's robbery attempt, that, if anything, the major had been acting as a "spy" himself to lure Russell and other conspirators into the open. He had died a hero, trying to protect his daughter and others. Sanborn probably didn't believe it, but he accepted Metairie's report, perhaps only for Becky's state.

"You didn't have to lie for Father," Becky told him again now that they stood alone beside the stagecoach.

"His last thoughts were of you, Becky," he said. "He never wanted you to get hurt."

"I know," she said. "I wish I had been a better daughter."

Gil let her grieve. John J. Rankin should have been a better father, he knew, but kept quiet.

"So . . . ," Becky said.

"So," Gil repeated.

They both smiled.

"I guess this is good bye," she said, and studied her shoes.

"For a little while," he answered, and she looked back at him. "Unless you want me to desert."

"I do," she said. "But I'll wait. You don't plan on reënlisting, do you?"

Metairie laughed. Actually General Pope had sent a personal plea to General Grant, asking that the 2nd and 3rd Regiments of U.S. Volunteers be reorganized into one regiment for one more year of active service on the frontier. The volunteers had once worn the gray, but they were damned fine soldiers and the West could use them. General Grant, bless his Yankee heart, denied the request.

The driver climbed on top of the stagecoach, and other passengers stepped inside the Concord.

"You remember?" she started.

"Julianne Moore," Gil said.

Becky Rankin fell into his arms.

"I would 'a' deserted," Arthur Bealer told him as they left the barracks on a bitterly cold November 7th 1865.

Metairie smiled. A 2nd Regiment captain began screaming at the sergeants to get their squads in order. Bealer returned to his men, shouting, cursing, as the soldiers fell in on the sprawling parade grounds, slightly covered with snow.

"Sergeant!" the captain yelled, and Metairie straightened, marching behind the officer to the flagpole where Colonel Caraher, Lieutenant Colonel King, and a handful of other regimental staff, dignitaries, and reporters waited. Gil tried holding his breath. He snapped to a halt in front of Caraher and sharply saluted.

"First Sergeant Gil Metairie," Caraher said, "you have earned the honor. Give out the final order of the Second Regiment."

After a click of his heels, Metairie spun around, facing the men he had served with for so long . . . in the Confederate Army . . . at Rock Island Prison . . . and now in the Federal Army.

Gil bellowed: "Attention!"

In unison, they stood erect. Metairie looked for a few friendly faces. G. W. Hardee remained in the post hospital at Fort Riley. He saw Goldy Michaels, wondering if the South Carolinian was about to break into a song, and next to him stood Arthur Bealer. Van Boskirk . . . Warren Fry . . . Pat Brock . . . Charley Scott . . . Phineas Jones. Gil thought about the missing faces, most of all Luke Murrah and old Peadar Flann. They should have been here to see this. Maybe they were.

"Gentleman," Gil said, and couldn't hold back his grin. "Stack arms!"

Seven months after Robert E. Lee had surrendered, the war for these men was finally ending. Really over. Gil Metairie and all of the officers and enlisted men of the 2nd Regiment were being mustered out of the Union Army. He heard the cheer, saw kepis and campaign hats fly into the dark, dreary sky. Men stacked their Spencer carbines on the parade grounds, hugged each other, cried. The war was over.

Metairie made it through a round of handshakes, and steadied himself against the flagpole. He was free to join Becky in Colorado, to start a new life together with her. He thought about Jim Lane, but the vengeance he wanted after Osceola had vanished. He'd let Jim Lane and those immoral jayhawkers answer to God, although Gil had no idea that God's justice would be swift and that Lane would kill himself in less than a year.

Caraher, King, and the others filed away, followed by the brass and reporters. But one reporter in a plaid sack suit removed one heavily chewed pencil from his mouth and, thumbing through a notebook to find a blank page, approached Metairie.

"Excuse me, Sergeant." He had to shout to be heard above the celebration spreading around them. "Stan Hollister, *Harper's Weekly* correspondent. Do you mind if I ask you a question or two?"

"Go ahead."

They went through the particulars, Metairie's name and how to spell it, where he had served in the Confederacy, how it felt to have his discharge papers, and if he had seen much action against the hostiles out West. After clearing his throat, Hollister tried his final question.

"Well, sir. The war's over, but I wonder if you and your men will be allowed to go home. Do you think the South, your friends and families, will forgive you for joining the Union Army? What do you think?"

Metairie had often wondered about that. He still wasn't certain. After a moment's reflection, he answered honestly: "I'm not going home, Mister Hollister. I'm going West."

"Good, sir." He scribbled something in his notebook. "Anywhere in particular?"

"Denver, Colorado," he said. "Julianne Moore."

"Julianne Moore? Is that your fiancée?"

"No."

"Relative? Friend?"

"Nope," — and Gil Metairie walked away, disappearing into the sea of blue-clad former soldiers, leaving Stan Hollister with a full notebook and a puzzled expression.

Author's Note

The character of J. B. "Wild Bill" Hickok as well as the other historical figures in this novel — Andrew P. Caraher, William F. Cloud, Jesse Leavenworth, Josiah King, William Mackey, and John B. Sanborn — are used fictitiously. Hickok did serve as an Army scout during the War between the States, and he is credited with bringing the news of Lee's surrender at Appomattox to Fort Zarah. But by that summer, he and other civilian employees were out of work, and Hickok left Kansas for Springfield, Missouri, where he killed Davis Tutt on July 21, 1865.

Many Rebel soldiers rotting in Rock Island and other Union prisons did join the U.S. Volunteers — with the pledge that they would serve on the frontier and not against the Confederate armies — and served nobly. Soldiers from the 2nd Regiment were stationed across the plains, including Forts Larned and Zarah, and Companies F and H took part in Colonel Jesse Leavenworth's show of force during the peace council on Bluff Creek. The 2nd Regiment was mustered out on November 7, 1865, at Fort Leavenworth.

For those interested in reading more about this topic, I suggest *The Galvanized Yankees* by Dee Brown. The conditions of prison camps, North and South, are superbly covered in *Portals to Hell: Military Prisons of the Civil War* by Lonnie R. Speer, and the best books on the Missouri-Kansas conflict include: *Gray Ghosts of the Confederacy: Guerrilla Warfare in the West 1861–1865* by Richard S. Brownlee and *Inside War: The Guerrilla Conflict in Missouri During the American Civil War* by Michael Fellman. Other sources for this novel include *Historical Times Illustrated Encyclopedia of the Civil War*, edited by Patricia L. Faust; *Firearms of the American West 1803–1865* by Louis A. Garavaglia and Charles G. Worman; *The West of Wild Bill Hickok* by Joseph G. Rosa; and *Forts of the West* by Robert W. Frazier.

Finally, I would like to thank Romona Newsome, reference librarian at the Great Bend Public Library in Kansas, for helping in my research on Fort Zarah and the Great Bend area.

About the Author

In addition to writing Western novels, Johnny D. Boggs has covered all aspects of the American West for newspapers and magazines ranging from travel to book and movie reviews to celebrity and historical profiles to the apparel industry and environmental issues. Born in South Carolina, Boggs published his first Western short story in 1983 in the University of South Carolina student literary magazine. Since then, he has had more than twenty short stories published in magazines and anthologies, including *Boys' Life* and *Louis L'Amour Western Magazine*. His first novel was *Hannah and the Horseman* (1997). Other novels include *This Man Colter* (1997), *Riding with Hannah and the Horseman* (1998) and *Ten and Me* (1999), this last a finalist for the Spur Award for Best Western Novel. His first nonfiction book was *That Terrible Texas Weather* (2000), a history of some of the worst natural disasters in the state from the 1800s to the present. After graduating from the University of South Carolina College of Journalism in 1984, Boggs moved to Texas to begin a newspaper career. He started as a sports-writer for the *Dallas Times Herald* in 1984 and was assistant sports editor when the newspaper folded in 1991. From 1992 to 1998, he worked for the *Fort Worth Star-Telegram*, leaving the newspaper as assistant sports editor to become a full-time writer and photographer. He is a frequent contributor to *Boys' Life*, *Wild West*, *True West*, among other publications. His photos have often accompanied his newspaper and magazine articles, as well as appearing on the covers of many Five Star, Thorndike, and G.K. Hall titles. Boggs lives in Santa Fé, New Mexico with his wife, Lisa Smith, and basset hound, Scout.